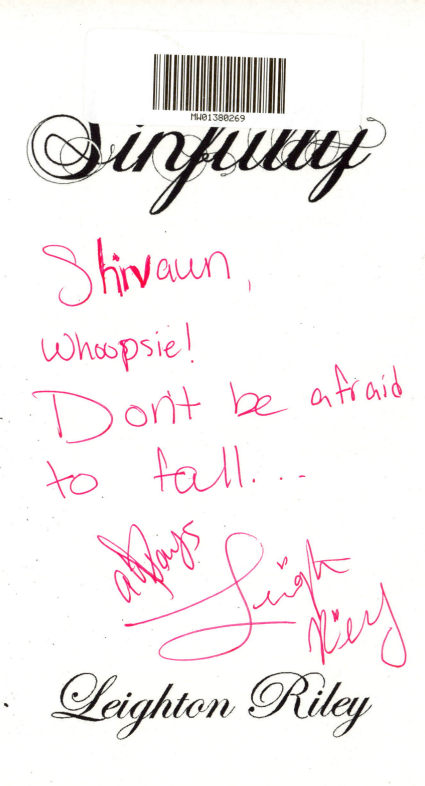

Copyright © 2014 by Leighton Riley

All rights reserved. No part of this publication may be reproduced, distributed, or transmitted in any form or by any means, including photocopying, recording, or other electronic or mechanical methods, without the prior written permission of the publisher, except in the case of brief quotations embodied in critical reviews and certain other noncommercial uses permitted by copyright law.

This book is a work of fiction. All names, characters, locations and incidents are products of the author's imagination. Any resemblance to actual persons, living or dead, locales or events is entirely coincidental.

Sinfully

ISBN-10: 1500105503
ISBN-13: 978-1500105501

Editor: Jenny Sims
Cover Designer: Cassy Roop of Pink Ink Designs
Cover photo: Andrei Vishnyakov
Interior Design & Layout: Deena Rae @ E-BookBuilders

Table of Contents

Chapter 1 1
Chapter 2 17
Chapter 3 25
Chapter 4 31
Chapter 5 45
Chapter 6 63
Chapter 7 77
Chapter 8 107
Chapter 9 121
Chapter 10 131
Chapter 11 153
Chapter 12 165
Chapter 13 175
Chapter 14 187
Chapter 15 201
Chapter 16 211
Chapter 17 215
Chapter 18 223
Sneak Peek — Regretfully I
Sneak Peek — Fatefully V
   Chapter 1 VII
   Chapter 2 XI
   Chapter 3 XV
   Chapter 4 XXI
Acknowledgments XXVII
Meet Leighton XXXI
Leighton's Books XXXIII

v

Chapter 1

Ryder

Loosening my tie, I set down another poorly written manuscript that had no depth or conflict. I had been searching for two weeks for my next new author. Every day I sifted through the stack of manuscripts sitting idly on my desk, looking for something different—edgy—something with raw emotions. I didn't want any of that happily ever after bullshit. Finding new talent used to be easy for me, and I really needed to get a handle on things.

I thought about getting out of the office and away from the real world for a few days. At twenty-seven, I missed the days where everyone headed down to the beach without a care in the world. I remembered spending hours surfing the waves just to clear my head and rejuvenate my soul. Editing was what I knew, but it wasn't the life for me. I had the talent but no passion for it anymore.

I had even sent an email to the one author who had piqued my interests but hadn't gotten a response. What self-published author wouldn't want one of the largest publishing firms behind them? I offered her an insane amount of money along with some of the best editors known to the publishing world *and* a guarantee of publishing three more of her books within the next two years. It was the offer of a lifetime, and yet, I hadn't heard a word.

I wasn't expecting to become so enthralled with Reece Edwards's book, but I couldn't put the damn thing down. A friend had recommended it to me after she saw it on a few blog posts with rave reviews. She was apparently addicted to indie authors and I told her I would look into it just so she would back the fuck off.

I wasn't planning on actually reading the book. I did, however, go online to read the synopsis, so that when asked, I would be able to tell her why I hadn't decided to pursue it. I knew I'd be able to find *some* reason why the book was just like all the others out there and not worth looking into. While on Amazon, I made note that the story had only been "published" for three months and already had over a hundred reviews, many of them being four and five stars. In that short amount of time, this self-published author should still be trying to get herself out there and struggling to *find* people to leave reviews. I was curious what was drawing the crowd and how she had become so…visible…in such a short amount of time.

One reviewer quoted from the book, *"I saw the questioning look in his eyes, asking if I'd heard him. He stalked over to me and grabbed my waist to pull me into him. I could feel how much he wanted me through his slacks and I was instantly wet."*

Adjusting my growing erection, I got comfortable at my desk to do some more research. Fuck, I needed to get laid. The writer's audience was primarily women, but *damn* if it wasn't hot. I had plenty of girlfriends who had told me about how much they loved their dirty books and how they could read them discreetly on their phones or e-readers, but I hadn't worked on many of those types of books before. Maybe they were on to something.

Once I got home, I decided I should probably give it a go. I one-clicked the book and opened it up on my phone, figuring I could do a quick run-through before I hung out with the guys.

About three percent into it, I took a beer from the fridge and got settled in on my couch. I told myself I would read the first chapter to fulfill my obligations. That, of course, led to needing to know what would happen in chapter two. With that chapter ending on a cliffhanger, I felt obliged to read chapter three. I considered myself a pro at skimming through manuscripts because of my job, and I only skipped over a few sections, the rest I read word for word. I was envious of how carefree and spontaneous the main character seemed to be.

I ignored my friends' request to join them at the bar for beers and instead stayed in to finish the book. Each chapter of the book was a different night with a different man. It seemed like there were multiple trips to the city. Most of them weren't storybook endings, either. Some of them ended in tears or clothes being thrown out the door while others ended with her having to get herself off after the man was gone. *Was it non-fiction?* The thought hooked me and I was sunk. Who would bare themselves to the world by telling their most intimate, and sometimes embarrassing, sexual experiences?

The, uh, *details* were so vivid it was almost like you were in the room watching. It was written from the woman's point of view, and from the description of her orgasms, foreplay, and overall thoughts, it had a feminine feel to it. I found myself lost in thought on numerous occasions while imagining what the scenario she described would really feel like. "Reece" had such an innocent yet powerful demeanor that you never knew what to expect from her. Sometimes she would be gentle and submissive, while other times she was downright kinky and domineering. My cock couldn't decide which persona he liked better, or maybe he chose both.

I couldn't get her nights with those men out of my head. Some were just casual encounters with men who wanted a girl's company for the night—those were the ones I was able to skim—but most were raw with passion and pleasure.

Before my only long-term girlfriend, Zoe, I was known for being a bachelor who had a different girl every night. I was young and having fun. What I did back then and what Reece was describing were two vastly different things. I fucked a girl just because it felt good, and didn't think twice when I told her to leave shortly afterward—no sleepovers was a rule of mine.

She'd seemingly just met these men as well, but there was a connection there that made it more than just a quick fuck. The way she presented herself to total strangers was personable and down to earth. She didn't go out looking for a hookup, but more so a guy who would be able to keep up with her and show her a good time. She wasn't looking to settle down or find a sugar daddy like most women these days. In her book, she judged a guy based on how he approached her and how he interacted with those around him. She made a point that if he was a douche to the cocktail waitress or dealer, he was a no-go.

In the bedroom, she dominated and was damn good at it, too. How did her nights seem to be filled with lust and passion with a stranger while mine seemed to be indifferent, no matter who I was with? Was I doing something wrong?

I used to be a big fan of one-and-done, but since discovering the possibility of deeper, more passionate sex without it lasting more than a night or two, I had to find out how she was able to have that kind of relationship. I envied her ability to let loose and enjoy life since what I'd had lately was the exact opposite.

I missed that look in a woman's eye that told me she loved me and wanted me. I missed those moments when I couldn't wait to get her alone so I could fuck her quickly and then make love to her slowly all night long. I missed the moans and screaming of my name with someone I truly cared about. The damn book was turning me into a pussy.

The next morning, while running on the elliptical at the gym, I tried thinking of ways to get this Reece Edwards to at least meet with me so I could persuade her into working with me. Her work should be available in major bookstores around the country, and eventually, all over the world. I had the experience to help her get to that point but could only help if she decided she wanted to take a chance.

Growing up with a father who was a publisher, I was constantly surrounded by books and I excelled in my literary studies. It seemed to be a natural fit to take over my father's company after college since he was itching to retire and finally get to spend uninterrupted time with my mother. Dad used to hand me manuscripts of unknown authors that were considered to be in the "other" pile so I could help him get through the massive stacks on his desk. It might not have been the most normal high school job, but it was what I had known my whole life.

While in high school, I had "found" two authors who later became New York Times Best Sellers. During college, I was able to continue to work for Warrington Strom while attending Ryker's University. Things had been going great for the last four years since graduating and I'd gotten comfortable, so to speak. I was used to working with multiple authors at a time with exciting new talents continuously sending me their manuscripts.

I'd been in a slump, not finding any of the recent reads that appealing. I didn't need a tear-jerker or sappy story, but I needed something with substance and appeal. Reece's book had both, granted the appeal was partially that of a sexual nature.

I decided I would drive out to meet her. She was in San Diego—only a few hours away. I couldn't help but wonder what she looked like. I had always had a soft spot for brunettes with natural curves, but with what I had read of her experiences in bed, I'd make an exception. I could only bang her, though, if she rejected working with me.

Reminding myself that I was not at all curious about her personal life and that I just wanted her book was something I had to do on multiple occasions that day. I had made a point to always stay professional with my authors so that our work relationship wouldn't suffer. I made the mistake of not following my advice once and learned my lesson.

Savannah Wilton was a steamy romance novelist who had a rather creative mind in the bedroom. Her books alone had my cock throbbing, but the fact that she was similar in real life, it was a dream come true. Our flirtations were innocent until she came by after-hours one night while I was trying to get some editing done. She said she was having trouble working through a scene in her head and wanted help getting through it. I let my authors know I was always willing to help out when needed, so I told her to walk me through what she had so far.

She proceeded to walk over to my desk and sit on it with her legs spread out in front of me. My black dress slacks began to tighten as I became aroused by the beautiful woman before me. Did I mention that she was wearing a black, scoop top dress that barely covered her ass? I stared at her, dumbfounded, for a few seconds before hearing her go over how her character couldn't get thoughts of being with her boss out of her head and wanted to satisfy her craving.

The way Savannah moved my rough hands from her voluptuous hips, up her tiny stomach, and massaged those store-bought tits while she discussed the scene was enough for me to not think clearly. I took her on my desk and learned a couple things from Savannah that night: 1- that I should make sure the door is locked before going at it in my office since the janitor walked in on us and stood there in fucking awe and 2- that I should never work with authors of mine because our night ended up in her next book and she was very detail oriented (including my birthmark on my left hip bone and tattoo on the other).

It had been a while since I had to go out and search for a new author, but I had a feeling this one would be worth it. Over the past few years, Lorelei, my assistant, had found a few knockout authors and the rest I had practically begging at my door. I could go and meet with Reece, maybe go down to the beach together and go over her concerns and questions about coming on board with me. It would be an easy in-and-out situation and my slump would be no more. *Wait, my personal slump or professional? Head in the game, man, this is going to be strictly a professional pursuit.*

After I finished my workout, I got cleaned up, changed into a black Armani suit with a gray shirt and a dark purple silk tie, and headed into the office to set my plan in motion. Lorelei could handle most of my normal work and was great about emailing me or texting me when something important came up. I was thankful I

Leighton Riley

had hired her instead of the blond Barbie who I was tempted to, but then realized it probably wasn't the wisest business decision.

Payton

Sitting at the local Starbucks, I couldn't believe what I was seeing. No matter how long I looked at the email I had just received, it didn't make it any more real. Why would anyone want to have my story published? I wanted to get my story out there but hadn't intended on anyone but a handful of friends actually reading it. After staring at my laptop for what must have been a solid five minutes, I finally shut the screen, packed up my journal and notes, and threw away the now cold coffee that I had been looking forward to. I came here to brainstorm different ideas of what I wanted to write next but was distracted as soon as my email popped up on the screen.

On my walk back to my car, I could only focus on that one sentence, "I look forward to meeting with you soon to discuss details of having your phenomenal work published by Warrington Strom Publishing Agency." I was an unknown author for the most part and my fan base wasn't that impressive. Where did they find me? The email was from R. Strom—not that I knew who that was, but assumed by the last name and status as 'Vice President and Senior Editor' that they were probably an old and important guy who needed to get laid. The way he addressed me was too arrogant and cocky to be a woman. I wasn't sure how he found out about my book and was even *more* unsure as to why an actual publishing company would want to read about my sex life.

When I started writing my personal stories, I didn't really think about what could happen if people liked what I wrote. I felt it was okay to leave in the "juicy" parts and didn't really feel the need to embellish what happened. It helped that no one knew it was me who wrote it, since I didn't have the courage to use my real name when I wrote the story. Some things were just too personal to put out there in the open. Plus, if the guys I were with ever read it, they wouldn't be able to connect it as easily. They all knew me as Payton.

Even though I might have embellished on my life story with some of them, I was still me with them, not Reece.

My Lips are Sealed was almost like a diary of the fun I had during my frequent trips to Las Vegas. I considered myself a pretty good judge of character, and realized during one particular trip to the city of sin that I could have flings with men in town for business without getting attached. I could meet a handsome man at a bar and let him know as much—or as little—about me as I desired. I had the control of letting the relationship go to the next level—meaning as far I wanted to take it in bed.

By the time we started getting more personal with each other, their business trip was usually over. It was the perfect way to have fun, meet new people, not get attached, and be free to kick them out afterward without feeling guilty. In the morning, I could move on to my next craving; finding the flavor of the day was never a challenge.

These encounters started off without even realizing what I was really doing. It was only when I got back to San Diego that I realized what I had done and how much I wanted more of it. I craved going back and meeting someone new. Just the thought of it made my core tingle and my nipples deliciously hard.

I missed being affectionate with people and didn't go out enough while home. I enjoyed being a children's author from home and going to bars with friends didn't have the same appeal that it did in college. It was the same guys at the bar each week and I needed a little more spice in my life. I knew it sounded bad, but I hated picking up men in my hometown. Once we ended—which I planned on happening—there was always the chance of seeing them again, and well, that was awkward.

I learned from an early age that if you didn't really let people into your life, the less it hurt when they left. Being adopted by my loving parents at the age of seven was supposed to be my dream come true, along with my forever home. Little did I know that they would be taken away from me six short years later.

Reports said a drunken teenager was behind the wheel of the car that hit them, but what wasn't said—due largely because of my family's lawyer—was that my father was also drunk behind the wheel that night. My parents were used to going to big parties of the most affluent couples in San Diego. Drinks flowed freely and my parents weren't ones to say no to any offerings. Being lawyers themselves allowed me to have a hefty trust fund when I turned eighteen.

My Aunt Katy took me in when my parents died so that I wouldn't have to go back into foster care. This was mainly because my best friend Chloe's parents agreed that I could stay with them during her overnight shifts as a nurse.

I met Chloe right after my adoptive parents took me in and she's been there right beside me ever since. Kids in my class thought I was weird because I didn't want to play with them or talk to anyone. I was so worried that I'd mess something up and get sent back into the system. Chloe, a blond-haired girl in my class, was the only one to walk around the playground with me at recess and talk to me about anything and everything. It was almost a week before I broke down and started talking back. She never asked questions but always listened. We slowly became best friends and she'd always been there for me since that day on the playground. Her parents welcomed me into their house and treated me like their own daughter. Chloe seemed more like a sister to me, anyway, so it made sense. All throughout grade school, she was the one constant in my life.

After I graduated high school, I moved into a place of my own by using a small portion of my trust fund. It was a nice, three bedroom, three bath with a bonus room upstairs that I made into a media room. It had a cottage feel to it that I fell in love with instantly. It was enough room for me and it had been my home and safe place ever since.

Chloe's house was less than a mile away from me, and a lot nicer than mine, but she only stayed there when her boyfriend stayed the night, too. Most other nights, she ended up at my house, making the media room her makeshift bedroom. She hated staying alone and I didn't mind the company.

Chloe had been pestering me for months to put my experiences from Vegas on paper since I had told her a handful of my encounters while there. Everyone assumed it was always prostitutes and strippers galore, and for some guys it was. I had found some of the most intriguing, admirable, and sexiest men while vacationing there. So what if I felt like it was my home away from home? I could privately fly there and be in my suite two hours after leaving my house in San Diego. A select few knew me there and it was the only time I could really feel free to be me. Although I took my girls with me on occasion, Vegas was somewhere I could go to relax, let go, and have fun without having to get too personal.

Being best friends since we were seven gave Chloe and me the ability to talk about our sex lives with each other and provide advice and encouragement when needed. She and her boyfriend of three years had a stable, yet boring relationship. She said she needed to hear my stories from my trips to Vegas to spice up her love life.

I was not sure anything would help Grayson, her accountant boyfriend. Traveling was a normal part of his job and Chloe didn't mind him being away for days on end. She used that time to catch up with girlfriends and have some time to herself, away from the douche she called her lover. He was the typical arrogant frat boy who had the charming looks, pedigreed to take over his father's company, and was the 'right guy' to settle down with. What she saw in him, I hadn't quite figured out yet. When we hung out together, Grayson was always flirting with me in a non-discreet way right in front of Chloe. He was disgusting.

While Chloe and I had quite a bit in common, taste in men was something we agreed to disagree on. She went for the well-kept, polo wearing, ivy-school grad who was destined to be a CEO in the near future. That worked for her since she was a cheerleader at UCLA and daughter to one of the top neurosurgeons in the country. Her five-foot-three petite frame with curves in all the right places, sparkling green eyes, and luxurious, wavy blond hair might have helped a tad bit, too. She worked for her father's office in reception and didn't feel the need in trying to achieve a well-paying career that she was passionate about. She figured she wouldn't be working long-term, anyway, once she got her MRS status.

I, on the other hand, played soccer for eleven years before quitting due to multiple ankle injuries. It gave me my lean yet muscular legs, ample booty, and toned stomach. I had been complimented many times on my "nice rack" and long brown hair that was "begging to be pulled" so I supposed I had that going for me. I liked my men tall and fit. It might be shallow, but the personality, humor, and everything else that mattered could come second. I wasn't looking to settle down; I just wanted to be free to be whomever I desired.

Out of the twelve trips I made to Vegas that went into my book, Tate's story was one that I always looked back on and wondered "what if?" During one of my monthly visits to Las Vegas, I became well-acquainted with the personal trainer from Chicago. Tate was built with broad shoulders, a narrow waist, jet black hair, and the lightest of brown eyes. Out of all the chapters in my book, his story was the most fun to write.

We met at the poker tables of a hotel a few doors down from mine and he was easy on the eyes. He had been talkative to the entire table and was generous to the dealer and waitresses. His left dimple would show when he had a decent hand—that was his tell—and I found it adorable. After he saw my luck dwindling, he offered to walk me back to my hotel. Normally, that would be a red flag, but he seemed genuine and I could always change my mind on the walk back if I started getting the creeps.

While at the tables, I learned that he became a personal trainer after injuring his ACL while playing football in college. He had a passion for tending to the human body—which would hopefully come in handy later that night—and training allowed him to help people make their bodies less prone to injury while maintaining his own scrumptious physique. He was also the oldest of three siblings, both sisters who looked up to him as the male figure of the house while growing up since his dad left them before they'd even entered elementary school.

Maybe that was why I seemed to be able to trust him? He didn't seem to have a goal in mind with taking me back to my hotel, although I secretly hoped he did.

My mind began to play out different scenarios that could happen as we headed into my hotel. He seemed sweet enough and I was curious to see his personal training skills in bed.

"Payton? Where'd you go?" Tate interrupted my explicit thoughts of us together upstairs and I noticed we'd stopped in front of security who was waiting for me to show my hotel key.

"Just thinking about how sweet and sincere you are," I responded, hoping I was able to disguise my blush while reaching in my wallet for my key. His crooked grin told me that he knew I wasn't thinking something innocent and the look in his eyes told me he wanted to devour me.

He placed his hand on my lower back, ushering me toward the bank of elevators.

Once we got to my room, Tate descended to the lower level and looked outside the window. "Ever think of being watched while you fuck?"

"We're on the thirtieth floor, Tate? I don't think anyone would be able to see anything." The image of him fucking me against the glass did turn me on. We could pretend that people could see us; it was almost like getting caught in the act.

He walked back over to me and guided me to the window. My hands were placed against the cool glass and his hips were aligned with mine behind me. He pulled my dress up and I was suddenly exposed. I was left waiting for him for a moment before he slapped my ass in one powerful swing. I jumped forward at the unexpected touch and instantly wanted more. "You're a dirty girl, Payton. I bet this turns you on—

Sinfully

thoughts of me fucking you so everyone can see how dirty you are?" My panties were instantly soaked and I wanted, no needed, him to touch me. Immediately.

I squirmed so that I could feel his erection pressed against my bared ass. I was craving his hand on me again.

"What do you want?" Would it have been inappropriate for me to ask him for all of the above? I wanted him to spank me again but the words failed to leave my mouth.

"You. Touching me. Everywhere," was all I could muster. I felt him staring at me with fire and want. He pulled the straps of my dress down and twisted my nipples with gentle force. I let out a gasp in response, instantly dying to know what would come next.

He started sliding my dress off of me in one quick motion and turned me to face him. My red lacy lingerie seemed to be a good choice, because for a few seconds, he just stared at me from head to toe, devouring me with his eyes. He began sliding his hands over my taut stomach and slowly dragged his tongue from my navel up to my breasts. Dipping his finger into the cup of my bra, he pulled the fabric down so he could look at my bare breast. He groaned in soft appreciation, letting me know that he liked what he saw. Starting on the left side, he massaged my breast with his firm hand while his mouth softly licked, sucked, and blew air over my pebbled nipple. Not wanting to treat one side better than the other, he slowly moved over to the right side. His hand slipped beneath my panties and teased me with his touch.

"Mmm, so wet…ready for me already?" Tate slowly slid a finger inside me while still paying close attention to my aching breasts. I tried grabbing for his pants but he swiped my hand away. "Let me feel you first." He continued stroking me with two fingers and the moment he curled his fingers upward, I came undone around him.

When I thought he was finally ready to unleash himself, he lowered himself and started lapping up my wetness. "Mmm, so fuckin' sweet."

I had already come once and he was about to make me climax again without him ever being inside of me. I found myself thinking, "Can I keep him?" but smiled at the outlandish thought.

"Hands on the glass, sweet girl, legs spread wide." I heard the distinct sound of a foil wrapper being ripped open and my patience was dwindling. I needed him inside me. Tate guided his fingers over my slippery core, coating me in my own wetness. Slowly, his hand was replaced with the head of his cock and he felt big, bigger than I was accustomed to.

"See all those people out there? They're all watching right now, seeing your perfect tits on display and your shaved, wet pussy that's begging for my dick. Your screams and moans will make each and every woman down there wet, knowing how well you're being fucked, while every guy down there will wish they were me, knowing how hard you like it."

I could feel his head nudging against my lower lips and I cried out in need.

"Let them watch me—us. That way they'll know what they're missing. Wouldn't want to disappoint the crowd now, would we?" Tate used that moment to slide slowly into me, giving me a few seconds to adjust, as his answer.

"Let's give them a show then, shall we?" He grabbed hold of my hips and pulled me toward him as he surged forward.

Fuck, he's huge, was the first thought that came to mind.

I tried to stay in place, but his pummeling was slowly pushing me closer and closer to the window, causing me to gradually straighten my body. Once I was nearly upright, his right hand swung around and started massaging my clit.

Picking up his pace, he applied more pressure to my overly sensitive nub and I fell over the edge, seeing stars as I climaxed harder than I ever had before. Screaming out his name, he picked up speed. His movements were becoming less controlled and I knew he was close.

"Fuck-k!" He slammed into me once more and stilled, breathing heavily against my back.

"Mmm, that was just what I needed, Tate." He pulled out of me and discarded the condom.

"So fucking good. I need more of that, soon." He walked over to his underwear and began sliding them on.

"Why don't you stay? A few more rounds sounds like the perfect way to end the night," I said as I made my way to the restroom.

Looking back, I saw him nodding in agreement, following me.

I had planned on just taking off my makeup but he had other plans. Tate turned the shower on and grabbed two towels off the rack. Realizing his motive, I couldn't find a reason to say no and stepped into the hot water with him following right behind me.

I woke up with Tate curled around me, still naked. The night before was exhilarating and exhausting. I was sure there was a trail of empty condom wrappers around the hotel room. Out of all the places he fucked me the night before, I think on top of the bathroom vanity was my favorite. After our rough romp in bed, he was gentle and sweet as I rode him. Watching our bodies as they intertwined from every angle in the mirrors was one of the hottest things I had ever seen. We took our time, memorizing each other as our skin glided together. He always made sure I came before he let himself go. I smiled at the memory and snuggled just a little closer to his warm body. I was sore in all the right places and thought I might make an exception and enjoy him for a few more days.

A stranger had never been more attentive to my wants and needs than Tate. Although we only saw each other one more time while he was on his trip, he made me feel wanted and loved. While the casualness of it all was what I needed, I still found myself thinking about Tate from time to time.

Chapter 2

Ryder

The drive from Los Angeles to San Diego was not enough time for me to figure out how to approach Reece. I was accustomed to having up-and-coming authors lie down at my feet, agreeing to whatever terms I saw fit. I never had to chase after an author and wasn't quite positive why I was going after Reece Edwards like she was the next big thing. I didn't have anyone at home holding me back from making the short trip and welcomed the change of pace.

After a little digging, *more like stalking*, I found out that she did kickboxing...I think? Her pictures were of the cover of the book she'd written, some downright sexy teasers, a beach photo—which included a pair of knockout tanned legs—and a kickboxing logo. I only hoped this meant she enjoyed actually *going* to kickboxing. Her photos were all I had to go off of so I had to start there.

When I searched what pages she liked, I saw that *Total Fitness 360* just happened to be in San Diego and had kickboxing classes every day at eleven a.m. It was a long shot, but if she was as much of a kickboxing addict as I was, she would be there at least two to three times a week.

I needed a drink, but it was just barely ten in the morning. I had been thinking about her all damn night and needed to get done with the bullshit so I could get back to my normal life.

Sinfully

Who was I kidding? My normal life had been hitting the gym before heading to work, working until seven or eight o'clock at night, making my way down to the bar, and going home to an empty apartment. Sure, friends were in the mix, but it wasn't part of the routine. I needed to get back out there and relieve some of my stress. I used to love quick fucks, and as soon as I was finished with Reece, I was going to treat myself.

I found a hotel close to the gym and hoped my plan would work out for me. It was a long shot, but I didn't know where else to start. I was just glad she didn't do some yoga or zumba shit because I didn't quite think I'd fit in there. I did kickboxing at home, anyway, so I wouldn't look out of place when the instructor started doing upper cuts, roundhouses, and burpies.

I changed into my workout clothes and made my way to the class. While the class was mostly women, there were at least seven men who seemed to take it very seriously.

Motherfuck goddamn motherfucker! I didn't know what she looked like. How did I miss that key piece of information? I couldn't just start calling out her name in class. *You're a smart one, Ryder.*

I didn't have time to figure out my plan of action because the instructor was already asking if they had any new people that day. I knew the names of the moves, so I didn't feel the need to raise my hand. No one had to know it was my first time here.

"I think we have a new one over here!!" I heard behind me on the left. *What the fuck? Who would do that?*

"Please don't be afraid to speak up, it's just nice to know if we need to go over how our class works so you'll be more comfortable," the barely legal bombshell of an instructor called out. I just waited until they realized I wasn't going to speak up.

"Becca, why don't we just start with the warm-up and I'll show him some pointers if needed. I don't mind at all," she said with a slight smirk while taking me in. *Was she checking me out? Ryder, stay focused! Turn off your pussy radar and get to work!*

Class began and I picked up on the speed and style of how Becca taught. She loved shaking her ass whenever possible. I wasn't complaining, but only a handful of the people in there should be shaking their asses. I caught a few quick glimpses of the mystery girl who called me out and she had to have been doing kickboxing for years. Her stance was perfect, hooks and jabs were at the right level and strength, and *damn* she shook her ass like a fucking pro. She caught me staring at least twice and I winked at her in acknowledgement. Her eyes were a deep blue in comparison to my light blue.

The hottie behind me stayed close enough to help if needed but let me do my thing. I hoped she'd realized I didn't need to be shown what to do. From the mirrors in front of me, I could see her watching me and I allowed myself to watch her, too. I mean, I was supposed to be learning this stuff, right?

After fifty minutes of turbo rounds, Becca began a cool down that allowed us to stretch before the class was over. It wasn't my favorite part since it felt more like yoga than stretching, but I couldn't make myself leave with the girl behind me still there. Seeing her stretching her hamstrings by spreading her legs apart and bending over, reaching the floor with her hands with ease, made me wish I was behind her. Her perfectly round ass in the air was begging to be squeezed and caressed. I couldn't get over the fact of how beautiful she was without trying. The workout had effectively managed to sweat off any of her makeup she might have had on and she was natural in front of me. While I was bent over, stretching as well, I snuck a peek between my legs to see her in a position that looked like a fun sex position. Thoughts of how flexible she might be flooded my brain and I had to work not to get hard.

I went through the whole class and had no idea who Reece was and if she was even here. That morning had been a waste of time and I wasn't sure what my next plan of action should be. I was grabbing my water bottle from the side of the room, getting ready to hit some weights, when I saw my new distraction walk up to me.

"I didn't mean to point you out like that. Most newbies who come in have no fucking idea what they're supposed to do and end up being a distraction from what is supposed to be going on. You didn't seem like a virgin out there, though." *So she isn't a total bitch. Huh.*

She was clearly in shape as I took in her lean stomach and killer legs. She had a feminine build that was clearly still toned and her luscious breasts were on display as she only wore black running shorts and a hot pink, front-zip sports bra. Her shirt was in her hand but she made no move to put it on.

"I understand. I'm just new to this gym. I'm actually in from LA on a business trip and thought I'd find a way to do my workouts while down here. I'm Ryder."

"Payton. Nice to meet you, Ryder. I'm about to head down to Starbucks for a drink if you want to join me." Her juicy, pink lips were wrapped around the top to her water bottle as she replenished herself. I blatantly watched before processing that she had asked me out. *This is going to be easier than I thought.*

I obviously wasn't going to get to meet Reece, so I figured there was nothing to lose. "Sounds like a plan."

Walking into kickboxing with a TDF in front of my normal spot made me grin like the Cheshire cat. "Mr. Tall, Dark, and Fuckable" had a lean waist with basketball shorts hanging low. His loosely fitted black t-shirt showed off his muscular arms. I knew he was new because I would remember that gorgeous face from anywhere. When he turned to see who had walked in the door, I noticed his striking blue eyes that left me stuck in place for a moment.

I wanted to see how he'd react when I called him out for being new, but he didn't buy into it. I figured he'd take me up on my offer to show him some of the moves just so he could be near my chest, but he didn't take that bait, either.

Ryder waited for me while I threw on a t-shirt and grabbed my bag. I really wished I had taken a shower or put on some lip gloss or mascara before my workout, but I figured I was about to sweat my ass off and wasn't expecting to see such an incredibly hot man while I was here. I had been at that gym long enough to know which guys were married, who were players, and who to stay away from. I had a few good guy friends from the gym but none of them sparked my interests. I never thought twice about how I looked when I got ready for the gym. It was close to my house and I usually headed straight home afterward, anyway. I made an exception that day by going to Starbucks since it gave me an excuse to stare at him openly as we got to know each other a little.

He let me lead the way out of the gym, saying bye to a few friends who were doing weights by the exit. I liked having a few friends who were always at the gym with me. They motivated me to push myself a little harder. As we walked down the street to the coffee shop, I decided to get to know Ryder a little better. No harm, right?

"Twenty questions. How old are you and where did you grow up?"

Sinfully

"Do you not know the rules of the game? You ask one question, I answer, then I ask you one, but I'll let it slide this time. Twenty-seven and Los Angeles my whole life," he said with a chuckle.

"Well, we're modifying the game. Is that okay with you? I'm twenty-eight and San Diego born and raised. We're kinda boring."

"I'm pretty sure the question was what made it boring. Where is the most embarrassing place you've had sex?"

I stopped mid-step and glared at him with my mouth open. He was laughing at my expression but did he really just ask that? I should have been appalled but I was slightly relieved. He would be my type of guy.

I wasn't looking for something serious, and with him being from Los Angeles and only here for a short amount of time, I didn't have to worry about him wanting more than a sexual relationship. With his body and personality so far, I was completely up for that.

Thinking for a moment, I decided on, "The dugout of a baseball field before a game in high school. I thought I'd get him ready for the game by surprising him with a kiss before he had to meet up with the team in the locker room and ended up with a little more than a kiss. You?"

"In the mosh pit of a Smashing Pumpkins concert. Everyone was hot, grinding up against each other and my girl at the time and I figured why waste the opportunity. We had music in the background that set the tempo, and at the time, I thought I had been pretty discreet about it. Everyone was so close; I wasn't the only guy with his front pressed up against a girl's ass. Looking back on it now, it was obvious what we were doing."

I cheered internally as I realized he was indeed straight. Maybe he was just focused on working out. I ordered my grande chai tea latte and he ordered the same. I was not expecting anything that came out of his mouth. I liked it.

"How long are you in town?"

"I haven't decided yet. Depends on if I can find what I'm looking for and secure it."

Well, wasn't he just a bit of mystery?

"Tell me something that no one else knows about you." Oh how I hated that question. If I haven't told ANYONE, there might be a reason!

"Umm, well, I used to think that when people were talking about 'big egos' or 'egos' in general, that they were...well, talking about penises. I thought that was its name and always acted like I didn't know what they were talking about and tuned out of the conversation." That wasn't so hard to say. Until I looked up and saw Ryder covering his face to hold back the laughter. Yep, I thought I had made the right decision in not talking about it to anyone.

"No shit! How long did it take you to figure out that little boys weren't trying to show you their goods? What if they were talking about a girl and her...ego?" He was still fucking laughing.

What a dick.

"That was the confusing part to me. I just kinda assumed they were talking about our hoo hoo's. Yes, I called them hoo hoo's when I was younger, so shut it. And I was, like, nine or ten when I finally figured it out."

"I was not expecting that to be what you confessed to not telling anyone but I understand why. It's okay, the first time I got a stiffy, I thought it was an accomplishment, so I tried over and over to get it to happen again. I was, like, six and thought I was something special. I remember my mom telling me to not bring it up to people again and my dad high-fived me. I was in hysterics because when my mom said 'not to bring it up again' I thought she meant my dick. Because she told me that, I may have 'brought it up' a few too many times and my dad finally had to have a talk with me about a man's parts."

"That's pretty funny! Kids get those that young? I never had brothers around so I guess I never had to hear about that." He was pretty damn cute.

Sinfully

Over the next two hours, and another drink for each of us, I felt like I had known Ryder for weeks or months. He was kind—flirtatious with a hint of mystery that kept me wanting more.

Something about him made me want to let my guard down. He was easy on the eyes but even easier to talk to. I was so used to letting people know only the basics about me and nothing deeper that I was pleasantly confused by my actions. I briefly wondered if it was because he was still only in town for a short period of time that I felt so at ease. Nothing would come of our lunch date so why not have some fun with it? Plus, if nothing else, I bet he was a rock star in bed.

He seemed to be contemplating something but I couldn't figure out what that might be so I decided to take a chance, "What are you thinking right now?"

"Is that your next question?"

"I guess it is…"

"I was trying to think of the best way to ask you to dinner and if tonight was too soon to see each other again." He said that as if he couldn't get it out of his mouth fast enough. Was he nervous?

I had to at least *act* like I didn't want to jump his bones right then. Ah hell, I never seemed to play the innocent girl very well, so why not go with what I knew?

"I'd love to go to dinner with you, although I didn't realize our time right now was done. Want to head down to the beach and talk a little more?" He stared at me for what seemed like a full minute with almost sadness in his eyes. *What is going on in his head right now?*

I couldn't help but laugh when I saw his face change to a dimple showing grin. I wanted to ask why he froze when I asked about going down to the beach but thought better of it.

Chapter 3

Ryder

The chick had some balls. We had just met, yet it seemed like we had known each other forever. It blew my mind that she wanted to continue our time together. Most girls would play hard to get and go to dinner then wait a few days before seeing each other again. It was a refreshing change to feel so carefree. She was fun and flirty without being obnoxious. I couldn't help but let my guard down with her.

While strolling down to the beach, I found out that she wrote children's books and was happily single. We talked about favorite foods, movies, and worst date experiences.

I assumed we would just walk along the beach and maybe get our feet wet. I hadn't been to the beach in almost a year, but was surprised when I didn't feel the urge to leave, or be alone for a few minutes in the sand.

I noticed that Payton was taking off her shoes while walking down to the sand so I followed suit. When she started taking off her shirt, I stopped dead in my tracks and just watched the sight before me. *I really need to stop staring. I'm becoming a borderline creeper.* When she turned and motioned me forward with her finger, I moved with a start toward her.

Please don't be a tease, please don't be a tease!

"Catch me if you can!!" she screamed as she raced into the water. *Who is this chick and where has she been all my damn life?* I didn't

Sinfully

want to leave her hanging but felt a sense of dread bubble up in my stomach and I wasn't sure I could go out there with her. She would think I was a pussy if I didn't follow her in. The day was not what I had envisioned at all, but I decided I needed to go with the punches when it came to her.

I stripped down to my sliders and jumped in to get to her. *Shit fuck that is cold!* She was waiting for me about twenty feet out with the most devious smile I'd ever seen. Still nervous, I headed out further in the water and hoped she didn't want to go much further. I would draw the line if we got out to the area surfers would be.

"Is this what you expected when you agreed to coffee with me?"

"I have a feeling this may be the best business trip I've ever been on, hands down." My balls were so fucking cold right then and I craved to have her warm me up. She was looking at me with want and desire in her eyes. I wanted Payton and I didn't want to wait.

We floated together in the water for what seemed like hours, just grasping to hold the other close. Words weren't needed between us. I felt her pebbled nipples up against my chest and slid her down just a tad so she could barely feel my excitement.

I pulled her closer to me and laid a kiss on her neck. *Atta boy, test her out and see if she's on the same page.* As I pulled back, she ground into me with that devious smirk I'd grown accustomed to in such a short amount of time.

"Kiss me. Now. Please." *Could she be any sexier?* She was demanding yet submissive. *So damn adorable.*

Our kiss was slow at first, as if figuring out the other's wants and needs. With her legs wrapped around my waist, there was no doubt she didn't realize how much I wanted her. Hell, even with the freezing water, I had a raging hard on. She messed with my hair and pulled herself tighter to me.

"You, my dear, are driving me crazy." She kept a slow, steady rhythm with her hips, causing me to let out a deep groan. Fuck, she felt good.

26

Leighton Riley

That kind of thing was supposed to happen *after* I had found Reece and signed her, but maybe things could be rearranged. I was not letting Payton go after one night. There were too many things I wanted to do with her.

She seemed so innocent with her children's books and being close to me would only damage her. Inevitably, she would find out what kind of dick I was and run as far away as her long, toned legs would take her. Fuck, a gorgeous woman was pressed up against me, practically fucking me with her eyes, and I was *already* thinking about her leaving.

"You like it. I can see it in your crystal blue eyes. You want me but you're trying to fight it. Let go and just feel," she said with such confidence, pulling me out of my own thoughts.

"You think you know me so well, huh? When I take you, I am going to make you scream so loud the neighbors will know my name."

Sinfully

Payton

I knew I was a whore face, but Ryder was hot, so it cancelled the whore-ness out, right? After swimming…err…floating together for a while, we both realized it was butt-ass cold and we should have never decided to go into the water. Oh well, it was still totally worth it.

I still couldn't figure out why I felt so drawn to him. All my instincts and rules for talking to men were thrown in the trash when I met Ryder. He made me feel like a girl who'd just been asked to prom by the quarterback. Feeling his rock hard abs against my softness and his arousal grinding against me in the water was enough to make me wet, and not from the ocean.

We headed back up to the beach to grab our randomly dispersed clothes and I noticed a new text message.

Ryan: Can't wait to see you tonight. Thanks for agreeing to meet with me after all these years.

Fuck my life. I meant, really, I agreed to meet up with Ryan a week ago and it was only to get him to stop bugging me. He was determined to prove that he was 'the one who got away' and how he hadn't stopped thinking about me since we broke up, wait for it, six years ago. He was the damn reason I stopped seeing men from San Diego! Who in their right mind would wait that long and still think they found their soul mate?

I was pretty sure he had a head injury or something since we broke up because the relationship I remembered was lackluster at best. I had never let him in like a good girlfriend would and never let myself be truly invested in the relationship. We both ended up cheating on each other. I was young and dumb, and I couldn't even say it was fun while it lasted.

Ryan had convinced me that he had grown up, figured himself out, and wanted to finally settle down. I think he said that thinking I

28

would jump in delight that he wanted to settle down, but he was sadly mistaken. I sure as hell hoped he didn't assume I wanted the same thing.

"You look like you've seen a ghost," Ryder said, successfully pulling me out of my memories.

"You're going to hate me."

"Already? What have you done in the past two minutes that would be enough to make me hate you?" He seemed a little fearful of what my answer might be. I could make up a lie about where I was going. *Wait, it doesn't matter if he knows I'm going on a date because we are just a fling, and I met him less than twelve hours ago!*

"Well I, uhh, forgot I already have a date tonight. Don't worry, though, I don't even like him and it was something that I agreed to a week ago just so I could get him to leave me alone." *Good job, Payton, you really sounded smooth there.*

"So you're going on a date with him so that you don't have to see him again? Now it all makes sense. Does he get a happy ending with that package?" He seemed a little bit upset but was taking it well, I guess.

He started walking back toward the gym without saying another word. It didn't matter if I had a date with someone that night. He should know we were a fling. Temporary. It was what I needed to keep reminding myself—he was temporary.

Chapter 4

Ryder

I needed to focus on what I came here to do. I could have my fun with women after I secured Reece. Reece…why did she have to be so damn stubborn? I decided to send her another email letting her know I was in town and wanting to meet with her. Her response?

Mr. Strom,

I love your persistence. Do you spend this much time with all of your prospective authors or just the female ones? Thank you for coming all the way down from Los Angeles to San Diego, the trip must have been exhausting. I assumed that my lack of response to your past emails would have pushed you on to your next conquest. I never planned on My Lips Are Sealed to be such a hit and am humbled by your interest in my story but feel like I have reached my goal in getting my story out there and do not need your publishing agency at this time.

Sinfully,

Reece Edwards

Bitch.

Sinfully

Why couldn't she just meet with me for one hour? Was that so hard to do? I was in her city and was practically *begging* to meet her and she didn't seem to care. I wasn't leaving San Diego until I had signed Reece.

Ms. Edwards,

I don't mind being exhausted as long as my reward is securing you with my agency. My ability to satisfy my authors' wants and needs is something I work hard to achieve. When we meet, I can go over your terms, benefits, and any questions you might have. Having me behind you will make everything worth it.

Until Then,

R. Strom

As I lay waiting for her response, I decided to text Payton to see how her non-date/date was going.

Me: I hope you remembered to shave. Wouldn't want to disappoint

Payton: Fuck you... I wax

Well, that's what I'll be thinking about while rubbing one off...

Me: Really now?

Payton: Mhmm. Btw, kill me now... He's talking about saving money on health insurance by getting married... WTF??

Me: Say the word and I'll come rescue you from the douche-nozzle

Payton: I don't need a prince, I just need a real man who has normal guy problems

32

Leighton Riley

Me: Tell him you have to get home to BOB and cut the night short. By the time he realizes what you're talking about, you'll be well on your way to orgasm number 2.

Payton: You're not offering your...time and services? You're passing me along to fucking BOB?

Me: In due time, sweetheart

I knew I could be a dick, but there was something about Payton that intrigued me yet kept me at an arm's length away. It was like she was holding back from letting me get to know her. Hell, I knew I wasn't going to let her all the way in since we would probably only see each other another handful of times. The problem was that I wanted to dig deeper with her. I hardly knew anything about her, yet I was thinking about her in a hotel room all alone, when she basically told me I could have my way with her. I should have jumped at the chance.

Damn it. No, she needed to be a one-night stand—maybe two nights—but no more than that. What was I doing with her? I should have been out at a bar meeting women to have a little fun with and not have the obligation to talk to again since I wasn't from the area.

Two hours and several Jack and Cokes later, I was determined that my night at the bar was a waste. None of the women sparked my interest and I just wasn't feeling it. Sophia, the bartender, looked like she could have been one of Charlie's Angels with her dark brown hair, green eyes, and a perfectly round ass. With her subtle flirting, I was sure she was pulling in some serious tips.

Normally, I would have already chosen which girl I wanted to be with and be well on my way to making her comfortable enough with me to allow her to accept going home with me. My cock didn't twitch for a single one of them, and he had pretty good judgment, so I trusted him.

33

Sinfully

"There are quite a few women eye-fucking you right now, Sugar. Why aren't you taking your pick?" Sophia said as she handed me another Jack and Coke.

"They aren't who I want."

"You sure look like they're what you need. A handsome guy like you? A girl would be crazy not to jump at the chance." I thought she was just trying to make me feel better but I liked her attitude. She was hot enough and seemed like she would understand my need for one night.

"What time do you get off?" I figured why not give *her* a go.

"The first time or second?" she nonchalantly replied as she made six shots of tequila for a bachelorette party behind me. I couldn't help but arch an eyebrow her direction.

Yep. She will do just fine.

Payton

My mind did me a favor and apparently had made me forget about how much of a sleazy douche Ryan was. Not only was he boring, he was always trying to get out of paying for shit and made me feel bad for ordering chicken and shrimp. He told the waiter my food was undercooked and that it was unacceptable. That happened while I was in the restroom, so I got to go back to an apologetic manager and a waiter who looked like he was about to cry. I hadn't eaten it all, but I'd had more than enough to figure out it was cooked just fine. When I gave him my evil glare, he just shrugged his shoulders and said he'd handled it.

I was trying to come up with excuses to leave when Ryder texted me. I wasn't in a good mood and his texts weren't making it any better. He told me to fucking use my vibrator instead of going over to his hotel.

I hated myself for feeling a pull toward him. Every time I was with Ryder that day, I wanted to jump him. When he touched me, I felt the connection and it was so unnatural for me, I wasn't sure what to do with the new feelings. I needed to get a handle on things. After reading his texts, I knew I wasn't what he went for, anyway. I wasn't going to let myself fall for him.

I know I smelled bad after my workout, but I figured he would understand. He seemed to enjoy my company in the water, so what gave? After letting Ryan know what a friendly gentleman he was, I quietly excused myself and hailed a cab. He didn't have to know my leaving the table also meant leaving the restaurant, but I figured he would realize sooner or later that I wasn't interested. It was just easier on my end. I knew I was a bitch and should have let him know I enjoyed the night and politely let him know I was leaving, but Ryan didn't seem to deserve that politeness from me. He needed to realize how much of an arrogant bastard he truly was and I smiled at the thought that maybe I helped him reach that conclusion.

I was done with men for the night and just wanted to get home to a bottle of wine and my DVR recordings of *The Vampire Diaries*. I needed to get away from San Diego. Ryan had reminded me of why I didn't date, ever. Ryder had been around for all of one day and I was already out of sorts. Guys didn't usually get to me like he did.

I decided to still go to kickboxing the next morning even though I knew Ryder might be there. When I got to the gym, he was doing some ab work.

My oh my!

I went and did some leg work just so I could be behind him and ogle him. He gave me a head nod and a wink when he saw me watching him.

He could totally be one of my new book boyfriend guys. Channing Tatum, Scott Eastfield, and the almighty Ian Somerhalder were some of my repeat models for book boyfriends, but it was always nice to mix it up and get some *real* guys in the lineup.

The way his muscles bulged as he worked out was insanely hot. He had his Dr. Dre Beats on and was completely in the zone. What was it about guys in a cut off shirt with big ol' headphones that made a girl want to drop her panties?

Focus, Payton!

I didn't realize he had gotten off the bench and was making his way toward me. His shorts were hung low, and when he lifted his arm to get a drink of water, I could see his happy trail of brown hair along with the V that led down to his manhood. Upon reaching me, he asked, "Can you spot me?" I looked dumbfounded as I thought to myself, *Uhh, yeah, I already see you, dumbass!* I allowed myself one more gaze over his body but apparently I wasn't discrete enough.

"Earth to Payton, I need a spotter sometime today." He had that sideways grin that made my core tingle.

"Sure. Of course. How was your night? Do anything fun and exciting?" He gave me a questioning gaze as he settled onto the bench. Did I bring up something he didn't want to talk about?

"Nothing worth discussing. What about you?"

"Oh, it was just dandy. After leaving Ryan at the restaurant, I had quite a night with Damon and Stefan." Ryder glanced at me while finishing up a set and setting the bar back in position. He was breathing heavily and his arms were glistening with sweat. Even sweaty, he looked delectable.

"Sounds like it didn't quite go as planned. I thought you would have been out with Ryan later." He seemed nervous and a bit...upset? He was adding more weight to the bar for his next go around.

"Nah, I knew I needed to leave after the asshat embarrassed the waiter. I was trying to lighten the mood but he still seemed unsettled.

"Well, I'm glad you found something better to occupy your time with, Payton. You look like you had a long night."

"How sweet of you."

His eyes were a darker shade of blue than before and his fists were tightening and releasing at a rapid speed. "I forgot I've got to be somewhere. Good seeing you. Catch ya later, Payt." With that, he left without looking back.

I had a weird sense that he was upset with me but couldn't figure out what the hell I had done, or why I cared.

Kickboxing was already half over, so I decided to just do a little cardio and call it a day. I couldn't get thoughts of Ryder out of my mind. I wished I could say they were just sexual thoughts, but I wanted to see him again, wanted to see him smile, and wanted to feel close to him. I listened to *Bleed It Out* by Linkin Park on repeat during my run to try to get in the zone but it was a waste of time.

Shortly afterward, I realized my workout was useless and decided to meet up with Chloe to have a little girl time. We met at the nail salon and gossiped over which of our friends were getting engaged, which were rumored to be pregnant, and who the daddy could be.

It was what Chloe was good at—distracting me from my life by talking about how ridiculous the lives of our former classmates were. She was always in the know but could keep a secret when necessary. Thankfully, she knew how important it was for me to keep my book under my pen name and not have anyone find out it was me who wrote it. Maybe someday I'd come out and let people know I was Reece Edwards, but at that time, it was still my current life and I didn't have plans to change it.

I filled her in on meeting Ryder and how I couldn't stop thinking about him. Our talks were normally her telling me about guys who were worthy of dating because of their career, family background, and portfolio, followed by me shooting each and every one of them down. While she had been with Grayson for years, it didn't mean she wasn't looking to upgrade if she saw something better. Grayson was convenient for her and seemed to treat her well. He seemed a little fake to me, but she obviously saw something in him to keep him around for that long. She wasn't a saint, but she'd been there for me through all of my tough times, and I had learned not to care about her ways with men. She knew that I didn't really care about a guy's 'stats' since I wasn't exactly looking for a ring anytime soon.

"So, have you had a chance to ride the Ryde?" She couldn't even say it without snickering. Albeit, it was funny.

"That's not all that I care about, Chlo!" I joked with her. "I also like long walks along the beach and candlelit dinners." *Ah, fuck. I guess our rendezvous on the beach yesterday kind of counted as romantic, right?*

"He's kissed you from what it sounds like. So what? You're spending way too much time thinking about some random who isn't even going to be here in a few weeks, anyway. This is so unlike you. He should be the perfect guy for you since he doesn't live here and you won't have to see him after the fun is over. This is almost like Vegas being hand delivered to you! Have fun with him if you want, but don't let him get to you. If that doesn't work for you, why not just head over to Sin City and really get your mind off him? I could come with this time?"

She always offered to go with me, and I always turned her down. I went there to escape reality for a few days and relax. If I found a cute guy while I was there, it was a bonus. If I brought Chloe with me, we would have to go shopping, do touristy things, and only go to the newest and hottest bar. I liked to stay more low-key and go with the flow while I was there. Chloe was the opposite of that.

Chloe was right. I couldn't let Ryder get close to me, that fact I knew for sure. We could only be fuck buddies, and that would be it. That way, when he left, it wouldn't hurt. I could get away for a few days and Vegas was definitely the place to forget about Ryder. That was what I needed, but my body was calling bullshit.

When I got home from getting my nails done, I had already made up my mind that I would start a load of laundry, pull out a bottle of Moscato, and figure out where I went next with my writing career. I wasn't sure if I should just keep writing children's books or stick with fun and dirty writing. Children's books were fun, easy, and stress free, but it was hard coming up with stuff that hadn't already been written. It took me twenty-five topics to search for before finding one that hadn't been written about multiple times.

I hadn't planned on writing about different types of parents, but there weren't many stories talking about what kind of life I'd been through. My first book was about adopted children and how foster families could be just as loving as real homes. That was how my writing niche was born. My next book dealt more with losing a parent and how, in time, the pain lessens but didn't ever go away. I made sure to include how using the support of friends and family could help the process and things would start getting a little better every day. It wasn't my favorite topic, but I was knowledgeable on the subject and wanted to provide firsthand experiences.

I was curious how it would feel to write another 'adult book' but make it mainly fictional next time. I could write the characters to have their own quirks with some major plot twists that would grab the reader's attention. Since I used Tracy Lowe as my pen name for children's literature, I could still write under Reece Edwards for any new 'smut' books that I wanted to publish. The more I thought about it, the better it sounded. I liked the idea of creating my own path for my characters instead of one that had already been laid out.

After laundry was completed, I grabbed my glass of wine, my laptop, and my mail and settled down into my comfy recliner. I wasn't too fond of using my trust fund for anything but major purchases like my house and car, so I when I got my first decent size check from *My Lips Are Sealed*, I splurged and bought a chaise lounge and a recliner so that I had a place to read and a place to write.

If I was writing, I would also be drinking. A little alcohol allowed me to be more creative and open-minded to different scenarios that played out in my head. I opened up my mail, while I was waiting for my laptop to turn on, and skipped the bills to see if I had anything worth looking at.

Shit. Really?

I held yet another letter that had the power to make my heart skip a beat and checked to make sure the doors were locked. There was never a return address or postage on them which led me to believe it was purposely placed by hand in my mailbox. The first letter was sent to me a month or so before and it simply stated, "I know who you are." I took it as a joke but saved the note in my filing cabinet just in case.

Something about it gave me the creeps but it seemed harmless. The envelope that was in my hands had the same wax seal that the first one had. No one used wax seals anymore! That alone creeped me the fuck out. The wax was a shade of deep red and the seal was a simple but elegant R. Without even opening the note, I was freaking out a tad bit. Not many people knew where I lived and I made a point to not bring guys over.

I broke the seal and carefully pulled the letter out of the envelope. A Reese's Peanut Butter Cup wrapper fell out along with it.

SWEEt LIKE CANDY. BE CAREFUL Not to OVERINDULGE.

I dropped the letter along with the candy wrapper as if it were on fire. They knew who I was and knew where I lived. I expected a few people to find out randomly; I probably wasn't the best at covering my tracks, but I thought it would be innocent fans who I could give a paperback to and they'd be on their way. This seemed more dark and twisted. I felt like I should burn the letter but decided it was best to file it away with the first one. At least if I wound up dead in some alley, the police might find them and figure out who the sick person was.

Needless to say, writing was not going to happen after that incident. I checked all the windows and locks before setting my security alarm and curled up with a blanket and watched *Vampire Diaries*. I found myself able to think about the problems on the show instead of my real life problem. I could deal with it another day; I needed time to process what the hell was happening and didn't like the conclusions I was coming up with so far.

Ryder

Seeing Payton in her short shorts and tank top almost made me drop the weights I had in my hands. I wanted to see her again but didn't want to look desperate. I decided to work my arms since it would be the most noticeable immediately afterward. My arms always looked their best right after a workout, and I made a habit of doing a little arm work before dates. It was a trick I learned in high school and had just become routine for me.

I knew I was trying to impress Payton and wasn't even sure she would be at the gym. I also knew that I needed to meet with an old friend at some point while in town but wasn't ready for that yet. In the meantime, I thought I could at least see where things went with Payton, hence why I was at the gym two days in a row while out of town.

God, she was beautiful.

I tried to focus on my ab work while knowing she was behind me. The wall in front of me was all mirrors so I knew the instant she got on the machine behind me. I was curious why she didn't come up and talk to me, but this way I would be able to eye-fuck her as I worked out. Seeing her legs in short shorts never got old and her motivation and dedication was clear when you looked into her eyes.

After my night with the bartender, I knew getting Payton out of my system was not going to be an easy task, so I came to the conclusion that I should give in a bit and have some fun with her.

The dark circles under her eyes made it apparent she had been up pretty late. With the texting that occurred the night before, I had my doubts that she spent a great amount of time with Ryan. I knew I had turned her down last night, but I was conflicted.

Just seeing her tits squeezed into that hot pink sports bra made me want to take her on the bench in front of everyone. I was in a constant state of arousal around her.

I had planned on teasing her a bit and apologizing, but when she started talking about other guys, I lost it. While Sophia had amazing tongue and hip skills, she wasn't doing it for me and I kept picturing myself with Payton. I was finally able to get off when I started picturing Payton as the woman riding me instead. Then I instantly felt guilty for using her and rejecting Payton's offer.

Payton obviously had the same idea as me. I couldn't help but wonder if her flirting with me was just part of her normal personality or if she was at least attracted to me.

I didn't want to hear any more of how amazing her night was and had to get out of there. I wanted to hang out with her more but didn't know how to get past the jealous feelings I had going on, which by the way, I had no idea where they were coming from. The whole reason I went to the gym today was to get to see her again and I ended up leaving after thirty minutes.

Fuck.

I made the decision to give Tristen a call. I knew I should have talked to him months ago, but I just wasn't there yet. He probably hated me, but the longer I dragged things on, the further apart I knew we would grow.

I went back to the hotel to shower and tried to think about what I was going to say when I saw him. We had been best friends since first grade and used to talk or hang out a few times a week. I could only imagine the earful I was going to get when I got to the beach.

Chapter 5

Payton

I wanted to see him again. I hated that my mind kept wandering to thoughts about him, which was not okay. He seemed so genuine the first time we hung out and seemed to be a totally different person the day before. Before getting him out of my system, I wanted to at least spend a little quality time with him. After booking my room in Vegas, I decided to text him.

Me: Meet with me?

Ryder: I'm with an old friend right now, come by my hotel at 8? I'm in suite 3404. I'll let them know to let you up.

Me: That'll work, see you soon

I still had three hours before meeting up with Ryder, so I decided I'd check my emails and get caught up on my life on social media. I noticed I had an email from R. Strom about my book and would be lying if I wasn't smiling at the thought that he was still trying to get me to sign with him. He also didn't seem as old and boring as I'd originally thought.

I knew it probably wasn't the most professional email I could have replied with, but damn, he was flirting, too. I didn't really intend on ever meeting with him so I decided it could be fun to mess with him a little.

Sinfully

Whenever I was on Facebook, I tried to respond to any questions or messages readers had posted on my page. I had numerous questions about when and where I would be signing next but didn't have the heart to tell them 'never.' I always responded by letting them know I was working on research and didn't have anything coming up.

I was, however, generous in giving away copies of my books to bloggers and readers to help keep my name out there. I gave in by sending signed paperbacks to fans who requested them. That way, they got what they would want from me at a book signing, they just didn't get to meet me.

After getting ready to meet up with Ryder, I decided not to overanalyze the situation and to live in the moment. He'd be a welcomed distraction from the letter I received earlier. I would be leaving for Vegas in the morning and wanted to see him before I left. I knew it might be the last time I saw him but I wanted to at least know if the feeling I felt the day before was mutual.

Ryder

Meeting with Tristen had been harder than I thought. Seeing him brought back all the memories of Cami like it was yesterday. *God, I miss her so damn much.* Not a day went by that I didn't feel the guilt of not being able to help her. To be honest, the first time I'd been back in the water since that day ten months ago was the previous day with Payton. San Diego used to be our 'go to' spot and we could spend the entire day at the beach without even realizing it. So much had changed, yet it still felt like everything remained the same.

Tristen and I met at the beach at his request. He must have been more comfortable being out there than I was, but I didn't see a board around, so I figured he hadn't planned on going into the water.

"I forgot how much you look like her," he said, coming up and giving me a hug before sitting in the sand.

"I heard that happens when you're fraternal twins."

We sat in silence for what felt like hours. *God, I don't want to do this.* Seeing him was opening up emotions I'd kept hidden for the better part of ten months and I wasn't ready for them to come spilling all out at that moment.

"I miss you, bro. I know it's been rough for you and I'm glad you finally made it down here, man." Tristen had gone to college with Cami and me, but he officially moved to San Diego two years ago and roomed with Cami while I stayed in L.A. with the publishing company.

They had tried to persuade me to move down here with them, but I knew my life was set up to be in publishing and to take over the company one day. I was able to visit at least once a month and they visited me as well. It all worked out pretty well until last July when everything changed.

"Have you been out in the water lately?"

"Nah, man, lately I've just been coming down here when I need to get away from everyone else. I come here when I need

Sinfully

advice or need to get something off my chest. This is where I feel closest to her. I haven't surfed again, though. I really just come down and put my legs in and lie on the beach."

I could tell he spent a lot of time down here. Besides his shaggy, beach-blond hair, he had a deep tan that stood in stark contrast to his light green eyes. He wasn't a pretty boy, but he definitely got attention from women, even though he hardly ever reciprocated.

I swallowed the lump in my throat before attempting to respond. He seemed to realize it was going to take me a minute and waited patiently. Cami always loved that Tristen was so patient and relaxed.

"I'm sorry I haven't come to see you sooner, man. I've thought about you and how hard this must be for you, too. I mean, you lived with her and were as close as friends could be. I got in the car to come see you a few times but just never made it out of the city."

I forgot how easy it was to talk with him. He had that personality that got you to spill your guts without even realizing it. I used to hate him for that very thing but was finding it comforting at the time. I hadn't talked to anyone about Cami in a while and it was nice to know he had amazing memories of her just like I did.

He seemed lost in thought, trying to figure out the right thing to say. The comfortable silence allowed us both to reflect on how things used to be when we were all together.

"Ryder, jeez, why did it have to be her? She was perfect. She was one of the good ones. She was going to be a child psychologist; she wanted to help people. She was my everything." His head hung between his legs and I knew he was trying to hide the fact that he was crying.

"I know, I've told myself the same thing. She seemed so happy, I mean, even more than normal right before it happened. You know?"

Tristen lifted his head and looked at me as if I shouldn't have known that about her. It took me for a loop and I was a little confused.

48

Leighton Riley

"Did she ever talk about...us?"

"She was always talking about what the two of you were doing. You were inseparable, so of course she talked about you guys together." I still wasn't sure why he had a torn look on his face.

"Ryder, I meant, did she ever mention *us*?" It took me a second to register what he had been trying to tell me. I was such a bad friend and brother. How did I not know they were in a relationship? The signs were there but I never put two and two together.

I realized I still hadn't responded and saw sadness and guilt wash over his face. "She hadn't formally mentioned it, no. I didn't realize, Trist. I am so, so sorry, bro. I should have been here for you through this. We could have dealt with it together."

He seemed relieved for a moment then broke down again. In all the years I'd known him, I had never seen him cry like that. I was at a loss for words and didn't do the best in situations like that. I never knew the right thing to say or do. It was part of the reason I had been dealing with the loss alone.

"I am glad you came down here. I've wanted to talk with you for a while but never knew when it would be okay to talk about her with you."

"Tristen, you can always talk to me about her. She will *always* be a part of us and will always be watching down on us. I promise to be here for you from now on."

"Thanks, man, I appreciate it."

"I've got to get running, but why don't we meet up Friday down here? It's her...our... birthday." I hoped that wasn't too much on him, but I really thought we should spend it together, remembering the good times instead of thinking about her not being there with us that year.

Getting up and brushing the sand off his pants, he called out as he started making his way back up to the parking lot, "I had already planned on spending my day down here with her. See you then, Ryde."

49

I didn't even know what I was supposed to do. I knew I said I had to go, but I felt like I needed to spend a few minutes alone on the beach so I could talk with her. Tristen was right about the fact that I could feel her presence there. I missed her so damn much it hurt.

Feeling the sand slide between my fingers, I welcomed the grainy feel and relished having the sun beat down and warm the sand and my skin. The beach used to be my safe haven, but ever since the accident, it only plagued my nightmares.

Closing my eyes, I tilted my head toward the sky and began a conversation that was long overdue. Even before I began to speak, I could feel the lump in my throat growing bigger by the second, but I knew I needed to do it.

"Hey, sis. How ya hanging up there? I hope they have some of the biggest waves up in heaven for you to surf. I miss hearing your laugh and all the curse words that flowed freely no matter who you were talking to. I think Tristen really misses you, too. Thank you for watching over him while I wasn't around. It was shitty of me, but I know you've been looking down and keeping us safe, Cam. I'm sorry I haven't come down to visit you more. Can you believe we're going to be twenty-eight on Friday? I'll be here to spend the day with Tristen and you. I wouldn't be surprised if we saw some fireworks light up the sky at night. You always did like to go out with a boom. Goodnight, Cami. Sweet Dreams."

I ended up leaving the beach a half hour later and knew I was in no condition to be an active participant in hanging out with Payton. The problem was that I wanted to be near her and see her again already. I made it back to the hotel in no time and was in the shower at twenty minutes to eight. As I made my way out of the bathroom, my phone buzzed, indicating a message from Zoe.

Zoe: Long time no see stranger. I miss you, how have you been?

Ugh, I did not need her texting me at that moment. We hadn't spoken in two years and didn't really have anything to talk about.

Leighton Riley

Every time she and her latest boyfriend broke up, she would try to get in touch with me. I decided I didn't owe it to her to even respond but I highly doubted she would let up. I'd probably be getting phone calls and voicemails by the next day if I didn't say something. Needless to say, she was a cold-hearted bitch and I couldn't believe I wasted two years with that cheating whore. But hey, no hard feelings, right?

Me: Now's not a good time Zoe. Have a great life

I heard a faint knock on the door and realized I had gotten sidetracked and was still in a towel. Looking down, I knew she would be perfectly fine with me greeting her that way. I couldn't help but saunter over to the door with a smile on my face.

I swung open the door to find her fidgeting with the zipper of her purse and biting her lip. She smelled heavenly—floral with a hint of spice. When she looked up at me, her eyes gave her apprehension away. I wasn't sure what made her felt that way, but I was sure I'd be able to make her feel at ease as the night progressed.

"Hey there, sweetheart. Ready for some fun? Come on in and make yourself comfortable." I stepped aside, giving her free rein to walk on in, but she stayed in the hallway, not moving an inch. She gave me a onceover before looking back into my eyes.

"I was scared this wasn't your room. Uhh. Umm. Why aren't you dressed?" She was pretty cute. Payton was just openly staring at me and blushing red in embarrassment. She was fidgeting with her fingers, showcasing her nervousness.

"I was just about to; I lost track of time. Make yourself at home and I'll go change. Want something to drink? You can raid the mini bar while you wait."

"Nah, I'm good. This view is amazing!" She stepped in further toward the floor-to-ceiling windows, taking in the view of the city to one side and the beach to the far left. I watched her for a moment before heading to get ready.

51

Sinfully

"I'm flattered, really, but I don't think I should stay in just a towel all night. It would be a hassle trying to keep it closed." *I love fucking with her.*

She gave me that 'you think you're so clever' look and turned back toward the windows.

As I strode to the master bedroom, I decided to keep the door open, just in case she decided to walk on by. I dropped my towel while pulling out a new pair of boxer briefs and changed into them before looking for my black jeans and grabbing a white Henley shirt. Realizing that she probably wasn't going to be taking a peek, I met her back out in the main room and turned on some music before motioning her to have a seat on the couch with me. She seemed unsettled with being alone in my room with me but she was the one who spoke first.

"You left the gym in a hurry this morning. You seemed a little on edge. Is everything alright?"

I contemplated my answer to her question for a moment. I left the gym because I didn't want to hear about her and other guys, but also knowing that I had to meet with Tristen added fuel to the fire.

"I've just got a lot going on. Nothing to worry about. I'm glad you wanted to come over, though." I wanted to touch her, even if it was just on her thigh, but I didn't want to scare her off. From the look in her eyes, she looked like she was ready to run. I moved my arm so that it was draped over the top of the couch as an inviting gesture but she stiffened immediately.

"It was probably stupid for me to drop by. I'm not really sure what I'm doing here. I should go."

I noticed her glancing between my eyes and lips and wanted to taste her so badly. In the dress she wore, her perky breasts were just begging to be grabbed, nibbled, and sucked. Oh the things I could do to her. She wanted me, but was scared for some reason. I could see the war going on behind those deep blue eyes. Her passion and desire were trying to be tamed by logic.

I needed to kiss her. She was waiting for me to tell her to stay or go and her leaving right then wasn't an option. Her lips had a slight gloss to them and I lost all coherent thoughts. Leaning toward her, she instantly followed suit and moved an inch closer as well. Payton looked up at me with questioning eyes. I grabbed the back of her head and brought her within an inch of my lips, feeling her breath against my skin.

"I think you should stay," I whispered right before my lips touched hers. A shiver coursed through her body and the sensation drove me insane. She let me lead the kiss and opened her mouth with no question when my tongue traced against her lips. She moved closer to me with one hand playing with my hair and the other on my thigh, teasingly close to my swelling cock. She didn't move that hand any further up but it was close enough to drive me crazy. She moved toward me with motive, straddling me on the couch as she rubbed herself against my hardness. *Oh, sweet Jesus.* I could feel her warmth and smell her arousal. She began kissing me passionately all the while grinding herself against my cock. My raging hard-on was pressed uncomfortably against my jeans and I didn't know why I bothered changing out of the towel. All I could think about was tasting her, making her beg for it, and then finally taking her.

My hands began at the edge of her dress and slowly started massaging her thighs, working my way inward. I loved how toned her legs were and thought about them being wrapped around my waist, tightening as she came for me. Before getting to her wetness, I glided over her toned stomach and took her succulent breasts into my hands, all the while kissing her neck and moving my lips lower to her chest. I wanted to get her out of those clothes and devour every inch of her body. The noises coming from her were so fucking sexy I would be glad to last two minutes, but that just meant there would be a few rounds that night, of which I was game.

Before I could get her dress and bra off, Payton had moved my hand back down between her legs, showing me what she really wanted.

Holy hell, she isn't wearing any panties. I looked up and she shrugged her shoulders, all the while smirking deviously.

I wasn't expecting that. I was happy to oblige. I wasn't used to a girl showing me exactly what she wanted and *fuck me* it was a turn on. She continued kissing me and riding my hand as I slid two fingers into her tight, wet pussy. She was slick with want and having her pulse around my fingers was incredible.

"Fuck, you're wet for me, baby. Is this what I do to you?" Her response was a moan and I accepted that answer. I could feel her tighten around my fingers, so I slowed up a bit, drawing out her pleasure.

"Oh, Ryder, please don't stop. I need this." She opened her eyes slowly, showing the desire and want she had for me.

"Mmm, Payton, I need to taste you. I'll let you come, but not until I get what I want." With that, I took her in my arms and laid her on the couch with me still between her legs. She wasn't lying when she said she waxed. It was magnificently smooth and slightly swollen with want, just waiting for me.

Using my tongue on her clit to form slow circles and sucking occasionally, I inserted my fingers and curled them just a little to reach her spot. I was able to feel her birth control ring and silently cheered for that. The arching of her back gave me the idea that she was enjoying it as much as I was. I wanted to be inside her so damn badly that I was actually in pain, but I wanted to feel her pulse around my fingers and taste her as she came for me.

She began writhing against me and pulled my face closer to her clit. When she started coming for me, I switched my fingers for my tongue and kept pressure on her clit with my thumb. She tasted so sweet and was screaming my name as she rode the wave. I licked her sweetness clean, and when I looked up, she had the most content look on her face. No other woman had ever tasted so delicious that I wanted to go back for more the moment I brought her to ecstasy.

Without saying a word, she moved between my legs beneath me. I was pretty sure she was the most amazing woman in the world. I didn't have to say a word about returning the favor, and just seeing and feeling her come undone was satisfaction enough for me. Not saying that I was going to turn down what she was about to do to me.

After unzipping my jeans and sliding them down just a little, she helped me spring free from my boxer briefs. She licked her lips as she stared at my dick. Payton started at the bottom of my cock and licked her way to the head, twirling her tongue once she got there. Her mouth felt incredible, so hot and wet as she stroked me ravenously in and out of her mouth.

"Oh fuck, that feels good." Her hungry gaze was on me the entire time which was almost enough to make me come on the spot. One hand was playing gently with my sac while the other grasped my shaft, firmly moving in a steady motion up and down as she flicked her tongue along the rim of my swollen tip. She took nearly all of me in and feeling the back of her throat was about to make me explode each time it happened. She was making little noises as she took me in over and over and the vibrations felt beyond amazing. Every now and then she would make that *pop* sound when my cock came out of her mouth and she must have realized it was turning me the fuck on. I couldn't help but think that she was enjoying it, too.

I held back as long as I could, and as if she could sense I was about to blow, she grasped onto my hips and started sucking fervently with need. I had no choice but to come in her mouth, and feeling her swallow around my sensitive head was unreal. Sweet Jesus, I couldn't tell you how much better it was feeling her warm mouth around me as I came instead of creaming on her tits or ass. Sure, that was a nice visual, but feeling her warm throat against my head as I came was unbelievable. Only after the spasms subsided did she look up at me with pride in her eyes and a naughty smile.

"Let's play a game, shall we?" There was a hint of mischief in her eyes as she said it. I figured that would be all the fun—for at least a little while, so we could both recharge—but she was already ready for more it seemed.

"At this point, I'm game for anything." I really hoped it involved finishing what we started.

Sinfully

"Poker. Texas Hold 'Em specifically. Whoever loses the hand has three options. They can take off an article of clothing, take a shot, or tell the other person something personal. I saw you had a bottle of tequila on the table and we'll have to make do with the glasses they gave us to do the shots. You still game, Ryder?"

"And you just assume I have a deck of cards that I travel with? Or did you come here prepared, Miss Payton?"

"I'm *always* prepared."

"Deal me in." I took a look at her outfit and counted that she had on three articles of clothing and her heels. I might not be the best at poker but I had on, shit, three articles of clothing. Why didn't I put on socks or an undershirt? Oh well, it just meant that we could get to more... pressing matters sooner which was completely fine by me.

An hour later, I was in my boxer briefs and she was in her bra and we were considerably drunk. I found out she once almost got together with her friend Chloe while drunk and they decided to see what was so amazing about being with another girl. She let me know that kissing and playing with each other's tits was as far as they went because they were both grossed out when they realized they were about to see each other's pussy.

I might have told her that I once called a girl I was having sex with by her sister's name in bed because I had really wanted her sister but settled for the next best thing.

She was currently lying on my lap while I played with her tits in one hand and her hair in the other. She had the silkiest brown hair that would be perfect for pulling. She was almost asleep and kept mumbling about how much she wanted me and needed to leave early in the morning. I didn't want to wake her up and I was content lying on the couch with her. It was the closest I had felt toward a woman in a long time. I was strangely at peace when I laid my head back on the couch, closed my eyes, and hoped the feeling never ended.

I jerked awake when I heard my cell phone going off. I must have dozed off at some point. Getting up and finding my phone in

Leighton Riley

the jeans that were in a pile on the floor, I noticed I had two missed calls from the office. I wasn't too worried about that at the moment, they could handle whatever the problem was. Where did Payton go? I remembered her being in my lap last night but didn't hear or see her anywhere.

Then I saw a piece of paper next to the bottle of tequila. Notes were never good.

Ryder,

I had a blast with you last night. I've never felt the way I feel when I'm with you and it scares the hell out of me. I feel like a 16-year-old with a mad crush on you but I know it's crazy. I think about you constantly and want to jump you every time I see you. I decided to head out of town for a few days to get away from everything and think. I don't know how long you'll be in town, but I'll text you when I get back. By the time you read this, I'll probably already be lounging by the pool or hitting up the tables.

Sinfully,
Payton <3

I stared at that fucking letter for a good five minutes, just reading it over and over. Lounging by the pool. Hitting up the tables.

"Sinfully...sinfully," I said to myself out loud. *Who signs a letter that way?*

It seemed familiar, but I was more concerned about the fact that she said she wanted me but still left. She didn't even tell me where she was going or how long she'd be there. With having no more clues of finding Reece and not yet ready to spend day after day around Tristen, seeing Payton was a highlight of my day. *Wait. Oh my fucking hell, what the fuck? No. No. No. Really? No.*

Sinfully. Reece signed her emails with 'Sinfully.' Payton said she wrote children's books and *My Lips Are Sealed* was definitely NOT a children's book. I meant, hell, I had a hard-on from just *thinking* about the book. How did it not come up in conversation? Did I ever tell her what my business trip was for? I couldn't even remember.

Reece had been so adamant about not meeting. Was it because she was really Payton? Why would Payton want to hide such amazing work and not put her name to it? Oh fuck, was Payton going to Vegas to get away from me and find a different random guy to pleasure her for a night?

My head was starting to hurt and the more I thought it out, the more pissed I was becoming. She lied to me. Well, maybe she just failed to mention her other type of writing, but still, I would have liked to have known Reece was fucking in front of me the whole time.

I thought we were just having fun with each other, so why would she feel the need to run off? Did I just let my prospective author slip out of my hands because she didn't want to be around me? Yet another confirmation that I couldn't involve my dick when working with authors; it never ended well for me, or him.

I needed a drink. Looking over at the nearly empty bottle of tequila, I poured what was left into my mouth before realizing it was definitely more than a shot or two. I felt like I should go for a workout to clear my head but I didn't want to go to the same gym Payton went to. I knew she wouldn't be there but I just didn't want to be around it right then.

The beach. *I could go down there again, I think.* I knew I was going the next day to celebrate my and Cami's birthday, but that was a little different. I had avoided the beach like the plague for so long; I missed the comfort I felt when I was there.

Leighton Riley

I threw on some black cargo pants and a green V-neck shirt and headed out. I had yet to surf again after Cami's accident and sure as hell didn't plan to start again. The furthest out I'd gotten was chest high in the water with Payton. She seemed to relax me and I wasn't consumed with thoughts of Cami when I entered the water.

I stopped by a taco truck in the parking lot before heading down near the water. Cami loved shrimp tacos and I hated them; I always went for the grilled fish with the special sauce on them. I ended up getting two fish tacos and one shrimp taco. Not quite sure why.

Being in San Diego had brought up so many emotions that I had hidden away. For twenty-seven years, I had my best friend and partner in crime right by my side. Even when we got older and weren't always in the same place, I never felt alone because I had my sister to go to. She was the one who cheered me on while playing soccer and helped me get my first girlfriend by playing up how awesome I was. She was one of the guys when we were out in the water surfing and she grounded me when I was being an idiot.

I wished she was here with me. I needed her advice on Payton. They would have loved each other. Cami was calm and down to earth while Payton was a little more feisty and mysterious. I tried to think of what Cami would say about the situation I had gotten myself into. She probably would have told me that only I would chase after an author who I didn't know a damned thing about and end up falling for her and making her run within a matter of days. She'd probably also have told me not to give up so easily and to go with my gut and find her.

I would be lying if I said I wasn't upset with Payton. Granted, she didn't know who I was and didn't have a reason to tell me she secretly wrote about her sex adventures in her spare time. But I was pissed that she left. From what I had read in her book, she didn't like relationships and just wanted to have fun. I thought we were having fun and never said anything about a relationship so I wasn't quite sure why she would run.

I watched the waves roll in and it instantly calmed me. I was feeling better about going down there and felt like I had been making progress with dealing with the loss of Cami. I just needed to figure out what to do about Payton. Although she left me abruptly, she didn't make it sound like it was a 'forever goodbye', so I took that as good news. She would never expect me to follow her to Vegas because she hadn't even told me where she was going. I was, again, going off a hunch that I felt had to be correct. So far, I hadn't been wrong about where I would be able to find her.

How long would she be in Las Vegas? Was she planning on being intimate with other guys? The thought made my stomach churn. I hated that I was falling for the chick but felt the need to be close to her all the damn time. *Fucking pussy.*

When I was with Zoe, what I thought was love was really just lust and acceptance of the other. We had grown up together and after college we were still friends. One night of drunken sex was what started our relationship. We were both attracted to each other and knew everything about the other person so it just kind of worked. I was never *in* love with Zoe and her heart had always belonged to someone else. Apparently she had met her soul mate in college and I was the consolation prize. I found them in our bed together and wasn't really all that angry about it. I was angrier that the man was in *my* bed getting *my* sheets dirty than where his dick was.

I had been without Payton for a total of two conscious hours and I already felt the need to be with her. I knew I was going to end up going to Vegas to try to find her, and in her book, she hinted at two bars which she frequented. I had to stay in town 'til the next night so that Tristen and I could pay our respects to my sis. I could leave afterward and the flight was only an hour or so. I might still be able to catch her at a bar depending on how her night was going and how long it took me to get to her.

I wasn't going to just swing by and let her know that I figured out who she really was. That would be too easy and I wanted to see her in action to really see how "Reece" was when she was in Vegas.

Payton and Reece were two very different individuals and I was curious to see which side I liked more.

Chapter 6

Payton

The drive to Vegas usually involved me being overly excited and singing girl power songs at the top of my lungs. While it was a particularly boring drive with mountains surrounding me the majority of the time, I knew it would only be a few hours before my escape from reality started.

I knew I had to get away from Ryder. I was starting to feel too much for him. There was something about him that told me there was more to his story than he was letting on.

I hated that I wanted to get to know him better. I wanted to cook dinner with him and wake up next to him after having mind-blowing sex and snuggling together as we fell asleep. I wanted to know who his friends were and what he did on Saturday mornings. That scared the hell out of me.

The drive usually helped clear my mind, but this time, I kept thinking more and more about a man I shouldn't be with. I had only had one relationship before but it shouldn't even be labeled a relationship. I wasn't close to loving him but felt like I should try out dating just to see what all the hype was about. I wanted to be normal. After Ryan, I never felt the need to get into another relationship or have any of the guys from Vegas become more than flings. They were sweet but I rarely thought about them after I got back to San Diego.

It wasn't about sex with Ryder. Let me rephrase…it wasn't JUST about sex with Ryder. I knew I was falling for him and had no idea what I should do. I had been so good at being independent without having to think about anyone else. What scared me the most was that I wanted to tell him about me and my past. I wasn't about to tell him about the non-children's book I wrote, but I wanted him to know where I came from. The only other person who knew was Chloe and I hated when friends asked about my parents or my childhood.

Growing up for the first seven years of life, I never once felt wanted. When I was around four, I realized all the other foster kids were going away to permanent homes but I was still there. My foster parents weren't bad people, but they didn't *love* like parents should. I watched kid after kid get picked and I was left wondering when it would be my turn.

I didn't find out why until I was twelve, when my adoptive parents told me that my mother was a murderer and my father was the victim. I was three weeks old when my birth mom caught my dad cheating on her and shot him and the girl he was with in their bedroom. I always assumed she didn't really love me or else she wouldn't have taken her own life the next day.

Neighbors heard my wails and found me in my mother's limp, lifeless arms. She had taken a bottle of pills and held me while she waited for her life to come to an end.

That information was supposed to be secure, but somehow all the prospective parents knew about my past, while I was clueless. When my adoptive parents finally adopted me at the ripe age of seven, they were loving, but always had that look of pity in their eyes. Being lawyers, they were always working and had help to raise me. I had assumed the help didn't know about my past because my parents were the only ones to look at me that way. I always kept to myself since I was scared they would leave me one day. It kind of made sense that they were taken from me when I was thirteen— everyone else had been.

My adoptive parents said they felt the need to let me know in case some stranger ever brought it up. They didn't want someone else to break the news to me and leave me alone to process what they had revealed.

It wasn't hard to do the research and find the news articles. Soon, I knew all too much about the baby found in the hands of my dead, murderous mother. I couldn't believe the details that they had written in the papers. My last name had been changed to that of my adoptive parents but we still lived in the same city. As I got older, people had seemingly forgotten about who I was and I was able to get by with telling people I didn't know anything about my birth parents since I honestly didn't, except for what the articles said.

Before my adoptive parents passed away, Chloe and I were best friends without a care in the world. We rode our bikes around the neighborhood, went swimming at the beach, went to the movies, and had fun without having to think of how cruel the world around us was. After the car accident, I had come to the conclusion that I would lose Chloe one day. She was the only one left in my corner and fate had a shitty way of reminding me of that. I changed that day. I freaked out if she didn't answer her door when I went over to her house, assuming the worst had happened. When we would go swimming, I only let us get waist deep for fear that something would happen to her.

It drove her crazy. She tried to convince me that she was going to be just fine and made a point to show how safe she was. Slowly, I became more accepting that she was there to stay but I always kept a close eye on her.

It was illogical, but I feared that something would happen to Ryder if he got close to me. I felt cursed. I knew I was damaged goods and no amount of rain could ever clean me of my past. I didn't deserve to be with someone as normal and genuine as Ryder.

I wasn't going to allow myself to fall for Ryder any more than I already had. It was scary to think I wanted him to know everything about me and that I wanted to let him know the real me. He would run, anyway. Either way, I lost, so getting myself more invested would only hurt more.

By the time I arrived on the strip, I was exhausted. I usually couldn't wait to hit the poker tables or a bar, but tonight, I was so emotionally drained and I just wanted to be alone in my room. I took a nice, steaming hot bath and read the newest book in a motorcycle club series. I was finally starting to feel better when I heard my cell phone in the room alerting me of a new text message. I hated that I hoped it was Ryder.

I spent another fifteen minutes reading and soaking until I realized the water was lukewarm and I had been in there almost an hour. *I may just have to run another one of these later tonight*, I thought. It seemed to calm me and reading got my mind off of the sexy man stuck in my head. I grabbed a towel and padded over to the bed where my phone was lying.

Ryder: Got your note, was last night a parting gift? A taste of what I could have had?

I had wanted a taste of him before I left him. I felt bad that his conclusion was so accurate. That night was amazing and I had never felt that way before, both emotionally and physically. But I needed to stay away from him. I knew he would shatter my heart if I let my walls down. My feelings for him were dangerous and I knew I was doing the right thing.

Me: I am incredibly grateful for being able to spend last night with you. Thank you for that. I just need to be alone for a while though. I hope your business trip goes well. Night Ryder

I turned the phone off and went to look outside the window. It was amazing to see such excitement and activity no matter the time of day. The lights, street performers, and overall ambience truly allowed tourists to get away from their normal routine for a short period of time.

There were so many people down on the street with their loved ones, sharing the experience of Sin City yet I always went alone. I had never had a loved one. Vegas was a place where it was okay to be single and alone—someone was always around to keep you company and it was maybe for a few nights at the most. People were laughing, hugging, kissing, and having a good time while being carefree. I wanted that so badly but was terrified of letting someone in. Who would want someone as damaged as me? I couldn't do that to Ryder. He didn't deserve to have to put up with my past and my inability to let people get close.

Behind me, I heard a faint knock on my door. I had set out my tray of food for room service to pick up in the hall so there was no need to be bothered. There was no reason for a complaint to have been made for me since I had been pretty quiet, although I wished I had a reason to be loud. I made my way to the door and I noticed in the peephole that one of the front desk workers was standing outside my door, waiting patiently. Tightening up my towel around my chest, I cracked the door open ever so slightly.

"I have a letter for you, Miss Davenport. I was told to hand deliver it to you to ensure you received it." He seemed…nervous? I thanked him quietly, taking the note and shutting the door behind me. Out of instinct, I locked and bolted the door.

A feeling of dread rose up in me as soon as I was alone in my room again. I wasn't that interesting of a person and didn't know what I had done to start getting those damn letters. They were obviously meant to deliver a message but I didn't know what I was supposed to do after reading them. Going on with my life like normal obviously wasn't what the creep wanted or else the letters would have stopped. I had lived in fear my whole life, but this was a totally different level of fear.

I walked over and gently sat on the bed, crossing my legs Indian style. I flipped the letter over and saw the familiar wax seal. *Fuck my life. Why couldn't I be more boring so no one would care to stalk me?*

As I broke the seal and pulled the letter out of its casing, red and white rose petals fell around me. Normally the thought of someone sending me roses would be a sweet gesture but I knew there would be some type of sick twist to it. I unfolded the letter and my mouth dropped as I read it.

ALL ALONE IN THIS SUITE. WHAT A SHAME DON'T YOU THINK?

I hated that all of the letters were short and could be nothing but a prank or something extremely possessive and scary. I lay in bed, thinking of what the letters meant. *He knows who I am. Be careful not to overindulge. Being alone in my room.* Did it have something to do with my time and activities in Vegas? I couldn't figure out who would know who I was and care enough to not want me to come here anymore.

I must have fallen asleep reading because I woke up and the towel was acting as my blanket when I woke up. The letter was on the pillow beside me and I had never gotten dressed to go to sleep. The sun was peeking through the curtains and I knew I had passed out cold for the night.

My mind wandered back to Ryder after exhausting a million different scenarios about the letters. I came here to get him out of my head, but found that he was who I thought of when I wanted to be comforted. I needed something to get myself out of my head for the night. I would go find a guy to be with later that night and hopefully he could help me forget my troubles for a while.

I went down to the spa for the day since I still didn't feel like being around crowds outside or in the casinos. I opted for the Himalayan salt room and the dry steam room, jumping in the whirlpool when I got too hot. While there were other women in the rooms, no one bothered me and it was peaceful. I got a massage and my hair cut afterward, figuring I could use a new style. My hair had hit my mid back and I thought going a little shorter could be fun.

Feeling like a 'new' me, I decided to go for a little shopping to find some new lingerie and an outfit for tonight. I headed down to the Caesar's mall, and four hours later, I left with three new dresses, four new sets of lingerie, a silk nightie, and a new pair of heels. Shopping always got me in the mood to go out and try the new clothes out, and made the weird feeling in my stomach lessen just a tad about what would happen.

I should be excited to be here, damn it! I went through my routine of getting ready for the night and decided on a black strapless dress that hit mid-thigh, thigh high stockings with lace around the top, and electric blue fuck-me heels. I paired it with a simple set of diamond earrings and matching bracelet. *This will do for tonight.*

I set my sights on some Texas Hold 'Em against the dealer at The Venetian. It was my go-to hotel when I was here and I wasn't planning on changing. I ordered a Colorado Bulldog and began scoping out the area. Luckily, the dealer was flirty, so I didn't mind hanging out at the table until I found someone who sparked my interest.

Sinfully

Ryder

After lounging around the beach for the majority of the afternoon, I decided I probably needed to get some work done. Back at the hotel, I went through emails and read through a manuscript that my assistant had passed on to me saying it was worth me looking at it. I loved the fact that I had an assistant who could find the rare gems just like I did growing up. Lorelei was my right hand man, and it was all because of her that I was able to put work on hold to do 'research' out in the field.

Lorelei would become one of my senior editors in a few years. I purposely gave her a full load of work each day to see her potential and to see how she handled the pressure. In the emails she had sent me, it seemed like work was going as usual and it gave me reassurance that I could be gone another week or two without serious damage. I wasn't sure what I was getting myself into by going to Vegas to find Payton. *Would she just run again?* I hated that I had to ask myself that question.

It was almost peaceful being back in San Diego. My avoidance of the city for the last year never allowed me to realize that coming back was healing for me. I was already starting to feel better about Cami's death. *Wait, I feel better about it?* That felt so wrong to say. Shouldn't I still be upset and sorrowed? I wondered how Tristen was really coping with things and if he was beginning to feel the same way.

It was almost nine and I thought about going out to a bar but thought otherwise. If the bartender chick didn't get my mind off Payton, I doubted anyone would. I needed to figure out my game plan for letting Payton know I knew her dirty little secret.

I was hoping to get there in time to catch her at the bar. If I did, I figured I would see how things went. I had no idea if she would be with some guy, or hell, if they had already moved on from the bar. I wanted to be pissed at her but had a feeling showing up angry wouldn't help. I had to play it cool, and I was secretly hoping

I'd find her all alone at the bar. She was way too sexy to be alone in a bar but it didn't deter me from hoping.

I ran through scenario after scenario about how confronting Payton would go down. I wished I knew her better to know the reasoning behind her actions. It would also allow me to better prepare myself for how she would react to me knowing she was Reece.

Her story was definitely on the sexy side of books and it was well written. I could understand how someone wouldn't want their sex lives written in detail, but she was the one who wrote them. She had to figure that *someone* would out her eventually. I wasn't planning on outing her to the world; I could keep it between us and even help keep her secret.

I kept asking myself whether I was going to Vegas to see Payton and try to get to know her better or if I was going to get 'Reece' to sign with me. I knew the answer I should give would be work related but found myself conflicted. I worried that if I pushed Payton too hard to sign on with my agency, that I would lose all chances of being with her. If I really wanted to try things with Payton, I couldn't pressure her about the book. She also might think I was trying to be with her because maybe eventually I'd be able to talk her into saying yes. Could I let a great author like that go? What if some other publishing company swooped in and gave her a better offer?

I just wanted her to let me the fuck in.

When I woke up the next morning, I decided to pack up my things so that I'd be ready to head to the airport after spending the day with Tristen. I stopped by his house and noticed there were still pictures of Cami and him all over the place. I wondered how long they had actually been dating before she passed away. I made note to ask later on.

"What did you want to do today, man? I figured we'd head down to the beach this afternoon but hadn't planned on anything beforehand," Tristen hollered from the laundry room. I had caught him off guard by arriving so early, but I didn't know where else to go.

"I hadn't thought much about it. For the past few months I thought about getting a tattoo to remember her. I hadn't had the time to get it while in Los Angeles, but if you want, you can come with. Seems like an appropriate day to get it done."

I didn't hear Tristen say anything for a minute or two and figured he didn't hear me and would bring it up again once he was finished up. I had put on *ESPN* to kill time while waiting for him to get ready. When he finally popped his head out, he came over and had a seat on the other end of the couch with his elbows on his knees, leaning forward.

"I, um, kind of already got one for her." He lifted up his shirt, and on his shoulder he had the quote, *Sometimes in the waves of change we find our true direction*, with two dolphins. The larger dolphin had a fin over the smaller one while they seemed to nuzzle each other. I stared at it for a moment before inquiring more about it.

The quote was beautiful and must have been hard to settle on. I wondered what his interpretation of the quote was. "Are the two dolphins you and Cami?"

"No. Listen, I wasn't sure if I should or how to bring this up with you, man." He cleared his throat and fidgeted with his hands, seemingly contemplating how to go about the conversation.

"Take your time. We have the whole day, Tristen. I know I haven't been around as much as I should have been, even before her death, and I know there was more to your relationship than I knew. I'm okay with it, man. Were you in love with my sister?"

Hopefully that would give him the nudge he needed to open up a little. I wasn't sure why he was acting so nervous; he had already told me about them. He was a good man and would have been great for my sister.

"Cami was pregnant."

I was pretty sure the world just stopped spinning. I couldn't have heard what I thought I just heard. "*What?* What do you mean Cami was *pregnant?*" I shook my head in disbelief. He had to be lying or had his facts wrong. My sister did not die while she was pregnant with my niece or nephew. God wouldn't do something that cruel; it wouldn't be fair.

"She had just told me three weeks before the accident. She didn't want to tell everyone until she was closer to three months. Apparently, you're most likely to miscarry in the first three months and she didn't want to get everyone's hopes up just in case anything happened. She was about two and a half months when she passed away. We were planning on letting everyone know that next weekend.

"After she passed away, I couldn't bear to tell people about it. Only a handful of people knew we were dating and I didn't feel it was right to give them another loss. I know I should have told you, I just never felt like it was the right time. The little dolphin is our little girl and Cami is with her, protecting her. Cami thought it was going to be a girl."

I couldn't stop the tears from forming. My sister was going to be a mom. My best friend would have become family and it never happened. I mourned for Tristen and the loss he must have felt. He lost his perfect family in an instant. I couldn't even *begin* to imagine the pain he must have gone through. I went and hugged him with all my power and we cried together for what felt like hours.

We ended up spending the rest of the afternoon talking about memories and thoughts of Cami. I found out Tristen heard Cami talking to her belly one day and used the name Ellie. They hadn't been planning to have a child but were in love and knew they would make it work. When I asked him if he had tried dating again, he changed topics so smoothly that I didn't realize it until minutes later. He was always quiet when it came to relationships, but I wasn't sure why he would be now. Even though she was my twin, I didn't expect him to never get back out there. I wanted him to find happiness again. He was so strong. I wasn't sure what I would have done; losing my lover and unborn child in the same day had to be devastating. He would never get to hold his child, never get to teach them how to ride a bike or see them off to school. Even if Tristen wasn't dating yet, it seemed like he had come to terms with Cami's death, which was a major step in the right direction.

I knew Tristen would make a great father and husband one day; there was no doubt in my mind. I didn't know if Cam and Tristen were soul mates, but I sure hoped he ended up happy down the road. He truly did deserve it.

We took calla lilies down to the beach with us in remembrance of Cami. By that time, Tristen and I didn't need to say anything. We had already talked about everything we needed to and just spent the time silently sitting on the beach, watching the waves crash, and paying our respects to my twin sister. Every day that week, I felt like I had made progress in accepting what had happened. There was no doubt in my mind that Cami and Ellie were looking down over us and protecting Tristen and me.

Tristen and I said our goodbyes and I promised to return soon. I had filled him in on my situation with Payton and he understood why I was heading out to Vegas.

I made my way through security and boarded the plane on autopilot. I couldn't tell you the gate number or how long I waited before boarding. I just kept replaying what Tristen had told me just hours before, trying to process my feelings. I felt a whole new level of pain and kept imagining how different life would be if Cami hadn't been pulled under. She would have a newborn and I would have been the best damn uncle ever. The fact that I would never see my sister again or meet my niece or nephew made me sick to my stomach and I suddenly felt so alone on a plane filled with seventy people.

I *wanted* to see Payton which was a feeling that I'd never experienced with any of the other women I had been interested in. I didn't know what my grand plan was going to be when I found her, but I certainly didn't feel like being a dick to her when I saw her. I just hoped I was there in time and she hadn't already moved on to her next conquest. I wanted to feel her silky skin against mine and hear her moans as I moved in and out of her perfect, made-for-me body. *Really, Ryder? Get a hold of yourself.*

Leighton Riley

I checked into one of the hotels Payton had hinted at staying and clubbing at while in town, dropped my bags off, and changed shirts before heading down to the casino floor. Hearing the bonuses of the slot machines and seeing the bustling attitude from all around me got me into the right mindset and I headed down to one of the bars where I figured she would be. The urge to see her was so strong, I couldn't think of anything but feeling her against me again.

Chapter 7

Payton

I was up three hundred dollars for the night so far. There were some pretty cute guys playing blackjack but I always got bored within a hand or two of that game. I noticed it was always the tourists who set their sights on the blackjack tables. It was simpler than Hold 'Em, Let It Ride, Mississippi Stud, or Three Card Poker, so it attracted the beginners much more. I didn't see the skill needed to play the game and the odds of the other games were better. I could only be found at blackjack if the guy playing was TDF, with 'tall' and 'fuckable' being more important than the 'dark' part of the acronym.

While playing Texas Hold 'Em, I ended up talking with a slightly older gentleman; I was guessing he was pushing forty. He was at least able to get me to laugh with his jokes about the game and his time in Vegas up to that point. He was from Dallas and was quite the charmer like most Texas men. I saw the wedding ring and knew he would be harmless fun for my time at the table. I hit a full house and a few flushes but Craig, my table companion, hit quads on a twenty-five-dollar bet. Needless to say, he was feeling very generous and offered to take me out to celebrate after we got finished at the tables. I politely declined and waited another twenty minutes before excusing myself from the table and cashing in my chips. I did not 'do' married men.

I made my way upstairs to freshen up and psyche myself up for heading to the club. Dancing would do me some good. I had already had three drinks, but figured once I had a few more at the bar, mission 'forget Ryder by getting drunk and finding a new boy toy' would be good to go. *Okay, so I know the name could use some work, but go with it.*

I checked myself out in the full-length mirror and made note of my assets and of course my flaws. I loved that I still had lean, toned legs that looked good in short dresses but hated that I had hips. Finding dresses that accentuated my tits and flat stomach without drawing attention to them wasn't easy, but I had found a style that normally worked well for me and stuck with it. I needed to hit the beach more often to get more of a tan, but in the dark room, everyone seemed a shade or two darker so I wasn't too worried.

I needed to focus on my positives. Looking myself over once again, I began to concentrate on my better areas. My lips were shiny with gloss and my hair tousled to perfection. My heels made my legs look even more toned and my ass looked amazing in the dress. With a seductive smile, I realized I could totally find a guy to make me forget about my troubles and I was ready to hunt.

I stepped out of my hotel room, making sure it was locked, and ran into a hard chest. I politely excused myself, before turning around completely and looking up into familiar eyes. *Holy shit, fuck a duck.* I hadn't seen him in almost two years and he had bulked up even more than last time I saw him. He was so damn hot it led me to wonder if he was here alone again. I crossed my fingers that lady luck was watching over me.

"Payton? I did not expect to actually see you here! Damn, girl, my memory does *not* do you justice." His grin made his dimple appear and I couldn't help but smile in return.

"Long time, Tate. Here on business?" I replied with slight nervousness. He had been one of the few guys who gave me butterflies in my stomach. He was also one of the few that I gave an exception for seeing more than one night.

Leighton Riley

"Bachelor party, actually. Not for me, for my friend. He's actually getting married here tomorrow. What brings you around? The usual?" He knew my routine in Vegas and he was fully aware he wasn't the only guy I had slept with in this town. When we were hanging out two years ago, he had point blank asked me if I had done that sort of thing before and I was upfront with how my vacations worked.

"Just felt like I needed to get away. I hadn't been here in a while and needed a change of pace." We both entered the elevator and went to push the button at the same time, hands overlapping each other. He grasped my hand and brought it to his mouth, giving it a chaste kiss. He had a grin on his face but didn't say anything in response. I'd forgotten how he could make me forget about the world around me when I looked into his stunning eyes.

He was adorably handsome. Two years had been good to him. His chest was swollen and his shirt was tight against his well defined arms. I wasn't quite sure what he was expecting me to say or do but I was not expecting to see him ever again. Sure, I thought of him from time to time, but wasn't prepared to see him that night. I had my mind set on fresh meat, so to speak, but I couldn't deny the strong urge to have him push up my dress and take me up against the elevator wall.

His hand slid to rest on my lower back but his fingers were creeping lower ever so slowly. This was the Tate I remembered. By the time the door opened, he was full on groping my ass, making his intentions clear. I assumed from his actions that he was single but couldn't be sure. Tate urged me out of the elevator first, with his hand moving up only slightly as an older couple walked by.

"Where are you headed to now? The guys and I are meeting up at Haze but I want to catch up. I could use a little arm candy for the night if you want to join me."

"I was actually headed to Haze myself. I'll walk with you, but don't want to keep you from your friends. Maybe dance with me once or twice, though?"

79

Sinfully

"Anything for you, baby. Those douchebags won't miss me anyway. I just have to make an appearance, and once they realize I'm gone, they'll assume I found some chick to take upstairs."

"Oh. Umm…" He cut me off before I could get my thoughts together.

"Not that that's the norm for me. They have one thing on their minds this weekend and it's pussy. Maybe money, also, but that definitely comes second. I don't expect that from you, doll."

By that time I was blushing furiously and had no idea how to respond. Did I want Tate? I felt the familiar attraction but didn't feel sure about it. He had gotten my mind off Ryder for a few minutes, though, so that was a good sign. *Fuck. I'm thinking about him again. I suck at not thinking about him.*

"It's okay. I know seeing each other wasn't expected and let's just see where the night takes us. Sound good to you? You can introduce me to your friends if you'd like." With that, he led me into the club with his hand on my lower, *lower* back and motioned me toward the VIP area where I saw eight just as handsome men taking shots with barely clothed women scattered between them. Of course he would have pretty friends. I was betting they were all personal trainers or models by the looks of it.

He motioned me to have a seat and immediately sat right next to me with his thigh rubbing against my own. We knew each other's triggers and subtle public affection was one of mine. No one around us knew how turned on I was by his simple touch and I knew he would become more confident in his moves if he got away with it from the start. He liked the risk of being seen, as well.

Last time we were together, he led me to what I thought was a set of elevators to head upstairs—but it ended up being a hallway used for employees—and began unzipping his zipper as he pushed me against the wall. I had already been ready for him to take me— upstairs in the confines of his room—but couldn't protest when I felt his hard cock slide against my slippery entrance. He could be such a loving, passionate lover at times but was also rough and dominant just as often. After pulling out a condom and wrapping himself, he lifted me up then let me fall all the way down his shaft, inch by inch, filling me all the way, and I couldn't stifle my moans. His long length and exquisite girth wasn't something I had just found out about, yet it always took me by surprise. He never let up until I felt him jerk inside me when my name escaped his lips. Just as he started to pull out of me, a slot machine technician walked by with a huge-ass grin on his face. I couldn't tell you how long he had been there, but he didn't seem like he would be one to stop us mid-session. Our clothes were haphazardly put back in place, my lips swollen from Tate biting and sucking on them, and the worker had the damn nerve to high five Tate. After the worker walked out of our sight, I tried being mad at Tate, but his cocky grin made me laugh and any negative thoughts were forgotten. I *did* have marks on my back for the next week as a reminder, though.

"I would be lying if I told you I hadn't thought about you, Payton. I know what I was for you, and will take what I can get, but I miss you." Tate's hand moved up my thigh and met the edge of my dress and lingered there for a while. He was such a flirt. I hadn't heard the banter going on between his friends, but realized they were attempting to bring me in on the conversation.

"Are you the infamous Payton? Man, I feel like I've known you for years, girl. Did you miss Tate enough to come back for more?" the guy across from me asked. Tate 2.0 was an ass. He looked so similar to Tate that he could have been his brother, but I knew from our past encounters that Tate didn't have brothers.

Why was Tate talking to his friends about me?

"Not cool, cuz. You've had enough beer and girls for the night. Why don't you just head upstairs and sleep it off?" So *that* was why they looked familiar. Tate 2.0 just smirked and flipped us off while he walked off to the dance floor to find his next victim.

"Sorry about Darren, he's kind of a dick. The rest of us aren't so bad. I'm Tyler, the groom, and the one responsible for bringing these meatheads down to Sin City. It might not have been my best decision ever." He was sweet. Blond hair, green eyes, and a laidback style made him approachable and I could see why some woman fell head over heels for him. He had one full sleeve of tattoos, and from the looks of it, he was probably hiding a dozen more.

The rest of the guys were preoccupied with their female companions for the night and Tyler suggested the three of us should hit the dance floor. I was a bit worried that maybe Tyler thought he could have some fun with us on his last night of freedom. Luckily, he must have been madly in love with his future wife because he danced around us but with no one in particular.

I began moving with the music and as soon as *Candy Shop* by 50 Cent came on, I was lost to the music. I loved that song and was surprised when Tate kept up with the moves. There was something about a tall, muscled man getting down with the music that was just downright sexy. I couldn't help but grin as I felt him dance behind me. He stayed behind me during the next song, *Dirty Dancer* by Enrique Iglesias, and he pulled me into his chest and kept a hand just below my breasts. He moved with the rhythm and I could feel his arousal pushing up against my ass. We didn't say a word to each other while on the dance floor and we didn't have to. He wanted me. I kept thinking that we could go back upstairs for a reunion, but a twinge of guilt was niggling at my brain. I brushed it off as nothing and tried to let the music drown out any unwelcome thoughts. I knew Tate would be a good time, and he was amazing in bed. I just hoped we could still have the same arrangement as two years ago without him wanting more. I was a bit worried after our earlier talk, but figured I would address the issue when it became one.

We separated a little as the song came to an end and I was able to give him a chaste kiss on the lips. A little encouragement never hurt anyone, right? He slid his hands from my shoulders down to my wrists and held me close. He kissed me with tongue that time and I could hear the beginning of *Gorilla* by Bruno Mars come over the speakers and I couldn't help but start dancing again. Turning back around so my ass was pressed against the bulge in his pants, I felt hands on my hips and a rock hard chest against my back. It was my favorite song at the time and I couldn't help but get turned on by the lyrics and Bruno's seductive voice. He ground into me slowly and almost intimately with the rhythm of the music. Looking up, everyone seemed to be turned on by the song as many were grinding up against someone.

I briefly lost his touch behind me but soon felt his fingers snake their way to my stomach, heading even lower, and I heard a growl as he skimmed over my pussy. He whispered so low, "Are you wet for me right now, baby?" Without putting much thought into it, I grabbed his hand and put it back over my mound and applied pressure to encourage him. I was so turned on that I couldn't wait to get back to the room, strip out of my dress, and lose myself in him.

He pushed his hips against mine with a thrust and I couldn't help but gasp. Through his jeans, I could feel his massive erection. I threw my head back and closed my eyes, wanting to enjoy the moment. His hands were all over me, moving in motion with me. He nipped my ear with his teeth, sucking on it gently afterward.

"Upstairs. I can't wait any longer to strip you bare and fuck you so hard you'll remember me every time you take a step tomorrow."

I know that voice. Ryder.

With how loud it was, in addition to me being consumed by the music, I wondered how long he had been behind me without recognizing the small differences between Tate's and Ryder's body behind me and his seductive voice compared to Tate's carefree one. My body responded before it registered with my brain and I was pooling with desire, yet frozen and unable to turn around. *It must be the alcohol. He wouldn't be in Vegas and sure as hell wouldn't be in the same club as me.*

I could feel his jaw clench against my ear when he demanded, "Now, Payton." He took my hand and led me out of the club. *How in the holy hell did he find me here? Didn't he know I left to get away from him?*

"Wh-What are you doing here, Ryder? Shouldn't you be finishing up your business trip?"

"My trip brought me to Vegas for the night. Show me to your room."

He was short with his words and something seemed to be bothering him, but I was too scared to ask what that could be. He held his hand along my lower back, guiding me even though I knew the way. I stayed silent as we rode up the elevator, leading him down the hallway to my suite. I fumbled nervously with my key and he finally grabbed it out of my hand to complete the task for me.

Someone was in a mood.

I made my way into the room, starting to walk toward the lower level where the couch was, but he guided me to the bed instead. I lay down, Ryder towering over me as he lowered himself on top of me. He was oozing sex appeal and pure masculinity and I was left feeling hot and bothered. I was close enough to see a single bead of sweat rolling down the side of his face. I wanted to lick it up, tasting the saltiness on my tongue.

I looked up into his eyes and saw pure anger and lust. I should have been frightened but just having Ryder near me made my core tingle. His hard abdominal muscles pressed against my stomach and I wanted to feel more of him. He kept working his jaw, seconds ticking by before he spoke up.

"Were you having fun with that fucker at the club? Did I ruin your plans to fuck him tonight? Is that what turns you on, Payton? Quick fucks and quicker goodbyes?" His eyes were a deep blue and I could see his jaw tensing up. I briefly wondered what Ryder had done to get Tate to leave without notice, but the man above me held my attention more than my questions about Tate.

"He's a friend from a while back. We were just having fun. I wasn't expecting him to be here." He looked away for the briefest of moments and I saw pain and anger in his eyes when he returned his gaze.

I couldn't stop thinking about his erection that kept grazing my thigh and writhed underneath him to feel more of him. I knew he was angry but I still wanted him terribly. Angry sex could be hot. He noticed my movement and pushed himself against me with more force than I was ready for and I involuntarily let out a loud moan which earned me a smirk from him.

"So you *do* want me. Why did you run, Payton? Worried I may find out your dirty little secrets? You can't deny what you feel for me. Hell, I can feel it when we are anywhere near each other. Everything about you gives you away—your eyes, voice, erect nipples. Your pulse has gotten faster, and the way you're breathing has changed since we got to your room. I know without a doubt that you want my cock deep inside you right now."

"Right now, I *do* want you, Ryder. I can't stop thinking about your fingers being inside me just like in your hotel room back in San Diego. I want you so badly I can't think straight." He didn't have to know that it would be our first and last time together. I had a taste of him the other night and was dying to get the whole thing. Just remembering the feel of Ryder's hot mouth against my clit—his moans as I took him in my mouth—I couldn't think of anything but him filling me with his hard length.

Wait. Dirty little secrets? Quick fucks and quicker goodbyes? What did he mean by that? I felt like I might have had an abnormal amount of dirty little secrets but why would he say the other? We hadn't talked about any of my tendencies while in Las Vegas.

I also doubted he had put two and two together about my birth parents and I didn't think he'd use 'dirty little secrets' as the terminology for that one. What could he have on me?

I came up with the conclusion that he probably thought Tate and I used to be intimate with each other since we were all over each other on the dance floor. Who cared if I had a past with Tate? Ryder didn't get to judge my past.

"My past is my past. I know these feelings I have for you are scaring the shit out of me, Ryder. I can't do a relationship. I can't let you in and tell you what made me who I am today. I'm not putting myself in a position to get hurt. I won't allow it."

He effectively got me to stop talking by crushing his lips to mine and moving his body closer to me so I could feel all of his hard body against my soft one. He kissed me with passion, anger, and lust. He moved to my neck and began kissing and licking right below my ear. I could hear his heavy breathing as he gently sucked on my earlobe, nibbling just enough to force another moan out of me. His hands roamed possessively over my body, caressing my soft skin. He shifted my dress to my waist and just the feel of his fingers skimming my panty line made me moan in anticipation. I was getting so wet just thinking about what it would feel like when his hand ventured over my panties. I wanted him so badly and didn't think I could wait much longer. He was so close to my sex and touched everywhere *but* there. This beautiful man was going to be the death of me. He was driving me fucking crazy and I just wanted him to fuck me!

His lips continued their unhurried, torturous journey downward, beginning with my shoulders and leisurely making his way to my ample breasts. He spent equal time massaging and twirling his tongue around each of my pebbled nipples, eliciting frequent moans from me. I grabbed his hair to hold him closer, not able to get enough of him. Ryder took his time getting to know my body, tugging my clothes off carelessly as he moved down my body. "I find your curves and firm stomach irresistible, Payton. I've imagined how your smooth skin would feel against mine all week." I wanted to touch the ridges on his chest and his oh so sexy V but he never allowed me the chance.

After devouring every inch of me, I finally felt him move down my body and heard his belt being unbuckled and his zipper sliding down. I looked up to see him pulling his pants off but his black boxer briefs were still on, his noticeable erection peeking out at the top of the material. His eyes were fixed on me as I lay naked in front of him, wet and waiting. Lowering himself between my legs, he brought my calves up and laid them on top of his shoulders. Teasing my pussy at an agonizingly slow place, he began by dragging his tongue up and down my wet entrance, and then slowly circled my swollen clit with the lightest of touches. Once I was panting with need, he flicked it quickly and rubbed it forcefully with the flat of his tongue. I squirmed with need as he inserted two of his fingers, moving in a 'come hither' motion once inside. He caressed me in the perfect spot, and just as I was about to come, he fucking stopped and started the whole process over. The cocky bastard knew what he was doing to me and loved the power he was holding over me at that moment.

"I need you inside me, Ryder. Please." I didn't care if I was begging. My brief encounter with his cock in his hotel room made me crave more. Just the thought of his rock hard shaft inside me was enough to make me come on the spot. Sliding his boxer briefs off with one hand while hovering over me, elbow propped up beside me, I was anxious for him. His chest wasn't as big as Tate's, but it was solid muscle, and his stomach was so well defined I could see all the muscle groups that ultimately led down to his impressive cock.

He pulled out a condom and I gave a quiet 'thank you' at the present that was wrapped before me. I was in awe as I watched him stroke his hard shaft while he rolled the condom on. I got on my knees to meet him at the edge and pulled him onto the bed first. I was tired of him being in control. I straddled him and began kissing him passionately, trying to show him how much I wanted him and missed him. I lowered myself slowly down on top of his shaft. I gasped at how full I felt and it took me a moment to move all the way down. I found his hands and linked our fingers together as I began riding him at a leisurely place. He looked up at me with desire in his eyes. He moved his hands to my hips to control my movements, guiding me higher before slamming back into me. He was thrusting upward, ramming into my tight pussy, as I continued to ride him. Sex had never been so hot.

We were both obviously used to being the dominant one in bed but I wasn't about to give it up that easily. I grabbed his hands and moved them above his head. He took my signal and put them behind his head, finally taking the hint. He felt so good inside of me. He was pushing into me, hitting just the right spot, when my first orgasm took me by surprise. I was tightening around him and trying to stifle my screams of pleasure. Ryder's eyes were alight with fire as he watched me writhe as I came, licking his lips and thrusting harder.

Ryder flipped me on my back and must have decided it was his turn for power. He played with my clit while pounding into me and I couldn't help but shout his name as he brought me closer to bliss again.

"I love how you feel inside me, Ryder. Fuck me harder."

"Yeah? You like that? I fucking love it when you clench your muscles around me. It makes you so tight it almost hurts. Come for me again."

"Oh…Ryder. Fuck, I'm about to…faster… right there!"

"I'm coming with you. Oh fuck! Oh, Reece!" He let out a load moan as he jerked inside of me, coming at the same time I did. We were both panting and out of breath as we lay there silently for a few minutes. He shifted to lie beside me and placed his arm comfortingly over my waist.

As I came down from my high, I finally processed what had just come out of his mouth. *Did he just call me Reece?* No, I was imagining that. He didn't know I was Reece.

"Did you…did you just call me… *Reece?*" I gave him a confused look, hoping I sounded crazy instead of being correct.

"I'm sorry. I thought you liked being called that when you're in Vegas hooking up. Or does it make you feel better when you give them your real name? I'd like to know proper protocol here."

It all clicked into place. How could I have been so naïve? *This is not happening.* I felt sick to my stomach and I was pretty sure the room was beginning to spin. I thought no one knew that I was Reece Edwards except for Chloe. The wax R. Ryder. How long had he known? More importantly, did he know that I knew he was the creepy letter sender? I needed to be smart about handling the situation, but I was so beyond pissed that I couldn't think straight. I took a moment to close my eyes and took a deep breath but that did no good.

"Get out. Right now. Get the fuck out of my room. Was this your plan…to manipulate me? Just because you didn't like what I wrote doesn't mean you should start stalking me, you sick fuck. Were you trying to get the real thing? Books not working for you anymore? It seems a bit much to fly out to Vegas to get the 'Reece experience', motherfucker." I was on the verge of tears and needed him to leave before they started flowing freely. I knew I shouldn't have gotten close to him. *I fucking knew it.*

"So you really *are* her. I mean, I had my theory, but holy shit!" He rubbed his hand over his face before trying to speak again. "I don't care about what happened in this city, Payton. I want to get to know *you*, not her. I just had to know if it was true or not." His words weren't making sense to me at that point but I didn't care to ask him for clarification.

"Who *are* you?

"Ryder Strom, or R. Strom when I'm addressing authors I am looking to sign. I didn't put the links together immediately, either."

I was done talking with him and said as much. "You were the publisher I was emailing back and forth? How could you keep that from me? Do you normally sleep with your authors or was this your way of negotiating, you jackass? What the fuck was with those letters? Do you like to scare the hell out of women? Is that what you need to get off? "

Yep, then came the tears. I wanted to be alone and curl up on the bed and cry myself to sleep. Why wasn't he moving from the bed?

"What are you talking about...letters? I didn't come here for Reece. We don't know each other that well, but I can't stop thinking about you. I go to bed thinking about you. I hated the way it felt when I read your letter. Was it a goodbye letter, Payton? You at least owe me an explanation as to why you left."

I wiped away the tears and looked up into his eyes. I was surprised at the amount of emotion I saw reflecting back at me. He almost looked hurt.

I hated myself for wanting to comfort him, to let him know I had feelings for him, but he had taken it too far. "Y-Yes. It was. You have gone above and beyond fucking up any chance you had to be with me. I can't even stand to look at you anymore. Leave, Ryder. Please." I hadn't decided that until it came out of my mouth, but I knew I couldn't be around him. I felt the pull to him as well and would be damned if I let it suck me in. I needed a clean break from Ryder. I just wished it didn't hurt so damn bad as I watched him walk out of my room with his broad shoulders lowered in defeat. He was muttering something but I didn't catch what it was, and I didn't need to.

Ryder

Upon walking into Haze, I realized it was going to take some time to find Payton with how jam packed it was. I started off at the bar, hoping to catch a glimpse of her alone having a drink. It wasn't probable, but I needed a place where I could see the dance floor in addition to the tables lined along the walls. I ordered a Jack and Coke and leaned my back against the bar, getting a feel for the place. It was dark with strobe lights lighting up the dance floor and waitresses had on deep red, form-fitting dresses with black heels. They fit in with the crowd, and if it wasn't for the trays in their hands, I would have guessed they were there for fun. There was a VIP area in the corner, but I wasn't close enough to see who was there.

After I finished my drink, I made my way through the tables, glancing at the dance floor when the chance was there. I knew it was just a hunch and had a sick feeling in my stomach that I was too late. I wasn't sure what I'd do if I didn't find her because that would mean she was probably already with some dick as 'research' for her sequel. I hated thinking about her with another guy, let alone some random tourist who was looking for a hook up while he was away on business. Fucker probably had a wife and kids at home.

I made my way to the dance floor, but as I tried to move past a group of clearly intoxicated cougars, I was grabbed and manhandled by two of them. They were pushing fifty and dressed as if they were maybe twenty-five. The blonde was in front while the redhead surprised me from behind and they started touching me, everywhere! It was so unexpected that I decided to just go with it. They seemed harmless and they were short enough that I could see above them for a glimpse of Reece.

Payton.

Fuck!

I thought I had caught a glimpse of her walking to the dance floor with two extremely well-built guys but I got distracted when I

Sinfully

felt a tongue on my now exposed chest. The blonde was tracing my abdominal muscles as if she was what I wanted. I shouldn't have consented to the MILFs in the first place, but I realized that a little too late. When I tried to pull my shirt down and move away from the duo, the redhead grabbed my ass and blurted out their room number upstairs, insinuating that I could watch or join in on their fun.

Yeah. I wasn't sure how to respond to that one so I just said thanks and walked away. They would find some other prey before the next song so I didn't put too much thought into it.

My attempt to find Payton was accomplished when I almost ran into personal trainer number one grinding up against my girl. *My girl? Shit.* They seemed comfortable with one another and I saw red. His hands were caressing her in intimate spots and he looked like he was ready to fuck her right then and there. I carefully moved up next to him so that Payton wouldn't turn to look.

"Hey, man. Just saw your friend over there get escorted out by security. He seemed really drunk and pissed. You may want to go check up on that." It was worth a shot.

He gave me a onceover and turned to look at Payton who was lost in the music and paying no attention to us whatsoever.

"Tell her I'll be right back." With that, he left quickly and I thought he must be really fucking stupid if he left her all alone with another guy at a club. Payton was hot as shit but didn't realize just how beautiful she was, which made her all the more irresistible.

I slid in his place seamlessly and I had my doubts whether she even realized it was a different body behind her. She ground herself into me and began moving my hands over her stomach and just a tad bit lower. Not able to stop myself from asking, I questioned if she was wet for me and her response was her hand placing mine over her warm mound. My erection was pushed against my jeans, just waiting to be freed. I smiled until I realized she could have thought I was still fuck-face and had meant to have his hand there. *Damn it!* She barely knew the guy and was clearly giving the go ahead for what he hoped would happen after the club.

Leighton Riley

I needed her alone. I couldn't get thoughts of her and that fucker out of my head, but her grinding against me was making me lose control. I was pissed and horny. That was not a good combination for me and Payton was about to take the brunt of it. After demanding she go upstairs with me, it seemed like she finally realized who I was. Knowing she hadn't thought it was me when she put my hand on her pussy made me enraged.

I knew she was confused and shocked to see me, but I didn't feel like I was the one who needed to explain myself at that moment. She was the one about to hook up with some stranger so she could add another chapter to her book. I just wished she didn't look so damn fuckable, so innocent as she fumbled with her room key. Being pissed and turned on made me conflicted as to what I needed to confront first—my needs or my questions.

My need to be with her was winning over as I stepped into the room. I was jealous and angry but I needed to touch her. After she was underneath me, I made myself ask about the other guy. I needed to know that he was someone random who she didn't care about. When she told me she'd known him for a while, I immediately knew she meant it was probably one of the guys in her book. I wanted to go back down to the club and punch his face in, but feeling her squirm against my dick was keeping me in the moment. I probably didn't approach her tendencies in Sin City in the most appropriate manner and felt bad immediately after asking about her quick fucks and quicker goodbyes. The woman made my head spin when I was around her.

Her skin glistened with a thin layer of sweat from dancing in the club. She bit her plump lip as I thought about whether or not I should make her suffer a little more or give in and have my way with her. She was *definitely* needy at the moment.

I needed to know if she really was Reece. I felt guilty going off an assumption without confirming it from the source, but all the signs pointed to me being correct. It was one of the few times I hoped I was wrong.

Feeling her push herself against my erection was my final undoing and I couldn't wait any longer to feel her warmth surrounding me. Once she was on top of me, I couldn't think of a single thing besides feeling her tightness enveloping me. She moved in sync with me and made the sexiest little moans I had only ever heard once before.

Her slick arousal made it easy for me to slide in, but she was so tight I had to concentrate on not losing control. Her tits bounced as she rode me with smooth, determined motions. When she looked into my eyes, I could see passion, hurt, and desperation all at once. I wondered briefly if she would be different with other men in Vegas. She had hidden her pain so well from me until that night.

She seemed to like the power of being on top, but I needed to be in control. I wanted to show her everything I couldn't say out loud. I knew once I told her I knew about her other book that everything would change. I wanted to *feel* with Payton before everything transformed into shit.

I was lost in the moment; us coming together was so fucking hot that I didn't even realize whose name I shouted. I was in a state of bliss until I heard her mention me calling her Reece. *Fuck. I'm a jackass.*

It wasn't the best timing but she needed to know. I had hoped that she could understand how I put the pieces of the puzzle together and hadn't realized who she was until the night in my hotel room.

Her reaction was not what I expected at all and I didn't even understand the reasoning behind her outrage. I wasn't planning on exposing her and didn't mean to find out the way I did. She mentioned something about some letters but by then she was full-on pissed. I was left dumbfounded since nothing I mentioned fazed her. I tried to let her know I wanted Payton, not Reece, but she didn't care.

I left feeling defeated and slightly confused. I was not expecting any of what happened to occur. I knew I needed to give her time but hated the idea of leaving there feeling as though I had lost any chance I had. She seemed too upset for me finding out she wrote that book. I didn't even care about her being with fuck-face anymore and I had no idea what my next move should be.

Payton

The trip was not turning out like I had planned. Vegas was supposed to be an escape from my real life issues, and instead, all of them were here with me. I came here to get away from Ryder, yet he found me. I didn't think the creepy stalker person would know I was here, yet *he* found me, too. My heart hurt watching Ryder walk out that door but I was so unbelievably pissed off at him and the situation that I didn't care about my heart at the moment.

He betrayed me. He knew who I was and decided to play a sick game with me. Those letters still scared me. *What if he's crazy and would do anything to have me for himself?* I didn't know him well enough to trust him and I hated that I had feelings for him.

After lying in bed for who knows how long, I decided he wasn't allowed to ruin the rest of my night. I wiped the dark smudges away from my eyes and reapplied my eye makeup, fixed my dress, and did a onceover in the mirror. I looked freshly fucked. My hair was wilder than normal, lips a plump red, and I tucked my bra strap that I didn't realize was showing back under my dress.

I contemplated stripping down and taking another hot bath and having a party for one in my room all night but decided that was just sad. I was curious as to what had happened to Tate and wanted to see if he was still down there.

Putting on my big girl face, I stepped out of the room and headed back downstairs. I walked past the poker tables and smiled, thinking that was another option if I didn't find Tate. The later the night got, the hotter and flirtier the men were. Glad I had a plan B, I walked back into Haze and went straight to the bar. Ordering a whiskey sour, I took a few minutes to calm my nerves and get a grip on my emotions. I could still feel the adrenaline pumping through my veins and was positive I would be doing something I regretted if I headed out to find the first hot guy on the dance floor. I needed to be in control. I hated the feeling that I had lost the power and hoped Tate hadn't been run off by Storm Ryder. Did he not realize how close his name was from Storm Ryder when you said it last name first? Ryder Strom. Strom Ryder. Storm Ryder. What a dick. I was grateful he took the hint and left. I wasn't too worried about him showing up at the club, since it seemed like he had left for good.

My drink was gone in less than two minutes and I stood to head to the dance floor when I felt a hand at my back. I froze at the touch and waited a moment before turning around. It was definitely a man's hand and I hoped it was Tate's. I could feel him leaning closer to me, to the point where his breath was on my neck. "Back for more, sweetie?"

Tyler. I turned around at the sound of his voice, and with one look, I could tell he was so far gone I was surprised he was still standing. "You look like you've been quite successful at celebrating, Tyler. Where are the rest of the guys?"

"Am I not enough for you, sugar? You gotta try out the goods before knockin' them."

Yep. He reeked of alcohol and would pass out as soon as he got upstairs. I wondered where the bride-to-be was. *She shouldn't see him like this.*

"I bet the goods are... good? Again, Tyler, where are the rest of your friends?" I was getting nowhere with him.

"Well, I saw Darren and two of my other buddies head out with some cougars a while ago. Johnny went back upstairs to be with his bitch-ass wife. I'm pretty sure Tate just left here with a petite little gymnast or something. She told us she performed in one of the shows on the strip and could twist into any position he wanted." He let me know the tidbit about Tate with a huge grin on his face.

"Really? Tate left already?" I had such shitty luck. I wanted him to help me forget about Ryder and didn't feel like finding someone else at this hour. That party for one in my hotel room sounded like my best option.

"Yeaapp. It's just you and me, baby. Were you ready to go upstairs, too? I think I might need a little help getting undressed and

Sinfully

my wifey and I have sep-sep-ret rooms tonight. I need yous, Payton." His arm was slung over my shoulders and his index finger was making its way from my lips to my chest.

"Tyler. I will help you upstairs and help you to bed, but nothing else. Got it? You're getting married tomorrow and I'm not about to fuck that up, too."

"Got it, sugar. Take me to bed." *Fuck my life.*

Remember what I said about all of Tate's friends looking like personal trainers, too? Yeah, Tyler was huge. He was able to walk, but kept swaying toward me and pressing into my shoulders, making me bear more than I could handle of his weight.

"Oof! Tyler, get off of me!" Douche-monkey had effectively fallen on top of me in a very compromising position. I was on my belly underneath him and he had his hips matched up with mine. It was in the middle of the casino floor and we were definitely making a scene.

"You like it rough, Payt? I prefer to start off with gentle lovemaking and then finish it off with some hardcore fucking. That work for you?"

Oh my God. I am about to get fucked on a casino floor by a man who is getting married tomorrow! Holy shit, no. No, Payton. Do. Not. Get. Turned. On. Right. Now!

"Get off me, Tyler, or I'll scream!" I heard his giggles and felt his hands over my ass. That was *so* not okay!

"Mmm, I love it when I can make a girl scream my name. Are you loud, baby?" Alright, I was done being nice.

"Tyler. I will find out what room your bride is in and will drop you off at her door if you do not get off me right this second!" It was getting really hard to breathe and the stares we were getting weren't friendly ones. Even if *I* had been his bride-to-be, this was not acceptable behavior.

"Fine, fine. You're so not as fun as Tate makes you out to be. Take me to my room and we can discuss what to do with the rest of the night." With that, he clumsily made his way to his feet and pulled me up. I was positive I had flashed a few dozen tourists, but at that time of night, most were slightly intoxicated so they weren't upset. I heard a few hollers and an "atta boy!" from the crowd. I got myself underneath his arm again, positioning myself to guide him through the rows of slot machines to the hotel elevators, when I saw Tate and Cirque Du Slut making their way in the same direction.

The karma gods must seriously hate me. Like really motherfucking hated me. I hoped Tyler and I were slow enough that we wouldn't have to stand awkwardly waiting for an elevator to arrive.

Tyler had seemingly found his rhythm and we were both at least on our feet, keeping a steady but leisurely pace across the creamy marbled flooring. Tate and the whore were almost to the elevators and we were at least thirty steps behind them so I let out a sigh of relief at dodging that awkward moment.

"Tate! Tate, over here, man!! You remember Payton, right? Yeah, she told me you're horrible in the sack and wanted to give me a go to make up for your lame ass. Said you were itty bitty and came in under a minute." Oh, for the love of god, why couldn't Tyler just shut the fuck up?

Blushing with embarrassment and jealousy, I tried to turn away from the beautiful specimen in front of me. "Get off her, Tyler!" Tate and his slutbag were making their way toward us and Tate seemed livid.

Ugh. Why did he have to notice me? I was perfectly fine hiding in Tyler's chiseled chest. Images of Tate and her fucking in all sorts of twisted ways entered my mind and I wanted to be sick.

"Who's your friend, bro? She looks like she'd be hella fun in bed. Details tomorrow, man!" Nothing out of Tyler's mouth surprised me anymore.

"Anya, this is Tyler and Payton. Payton and Tyler, this is Anya." While we nodded in her direction, she giggled and began rubbing her hand over his hard stomach. *Whore.*

"I was just helping Tyler to bed before going back to my room. Don't let us bother you two and your plans." He looked confused

Sinfully

for a moment, as if he was trying to figure out a puzzle. He kept looking at Tyler's arm that was swung over my shoulders and his hand that kept grazing my chest. I had gotten used to it during our stroll and hadn't realized how it looked.

"What happened to the other guy? You know, the one you went upstairs with a few hours ago? Not even five minutes after dancing and hanging out with me?" I hadn't realized he had seen me with Ryder. Was that why he was acting all pissy?

"That was a misunderstanding. He means nothing to me. It was nice seeing you again, have a good night, Tate." I was tired of figuring out the men in my life and just wanted to get to my room and be alone. Tyler was conscious enough to know that it was time for us to start moving again. I could hear Anya's squeaky voice telling Tate that she was glad he upgraded from me to her. I knew she wasn't worth my time but she was such a fucking bitch I couldn't help but be pissed. Tyler and I left Tate and Anya standing next to the Wheel of Fortune slot machines and headed toward the elevators once again.

"You care about him, don't you? He talks about you all the damn time. Hell, I figured he made you up since we never met you and his details were quite vivid." Tyler was rather observant for being inebriated.

"I guess in a way I do. Nothing would ever come of us two being together, though, so it's a casual caring if that makes sense. Maybe the girl he's with right now will be better for him than me. He deserves better than me."

I pushed the button, waiting for the next available car, and felt Tyler's fingers massaging my shoulder. It was a kind gesture that wasn't at all sexual. "That boy has it bad for you. He tries to compensate by finding other girls to occupy his time, but the only girl we ever hear him talk about is you. Why do you think he picked this hotel? He was hoping to see you again."

Wow, I didn't realize Tate had feelings for me. A few hours ago was the first time I found out he had talked about me with his friends. He was a sweetheart but I couldn't be anything more to him than a hook-up. "Thanks for filling me in, Tyler. I had no idea. You're going to be a handsome groom tomorrow, you know."

We stepped into the elevator and he pressed the thirty-fourth floor without me having to ask. He seemed to be sobering up some.

"I wasn't done trying to have my chance with you, Payton. It's my last night of freedom and I'm dying to know if Tate was true to his details. That little tongue thing you do? I want that." His smirk gave him away to let me know he was kidding, sort of.

I walked him to his room and laid out some aspirin and a bottle of water next to the bed, followed by shutting the curtains and setting his alarm clock for nine in the morning. I wasn't sure when he had to be up but hoped that was early enough. Tyler had made his way to the bed and was already snoring. I took off his shoes and set his phone and wallet on the nightstand as well. One of his friends was in the room but was taking a shower so I didn't disturb him. Before shutting the door, I looked back to make sure everything was okay in the room and smiled at how peaceful and innocent he looked.

When I finally made it to my room, I was drained physically and emotionally. Giving up on boys and turning into a lesbian or a nun seemed more appealing than it had a few hours before. I hated that I liked cock so much.

Stupid penises and the men attached to them.

Ryder and Tate both seemed to be decent, nice guys who I could have a good time with but now they were both gone. Tate made it clear that while it was nice seeing me again, I shouldn't get my hopes up for another go around with him. He'd apparently already had his fill of me and found something new and more flexible. I wondered how many different positions that chick could maneuver into. I instantly saw her in an inverted donut position with her neck and chest against the ground and her thighs and pussy in the air, waiting patiently for Tate.

I hadn't felt this alone in a while. Vegas was usually the place where I felt at peace and didn't have to deal with any of the bullshit that had occurred over past twenty-four hours. I took the hottest

Sinfully

shower I could stand to wipe myself clean of the day, followed by a luxurious bubble bath while I drank the bottle of Moscato I had bought to be shared with someone other than myself. I submerged myself under the water, holding my breath for as long as I could while I floated back to the top. It felt liberating being able to only hear the roar of the water, without noises from the real world getting through. I must have repeated the process six or seven times until it lost its fun. I didn't want to go home and I didn't want to stay there. Both places reminded me of Ryder. *I can't believe he ruined Vegas for me.* I had no idea where I would go the next day.

After the water started to turn lukewarm, I hopped out and air dried as I packed my bags. It felt nice to walk around my room, feeling the air against my cool skin. I was high enough that no one would see me when I walked close to the windows and the feeling of possibly being seen was highly erotic. I was packing my heels in my bag when there was a weak knock at the door. Turning suddenly, I had to wonder if it was meant for my door or maybe I was hearing someone knock next door.

I threw on a t-shirt and thong and stepped closer to the door. Just as I got on my tippy toes to see through the peep hole, I heard and felt another knock. Looking through the hole, I saw Tate walking away from my door. I opened the door without another thought and followed him, tapping on his shoulder.

Tate stopped, turned toward me, and then looked back at my door. "Were you planning on going back out like that?" He had a hint of amusement in his eyes.

"No, I heard you knock and threw the first thing I saw on to see who it was."

"So you weren't dressed?" His smile was full force.

"I was just packing to leave and hadn't decided what to wear for the rest of the night. Why aren't you with whore-face?" I didn't need to tell him I wasn't sure when I was leaving or where I was going. I hadn't quite figured it out.

"Ahh, the more important question is how you're going to get back in your room, doll. Seeing you strut downstairs to the front

102

Leighton Riley

desk with your tight little ass peeking out from under your very thin t-shirt might gather even more looks than you and Tyler got on the casino floor earlier. You *do* know he's getting married tomorrow, right?"

"You think I messed around with Tyler? That's pretty low, Tate. Since his good friends left him at the club wasted, I figured he'd need help getting back to his room before he passed out. Luckily, one of the other guys was awake in his room when we got there so I didn't have to babysit *your* friend all night!"

Looking back at my completely closed door, I thought to myself that I really had hit rock bottom. I didn't even mean to walk out in the hallway; it was more involuntary than anything. I was done making decisions and had no idea how to get back into my damn room.

He must have seen me pondering what to do. "Stop biting your lip, hun. I'm right down the hall. Let me call the front desk and see if they can help us out. Unless you wanted to just come over to my room with me?"

"I need to pack, sorry. Thank you, Tate."

Ten minutes later, I was introduced to Elijah, a decent looking hotel worker who appeared to be extremely nervous but was very polite—then again I was almost naked.

"Miss, I'm so sorry y-you got locked out-t of your room la-like this. Can I help you w-with anything else?" His eyes kept moving to my chest and I couldn't help but feel exposed in my shirt and panties. He got my door open quickly and checked my ID to make sure I really was the guest checked in to the room. In the meantime, Tate was staring him down and trying to keep Elijah's attention off of me.

"Thank you for your help, Elijah. I'll be able to take it from here." Tate shook Elijah's hand and gave him a tip. He then proceeded to shut the door and deadbolt it. "I would have tipped him more if he would have stared a little less at your rack."

103

Sinfully

I gave him a curious look. "Just in case he works up the nerve to ask you out. I wouldn't want him interrupting your, uhh, packing." *Ugh, he is such a flirt!*

I slid on a pair of shorts but that didn't stop him from staring at my chest. As I put my arms over my hardened nipples, I remembered why I was supposed to be mad at him.

"Was she a one and done girl?"

"You don't get to ask that. You went off with another guy without so much as a goodbye, and then I see you with Tyler an hour later! What the fuck, Payton? I sent her off in a cab, for your information. She had nothing on you."

He shouldn't care that much. From what I knew, he still thought about me, but I wasn't what he needed or craved.

"Tate, we have fun. I care about you but we aren't supposed to be more than that. I'm so surprised you haven't settled down with little mini-Tates running around lifting little baby free weights." At least that got him to smile. It didn't make me feel any less like shit, though.

"You're not out of your phase, huh? I had hoped the last two years had allowed you to heal from whatever happened to you. Guess I was wrong."

"It's not a phase. Everyone I loved has died. I have one friend who has been with me through everything and I can't handle letting myself fall for someone only to lose them. We can't get any closer than what we are right now. I'm sorry I didn't make that more clear initially." I was so done with feeling vulnerable.

"I've dated other women. The problem is that I compare all of them to you. I caught myself pretending they were you while I fucked them. You're different, Payton. You're confident, yet behind those dark blue eyes I can see the pain you try to hide away. I knew you weren't ready for anything serious back then, and neither was I, but you've changed. I am drawn to you and giving me a taste of you back then only made my thirst for you grow. You need to let yourself fall and not be scared of getting hurt along the way."

"You deserve someone who can give you everything. I'm too broken and fucked-up to be what you need and you'll see that someday. Tate, I just let the only guy I remotely saw myself changing for walk away from me. I pushed him away and he's gone now. Maybe I do deserve to be alone."

He walked closer to me and held me close to his chest without saying a word. Feeling comforted, I let myself sink into him and began quietly sobbing. I hadn't cried in...I couldn't remember how long. He didn't press the issue any further and seemed to know exactly what I needed.

Minutes later, he lifted me up, held me while he pulled back the covers, and laid me gently in the middle of my king-size bed. My eyes were closed but I could hear him unbuckling his pants and felt the bed dip as he slid in beside me.

I fell asleep with his arms around me, murmuring how beautiful and amazing I was. It would have been easier if he didn't care so much. I didn't want to leave the feeling of his warm arms around me but knew I needed to figure out my next plan of action. Tate knew what he was to me but he was still here, even after I confessed to caring about Ryder.

Chapter 8

Ryder

I ended up staying in Vegas for another night in hopes of her texting or calling me to meet up. When I didn't hear a thing from her, I decided to head back to Los Angeles to resume living my normal life, determined to find a new author. Lorelei had run everything so smoothly while I was gone that I didn't have much to go through before diving into the handpicked manuscripts she had laid on my desk.

"There are three authors I really think you should take a look at. One is a steamy new adult book with a billionaire and a librarian and the other two are love triangles of sorts. This is the stuff people are reading these days. The sex scenes in them are hot! I mean, they are very well written, sir. Please let me know if you need anything else." This was why I loved her as my assistant so much. She knew what was trending and jumped on it. She also had a habit of being brutally honest with things she liked or disliked, which I found amusing.

The new stories were good and would sell. The librarian one caught me off guard when the male character turned her on to a whole new world in the bedroom. I liked the idea of a shy yet beautiful woman becoming comfortable in her skin and exploring new desires. It would be my next concentration but I couldn't get Payton and Reece's story out of my damn head. *I'm talking as if there are two of them now.* I was starting to slowly lose my mind.

Sinfully

Three weeks later, I still hadn't heard a word from Payton. I held on to the hope that maybe she just needed some time apart to realize that I wasn't a horrible guy. Granted, I was known for being a dick at times and *did* call her out about her sex book while having sex with her. I wasn't the worst of them out there and wanted to prove it to her. The problem was that I had already run to her twice and wasn't about to again. If we ever saw each other again it would have to be from her initiative.

I was walking out of my office for the day—my mind already set on hitting the gym, working a bit at home, and then crashing early. I had been up late the last week, working until my eyes stung, and was forced to go to bed, alone. I had too much time on my hands and the distraction that work gave me was necessary at the moment. Once I was alone, my mind would wander to thoughts about Payton and how her beautiful body felt against mine. I was running myself sick and needed a night to catch up on sleep.

I had been looking down at my phone, checking how my stocks were doing for the day, and didn't even see the blonde at the bottom of the stairs. I ran straight into her, sending us both off balance with her being the unfortunate one to fall. She cursed as she landed on her ass, purse falling right along with her, and the contents spilling onto the cold marble.

I apologized profusely, quickly trying to gather the contents of her bag without being too nosy. I picked up her wallet, wintergreen mints, pink pepper spray, and a couple business cards that noted "Kylie James- Realtor" in addition to her company and personal information. "Kylie, I presume?"

As I helped her off the ground, she looked up and it was then that I realized how hot she was. She was young for a realtor, maybe twenty-five. My normal vision of a realtor was a woman who clearly looked like a mom or grandma with stuffy clothes. She had on black dress pants, black peep toe heels, and a white silk blouse. It was simple, yet sexy, and it worked on her.

"Yes, have we met before?"

"Your business cards gave me a hint. I'm Ryder Strom, Warrington Strom Publishing, on the tenth floor." She looked at me for a moment, as if she was still processing our encounter.

"You live in the same building as me—off Pearl Street and Jefferson. I've seen you jogging in the morning."

"Small world! I need to pay more attention to my surroundings apparently. Were you headed that way?" She was cute and could be a new type of distraction that I could find myself taking a liking to.

"I'm waiting on a buyer to show him some new construction right now, actually. I'm in 14A if you ever want to stop by. I wouldn't mind getting to know my neighbor a little better." Her smile was genuine as she turned to walk further into the lobby.

"See ya around, neighbor," I called out as she walked away, those heels making her legs look a mile long. She was definitely worth a shot.

I headed home after doing some cardio and legs at the gym, feeling a little more optimistic in general. Payton knew who I was and could find me if she wanted. In the meantime, I had plenty of options waiting to keep me company.

Lorelei had offered to have a drink with me if I ever wanted to and I couldn't forget Kylie who was apparently my neighbor. I usually didn't go out with coworkers but Lorelei was innocent. I could see her being a good friend and figured I'd be able to help her make a name for herself in the publishing world.

After sending a text to confirm meeting Lorelei for drinks at the bar down the street, I showered and decided to Facebook search Payton/Reece to see if I could find out how she was doing. Reece's page had generic posts about other books releasing soon but nothing personal on there. I wasn't sure of Payton's last name but looked through Reece's fans and found a Payton Davenport and the picture was definitely her.

"Who knew spending a few weeks at a beach across the world could make such a difference. Glad to be back home <3"

She was back in San Diego. I felt a little better knowing where she was and that she was safe.

Lorelei was easy to talk to but was more on a little sister level than any of the girls I talked to. I think she knew since she didn't think twice when she brought up her fiancé and how they wanted to start a family within the next few years. She was also the only girl I didn't mind talking to about my one-night stands and relationships. She knew about Payton, but not that Payton was also the author I was trying to sign.

"So, what gives? You're back here and from the sounds of it, aren't getting any. So what happened and how did you fuck it up?" Lorelei questioned as she took a sip of her Long Island.

"I didn't fuck it up—technically. I mean, I found out some stuff and confronted her about it. She didn't take it so well." I rubbed my neck, looking anywhere but at Lorelei. She knew my expressions too well and she'd know that I was torn up about not having Payton.

"And you're giving up or just giving her time?"

"Both? She got the wrong impression, and I know I need to fix it, but she ran from me. She needs to figure her shit out before we talk again. Plus, I don't think she'll want me even if I *do* try to get her back." I finally looked up and saw understanding in her eyes. *Thank fuck.* I didn't want her trying to persuade me to go after Payton.

"Just go with it. If she comes back, great. Don't stop being you while you wait, though. When you aren't getting any, we *all* know about it." Seeing her cheeky grin caused me to smile as well. She was probably right, I was an even bigger dick at work when I wasn't getting laid.

I left the bar looking forward to whatever was planned for me in the future. Whether or not it had Payton in it, I wasn't sure.

My mind kept wandering back to my earlier encounter with Kylie. Her nipples were erect and visible through her silk blouse, just begging to be licked. I considered walking up to her door and asking for a cup of sugar but came to the conclusion that was too lame. I needed a reason to talk to her. Real estate? I wasn't planning on moving anytime soon but maybe I could ask for a friend of mine who wanted to move closer to the area. It wasn't the most creative way to talk to a girl but it was normal enough that if she wasn't interested in me I wouldn't have to avoid her in the future.

I ended up waiting three days before making my way to 14A. It was enough time for me not to look desperate but not enough time for her to forget about our encounter. I waited until a little after seven to give her enough time to get home from work and errands and crossed my fingers that she was home.

I was about to leave after knocking twice with no response when I heard shuffling from behind the door. She opened the door with her elbow as she finished throwing her hair up into a messy ponytail. She had on black capri yoga pants and a loose neon orange tank top over a black sports bra. Even in workout clothes she was sexy.

"Sorry it took me so long to get to the door. I was just about to take a shower from working out and had to get redressed. Ryder, right? What's up, neighbor?" She still seemed pumped up on adrenaline from whatever workout she had just finished. Her cheeks were flushed and she was bouncing lightly on her feet.

"I was just thinking I could ask for some advice on real estate in the area for a buddy of mine. I didn't mean to interrupt you, though. I can come back another time." I still had no idea if she was into me or if she was even available. I wasn't ready to fully hit on her until I got a better feel for what I was dealing with.

"I'll only be a few minutes. Come on in and make yourself at home. I'm sure the layout isn't too different from yours. Feel free to grab a beer or water from the fridge; I also opened up some wine a little bit ago if you want." She was quick with her words, but at least welcoming, and had a bright smile that showcased those dimples I had thought about so often. She held the door wide open, waiting for me to make myself at home and I figured it would be alright whether or not we ended up as friends or more. Any girl who stocked her fridge with beer was okay in my book.

"Your place looks nothing like mine, but I'm pretty sure it has to do with the décor." I walked around her living room, mesmerized by the black and white photos that were similar to the ones directly above or below them. The first one I noticed was of a middle-age couple walking along the beach. Above it was a much older couple in the same type of pose on the beach. Below both photos was a photo of two children, maybe five or six years old, who were also walking along the same beach. Were they related to her? I made a note to ask her.

In the kitchen, there was the same setup of photos but of two women baking what looked like a cake or possibly cookies. One of the women had powdered sugar or flour on her cheek and both women were laughing. It was the same in the other two photos as well.

After browsing through a few other sets of photos and grabbing a beer, I went to make myself comfy on her loveseat but got sidetracked when I saw her bookshelf beside the TV. The books weren't classics by any means, some of them being self published by the looks of it. I didn't take Kylie for being a reader but was impressed by her collection. She had multiple books by SE Hall and also a handful from Jillian Dodd. I added their names into my phone to check them out later.

She dried her hair with a towel as she walked back into her living room, heading toward the bookshelf to meet me. "You found my stash I guess. I'm glad you haven't found my Kindle yet! I have hundreds on there but those are some of my favorites. I've met some of the hottest, most perfect fictional boyfriends in those books."

"Really now? How excited you just got telling me about them shows how much you love reading about them. They must be pretty amazing. I may have to go to you when I'm looking for a new author I guess. Are you sure I'm not stopping you from any other plans?" We had both made our way to the sofa and were sitting in a way that each one of our knees were touching. She seemed comfortable with me and it was nice to feel so trusted after just meeting each other.

"No plans, I promise. I try to have a night or two each week where I have nothing planned and have a 'me' night. No rules, no schedules, just go with the flow. It usually ends up with me in shorts and a t-shirt catching up on reality TV or shopping online but it's totally worth it. You were lucky enough to catch me on one of these nights."

"I'm glad I have luck on my side then. Am I lucky enough to find a beautiful woman in my complex who doesn't have a boyfriend also? If that's the case, I may need to go buy a lottery ticket." I couldn't help but add the cheesy lottery ticket phrase. She was smiling which in turn caused me to as well. I took that as a good sign.

"Buy me one while you're at the gas station since I, said beautiful woman, also found herself a handsome man a few doors down." Yep. We were both cheesy but it was fun.

"What kind of reality TV were you planning, or not planning, on watching tonight? I don't want to mess up any of your non-plans for the night." I scooted a little closer to her and made myself comfortable.

"One where there are a bunch of models living in the same house, competing to see who's best. It's fun to see the competitions and photo shoots. Girls are always having meltdowns which can be entertaining, too. I can make some popcorn and make a night out of it if you want to hang out a bit. Then we can totally talk about anything real estate related for your friend. I just need to unwind a bit first."

It wasn't on my normal list of shows to watch but I thought I could handle watching models on TV for an hour. What I meant was it would be difficult but I was up for the challenge.

After the show was over, I tried to come up with questions that I didn't need the answers to about real estate. I could tell she had a real passion for selling homes as her eyes lit up and she couldn't get a breath in when she was going over what was hot and why it was such a good time to buy. I went along with it, but after two questions, she just started going off on tangents so I sat back and ogled her. When she was excited about something, she would touch the back of her head, like she was fluffing her hair in the back. I counted and she did it a total of nine times that visit. We all have our quirks, and I didn't mind hers so far.

"Why'd you really come over here, Ryder? I know you aren't that excited about what I do for a living. There are a thousand different realtors in LA and San Diego I'm sure that could have helped your friend. Wanna spill?" I gave her credit for being observant. I also needed to work on my pretending-to-act-interested skills. I used to be able to get away with that shit with girls.

"You seemed to be someone I'd get along with and I was curious to get to know you a little better. I don't know too many people in the building, either, so if nothing else, I met a new neighbor." She apparently liked that answer since she scooted closer to me.

"I do like meeting new neighbors. You're completely single, right?" My thoughts immediately went to Payton. I missed her. I was nowhere close to being in a relationship with her but felt a twinge of guilt. I knew my chances with Payton were near zero and I needed something with Kylie. It would help me move on or at least distract me for a while.

"That I am. Did you have something in mind for how the rest of your unplanned night was going to go?" I could see her trying to make a decision, playing with her small pink sapphire ring on her left index finger.

"It's okay; you can walk me through what you're thinking. I promise not to laugh or judge. I can see your gears turning and am curious what your options are." Hopefully that gave her the nudge she needed.

"Well, I should call it a night and walk you out that door. That would be the good girl thing to do." She slid her hand over my stomach as she finished her thought. "What I am tempted to do is see if you want to watch a movie on the couch with me and hope you don't get the wrong impression about me. I'm not usually this comfortable with a guy, but you seem…comfy? Is that okay to say?"

I had never been called comfy before and was now on a mission to give her a new word to think of when she thought of me. Sexy as hell, man of pure awesomeness, dark and dangerous, or sex on a stick would have been my first choices.

"I would love nothing more than to watch a movie with you. I'm even okay with a chick flick if that's what you desire." I wasn't planning on watching much of the movie so it didn't really matter.

"*Varsity Blues* sound good to you? It's one of my favorites and I'm in the mood for a classic." I was in the mood for some whipped cream covered titties but I kept that bit of information quiet. It might not be the best way to get close to her.

Sinfully

Payton

I thought about leaving Tate with a note when I woke up but decided he deserved a real goodbye. Waking up with him next to me, I could see the sadness in his eyes. He knew how it was going to play out.

"Stay here with me. Give me a few more days with you, at least. You said last night that the other guy isn't in the picture anymore. Let me show you how amazing we can be together. I want this, Payton, more than anything." He motioned between us, scooting closer so that our naked bodies were nearly touching under the covers.

"I'm not what you need, Tate. I can't give all of myself to you. I want to, but it just won't work out that way. You are so genuine and driven, you'll always have a spot in my heart and I hope we can still remain close. There has to be *some* woman in Chicago who's worth what you have to give, though. When you meet her, you better damn well tell me, too! I'll give my stamp of approval for ya." I smiled slightly, but in reality, I hated having to go through that with him.

"Move to Chicago so that there *will* be a girl there who's worth it." He remained optimistic which crushed my soul. I fell for Ryder and he was the only one my heart wanted. Even though I had ruined the prospect of Ryder and me being together, my heart didn't give a fuck. It knew what it wanted and wasn't planning on letting anyone else in.

I pressed a soft kiss on Tate's lips and murmured, "I'll always be there for you and you'll always have a special place in my heart. Thank you for showing me how it feels to be loved." I swung my legs out of bed and headed over to my suitcase to get dressed.

I hoped that Tate would still want to be my friend but would understand either way. I really did want the best for him; I just wasn't *it* for him. He watched quietly as I got ready for the day and all I wanted to do was comfort him, but I couldn't.

"I should get back to the guys, wedding stuff, you know?" He looked everywhere but me as he started to slowly head toward the door.

That wasn't how our goodbye should be. I quickly ran over to him and gave him the biggest hug I could, kissing him on the shoulder because he was so much taller than me since I was barefoot.

"We'll see each other again, but let's do somewhere other than Vegas." I smiled at how completely over the city I was. "Stay in touch, Tate."

"I will, Payton. Hey, don't make that guy wait two years like you did me. Don't be afraid to get hurt or else you're only hurting yourself and the people who love you even more."

"Thank you, Tate. I'll see you around." I watched him walk down the hall, away from me. I had watched two amazing guys walk out of my life within twenty-four hours. I realized then that I truly was all alone. I hoped that time would fix the mess I'd created, because I wasn't sure what my next step should be.

I left Vegas later that morning and headed to the Bahamas with a stopover in Atlanta. I missed the beach but needed to get far, far away from the West Coast. I didn't mind traveling alone and welcomed the idea of having peace and quiet where no one could find me. I didn't bother telling anyone where I was going but sent Chloe a text saying I'd be back in a few weeks.

Nassau was a tourist city but lounging around on the beach all day and swimming in the aquamarine water was heaven for me. Having Atlantis nearby was also a selling feature when I picked the destination. Being able to gamble and lay out under the Caribbean sun all in the same day was just what I needed.

The shops were much of the same—selling shot glasses, gifts made of shells, and other tourist memorabilia—but they also had a wealth of designer named stores. I'd had my fill of Michael Kors, Chanel, and Tortuga rum cake within the first week of being on the island. I hung out near the docking area when new cruise ships unloaded passengers for the day. It was fun to find hot guys in their twenties who were out to have a good time. I often pondered the idea that it wouldn't be a bad place to do a little, uh, research for my next book. The men were there for a day or two and were looking for some quick fun with low risk.

I met a fraternity boy who had found his girlfriend in a compromising position with his frat brother on the ninth deck of the cruise ship he was on. He wasn't looking for revenge sex but it might as well have been. I could tell he was still torn up about being stuck on a ship, in the same room as his cheating girl- ex-girlfriend. His mind was elsewhere but he sure had stamina. I would give him a 'B' for effort and an 'A' for endurance.

Most of the time, I flip flopped between the poker tables and the beach. The warm white sand underneath me along with the soft crashing of the waves often lulled me to sleep. I dreamt many times of Ryder and how things could have turned out if I were a normal woman. Thinking about us together on a deserted island or tucked away in a cabin in the mountains seemed pleasant.

It was two weeks into my Caribbean vacation and I finally felt free and open to whatever I had to face when I returned to San Diego. I was done worrying about letting guys get too close to me. Tate and Ryder had shown me how good it felt to feel wanted and not only in a sexual way. I was curious to see how it felt if I fully let someone in. I knew I could get hurt, but hell, I was excited for the journey.

Tate was a sweetheart but there was something there that made me wary of him. I didn't know enough about his past or present for that matter but something was off. I was curious why he hadn't settled down.

Ryder was the one who I felt like getting to know better. I wasn't ready to forgive him for how he went about the whole Reece situation but I realized I didn't really give him a chance to explain himself. I needed answers from him. I couldn't get over the fact that he knew who I really was. Did he write those letters? I wasn't sure what to believe about Ryder anymore and hated how normal we seemed before I went off to Las Vegas. He came after me. Was it out of passion or possessiveness?

    I didn't have the answers and being in the Bahamas wasn't going to fix all of my problems. I wasn't sure if I would seek Ryder out but at least I was feeling more myself than I had been the previous few weeks. I was ready for a change and ready to get back to some normalcy in my so called life.

Chapter 9

Ryder

"Kylie is insatiable, man. Let me hook you up with one of her realtor friends down in San Diego. Apparently she was in a sorority down there during college and has a few good options for you." I had been keeping in touch with Tristen by phone and he seemed to be warming up to the idea of being set up with someone.

Kylie and I had hung out a handful of times and she was fun to be around. She never asked about my past and seemed to be content just going with the flow and living in the present. I knew she was happily single and moved to Los Angeles from San Diego three years before and had three brothers who were all younger.

She didn't mind watching football with the guys and me, even going as far as making game day snacks for us. Her booty shorts and cut off jersey were distracting to well, everyone, but no one complained and I didn't really feel too possessive of her. I knew she'd be with me after they left and she seemed to be enjoying herself.

She and I weren't a 'thing' but we were sleeping with each other. We didn't talk about relationships but hung out enough for me to know she wasn't seeing anyone else. It was convenient that we lived in the same building and had similar schedules.

Work was picking up significantly and I had signed a hot, new, up and coming author who wrote a book on a destructive bad boy who was tamed by the virgin next door. People ate up the bad boy/virgin story and the author was already working on a spin-off for the next book. New authors took up more of my time than my experienced clients but it was worth it when they became new bestsellers.

I was finally getting into a routine that seemed to work. Lorelei and I were an amazing team that saw eye-to-eye on most authors and that made work easy. Tristen and I were talking a few times a week and I was set to go down there a few weeks later. Kylie was someone I could talk to when I needed to vent and was the least clingy girl I had ever met. I was still not sure how she saw our relationship but I wasn't going to be the one to bring it up. I was finally getting to the point to where I didn't think of Payton every time I got in bed with Kylie. That was definitely progress.

Payton

It felt good to be back home. I'd missed Chloe and she was pissed when she found out I went to the Bahamas without her. She demanded that we have a girls' day to catch up on my whirlwind of a life. I met her at a boutique near downtown so that she could find a new dress for a fancy dinner Grayson was taking her to that night.

"Tate met Ryder? How did those two worlds collide?! Wait, how did Ryder find out about Reece? Tate doesn't know about the book, right?" She already had a handful of dresses in her hands within moments of walking into the store. Anything looked good on her so she didn't have to search for just one style that worked. *Lucky bitch.*

"Yes, they met, but they don't know who the other person really is. Ryder doesn't know Tate was in my book, and from what I know, Tate has no idea I wrote a book about him. Ryder found me with Tate and went all caveman. It was really kinda sexy. Then he dropped the bomb that he knew I was Reece. I was so pissed that I'm not really sure what words were said after that, but I'm pretty sure Ryder's been the one sending me the letters. They all were stamped with a wax 'R'." She made her way back to the dressing room and I was following her lead, hoping she wasn't going to spend an hour debating which one to get.

"Whoa. I still don't get how he found out or why he would bother with the creepy letters. It sounded like if he just kept his damn mouth shut, he could have had you. No offense, babe, I know you said you weren't giving in to him but I've seen you change since he was around then suddenly not. You like him, and even though you're upset at the situation, you still care." Chloe had tried on three dresses that all looked stunning on her. I was bored, sitting on the floor cross legged in the dressing room, checking my Facebook notifications while she tried on dress number four.

"It's over and done with now. I haven't gotten any more letters so maybe he's moved on. I have definitely worn out my welcome in

Sinfully

Vegas and doubt I'll be going back there for a long time. You should get the gray dress and play it up with some sexy heels and jewelry. It makes your tits look perky and we all know how much of a boobs guy Grayson is. Does he not realize girls can see him staring at their chest when he's talking to them? He does it all the time! Just because he's 'taken and isn't interested' doesn't make it okay to eye-fuck other women. I had to bend down to catch his attention the other day, Chloe. I mean, come on!"

"So what if he likes tits? If it makes you feel any better, whenever I catch him doing it, I make him go down on me and then am suddenly too tired to return the favor. He always seems to have that glimmer of hope that I may put out so he agrees. He goes to bed pissed but then it's the best morning sex the next day. I'm well rested and usually have already forgotten about his ogling to protest."

Gross. I didn't need to think about Chloe and her boyfriend being intimate together. "I'm walking away now. I'm heading over next door to get a chai tea latte. Want anything?"

"Sure, get me a shaken passion iced-tea lemonade? Love you!" she called out as I headed out of the store.

After Chloe got her new dress and we had drinks in hand, we made our way down the street to Swizzlesticks Bakery. It was actually a guy in his early thirties who owned it and made the best desserts in town. Adding liquor to everything, he gave a male twist to your normal desserts. I ordered a Whiskey and Coke cupcake while Chloe got a Buttery Nipple truffle. Thomas was quite the flirt and usually sat and talked with us for a while when we stopped by. He was a sweetheart and always wanted to know what we were up to. Most customers probably assumed he was gay, but after turning him down four times, I had determined he liked women at least a little. He didn't seem to have hard feelings about it but still brought it up on occasion.

"Payton, that tan makes you look edible right now. Where have you been the past few weeks? I've missed you coming by!"

"I needed to get away for a bit, you know? I am back to normal now, though, and you will be seeing me every week again. You know I'm addicted to anything you make, right? I'm surprised I haven't gained ten pounds from your alcohol filled, well, everything. You shouldn't be allowed to put my two favorite things together into a dessert, Thomas, it's just cruel."

I seriously had a problem because I never left there without a box to take home and said box never had less than six cupcakes, all for me. I would make myself feel better by just eating half a cupcake at a time, but might only wait an hour or two before getting my next fix.

"I have something special for you to try. I've been experimenting with some new flavors and would love to see what you think. I'll be right back."

"Man, I love when he experiments and lets us sample it. The amount of alcohol he uses in the new stuff is always more than when he puts it out for sale. I hope it's a Long Island ice cream or Mai Tai-ype of cake." Chloe was just as much a Swizzlesticks supporter as I was but was more disciplined. Whenever one of us stopped by to get a few desserts, we made a promise to get the other a couple pieces as well. I somehow brought them to her more often than she did to me, but I had seen her sneaking in here when she thought no one is looking. She would play it off like she only treated herself on occasion, but she couldn't fool me.

"What is your go-to drink in Vegas? Is it anything different than when you're here?"

"I stick with Chocolate Martinis or Colorado Bulldogs when I'm there. They make them extra tasty and I can't help myself when the waitress stops by and offers one. It's like I can't say no to them. Whenever I'm here you know I stick with Long Island Iced Teas or Whiskey Sours."

"Alright, ladies, I hope you like it. The first one is a Chocolate Martini bon bon and the second is a Whiskey Sour tart. I'm still working out the kinks but I think they taste pretty good."

Sinfully

Chloe and I stared at each other for a good minute, speaking volumes to each other without saying a word. Thomas was a sweet guy, but what were the odds that he picked two of my favorite drinks? We didn't know each other well enough that he would know my preferences and we had never gone out together. Red flags were going up, but I didn't know what to do about them. Thomas waited patiently for us to try his new desserts and I secretly prayed that we weren't being poisoned by a hot baker.

I slowly picked up the bon bon and smelled it before popping it in my mouth. I hoped Thomas thought I was smelling the chocolate—and not checking for a bleach smell—but it smelled fine so I figured the hell with it. Chloe followed soon after me. They tasted just like the drink and I was impressed. He was able to infuse the flavor without losing the texture of the product. I smiled up at him and gave a thumbs up since my mouth was still full of tart.

"It's awesome, Thomas. What was your inspiration?" I knew from the sound of Chloe's voice that she was playing detective. She was like a drug dog sniffing to find the hidden cocaine.

"I am very observant in what people enjoy. Making desserts from drinks is a way to express my love for a person. The whiskey and Coke cupcake y'all like so much was inspired by my grandpa. I get my inspiration from my friends now, but I try to please the people I care about." I could tell that wasn't a good enough answer for Chloe but didn't want to see how it would turn out if she kept questioning him. I needed to get her out of there before I found out something I wasn't prepared to hear.

"Come on, Chloe. We need to leave so we can make our appointment." I stood up, giving her the stare down, hoping she would take the hint.

"I don't have an appointment and want to keep chatting with Thomas here. Thomas, what's the first thing you think of when you see Payton?"

Before Thomas answered, I grabbed her forearm and starting pulling her away. "Thanks for the treats, Thomas. Bye!"

Once we were a few stores away from Swizzlesticks, I stopped walking and waited for Chloe to let me have it. I knew where she was going with her questioning and did *not* want to go there at the moment. She couldn't help herself in prying for information, though.

"What the hell, Payton! He's already had a crush on you and he just went into 'I'm a creepy stalker, here, want some candy, too?' territory. Did you not see all the red fucking flags? He *has* to be the guy sending you letters. I was close to finding out, too!" With how short she was, it really was amusing when she got fired up.

"Come on now, Scrappy Doo, let's get you home before Grayson has a fit about you being late. I'll stay and help you get ready so you can brainstorm ideas of how to get revenge." I needed a distraction from all the stalker talk and was hoping by the time we got to her place, all would be forgotten.

I loved going over to Chloe's house. As a high school graduation present, her parents bought her a Mediterranean style two-story, three bedroom home with a pool and gym that was located in a gated community. I didn't need anything that big or luxurious, but my eyes still lit up every time I walked in.

"You know it's him," Chloe nonchalantly mentioned as we walked into her place. We weren't done talking about it after all.

If I were to be honest, the idea of Thomas being my creeper was less nerve wracking than some of the other guys that popped into my head. At least Thomas was harmless. The other guys I imagined worked for the mob, just got out of prison, or wanted to do disturbing things to me since they knew about my sexual relationships. I could definitely handle Thomas. I had already let him down gently so I'd have to try another tactic, but I wasn't too worried.

We headed to her room and I could still see Chloe processing everything in her head. I wasn't sure why she was so caught up in it. "It'll be fine, Chlo. We know Thomas. If it was him, we just need to talk about boundaries, and hopefully he'll drop it. I know he's nosy, so we need to start being more careful about what we say around him."

"You mean to say we're actually going to go back to that guy's bakery after what we just found out? You are insane! He was always too kind for my tastes. I can't believe we didn't see it before."

"First off, we aren't positive that it *is* him sending the letters. Second, would you rather it be Thomas or my creepy neighbor who conveniently leaves his robe undone while getting the morning paper? I feel far more safe thinking it's Thomas, even though it may not be him. Stop thinking about it and let's get you dressed!" We rummaged through her closet for the perfect shoes to go with her dress in silence, both of us running through various scenarios in our head.

I helped Chloe style her hair so that most of it was up with just a few strands hanging down, allowing her diamond earrings and necklace to be the focus. She was putting on her makeup when I heard Grayson set his keys on the counter and head toward us. I loved Chloe but hated having to deal with Grayson.

"Hey there, Payton. Man, you look stunning as always. You ready to go, Chloe? You look fine, and I don't want to be late." It was like it didn't matter what she looked like to him; she was just the arm candy. He was already dressed in a suit and seemed to be bothered by the fact that she was sticking everything she might need in her purse, needing only another minute or two to be ready. I felt bad for her having to deal with his douchiness all the time. I felt his eyes on me and hoped we didn't have to chitchat while he waited. I was ready to bail if things got awkward.

"Haven't seen you around in a while, Payton. What have you been up to?" Sure enough, he was staring at my tits, even though I had on a t-shirt and jeans. What clothing I wore didn't seem to matter to him.

"You know, just having fun and taking care of me. I gotta run, Chloe. Have fun tonight, guys. Text me later, babe." With that, I picked up my purse and headed for the door. I couldn't get out of there fast enough.

"Bye, Payton! We'll talk tomorrow over breakfast. Newk's at ten thirty sound good?" I didn't have plans and still missed her from being gone so long.

"Sure thing. 'Night, girlie."

I went the long way home, enjoying the night air with my windows rolled down. I hadn't thought of Ryder once and was proud of myself. Baby steps.

Chapter 10

Ryder

"You ready to be back?" Kylie and I were driving down to San Diego to meet up with Tristen and one of her good girlfriends. Her idea was to get a feel for Tristen before trying to set him up with McKenna. Apparently, McKenna had particular tastes in men and Kylie was trying to make sure it wouldn't be a disaster by throwing them together. It was sweet and I felt the need to protect Tristen from another heartache if I could.

"I was down here a few months ago, actually. Got to catch up with Tristen while I was here. It feels good coming back, though; it's like my second home."

We were driving down in my SL63 AMG Roadster and Kylie insisted on having the top down during the drive. It was mid-October and getting cooler but still felt nice as long as the sun was out. Looking over at her, she had a smile on her face and legs kicked up on the dashboard. She was so easy to be around but I couldn't help but wonder why she was so content in our non-existent relationship. I wasn't going to complain; any guy would be lucky to settle down with her.

The fact that I would be seeing Tristen in a few hours was enough to put me in a good mood. I knew there was a chance I would see Payton while there but it was a big city so I figured the odds were slim. Although, if I were honest, I wanted to see her again. I wanted to see how she was doing and if she had moved on.

Sinfully

Did she ever think about me? I hated wondering 'what if' but damn it, I didn't get a fair chance with Payton—I had a thousand 'what ifs' going through my mind. What if I had never told her I knew? What if I hadn't walked out her hotel room, and instead, made her confront the issues she was spewing out? What if I had never seen her with that other guy?

"Where'd you go, handsome? I lost you for a sec."

"Huh?" I glanced over at her and couldn't tell anything from her expression since she had on those damn bug sunglasses. They covered half her face and I couldn't tell if she was upset, concerned, pissed, or happy for that matter. "I'm good. Just getting lost in the drive. I think we should take Tristen to dinner tonight and get him in a casual setting so you can see how he normally is."

I hoped that was enough to get her off my back. She didn't know about Cami, and I doubted that Tristen would bring it up. I noticed a mom and pop candy shop billboard that said it was just three miles off the highway and it seemed like a good spot to break up the drive and get my mind back on the lady sitting next to me.

Without saying a word, I exited the highway, taking a left at the stop sign. I could feel Kylie looking over in my direction and I just smiled in return. "Trust me."

"You better not be taking me out to the middle of nowhere to chop me up into little bits and pieces, Ryder. That was not what I signed up for." I couldn't help but chuckle at how nonchalant her statement was.

We pulled into the parking lot and the store looked like a cabin that had been there forever. The neon *Open* sign was lit and there were probably twenty cars in the small lot. I took that as a good sign and began getting out of the car, wondering if Kylie was going to ask any questions or just go with it. I could see it going either way, quite frankly.

"Oh, I hope they have rock candy and those vanilla cream caramel bull's-eye thingies!" She was skipping to the front door, leaving me a few steps behind her, and I couldn't help but smile. I wanted some gummy bears and something with chocolate and peanut butter but wasn't too picky. Kylie, on the other hand—she was on a mission for particular candy. I grabbed a wooden basket and made my way over to the barrel she was currently staring at. "Should I stock up? I mean, rock candy doesn't go bad, right? Oh my gosh, they have the dark red ones!" I could feel the basket getting heavier already. She had the biggest grin on her face throughout the whole store, stopping at barrel after barrel to get a little of her favorite things. I found some candy buttons that Cami used to love and grabbed a few strips, as well as some gummy worms that I would enjoy during the rest of the drive.

"Did you find your bull's-eye candies, babe?" I had lost her while filling up a bag of gummies and she had made it across the store.

"Uhh. Maybe. You're not allowed to judge me for this. They'll last me forever, and I haven't had them in a long time, and they're my most absolute favorite." She looked nervous with her hands held behind her back, looking like a sad puppy in the rain.

"No judging here. See, I grabbed some stuff, too. Come on, let's go check out and get back on the road. I got some stuff Tristen will probably like, too."

"I'll meet you there, just a sec." I watched her slowly move the bag that was behind her back around and placed it in the barrel. I contemplated what to do next. Her brows were scrunched together and her tongue was peeking out of her mouth. I watched in amusement as she put a few wrapped pieces of candy back in the barrel, but no more than three seconds later, she put a handful of the wrapped candy back in her bag. Picking it up, she called out that she was ready with a satisfied smile on her face. She was a tiny thing and I would have never guessed that she had such a sweet tooth.

I couldn't help but chuckle at the innocent look she gave me as she plopped the bag of caramel vanilla cream bull's-eyes on the counter along with my basket and her basket of bulk candy. She had decided shortly after getting the rock candy that she would need her own dedicated basket and I happily obliged. Mine weighed in at just under a pound with the gummy bears and hers was over four and a

Sinfully

half pounds. Granted, a lot of it was due to the caramels but *damn* that was a lot of candy.

Handing over my credit card, I received a chaste kiss on the cheek and a bear hug around the waist. Glad she was easy to please. We walked back to the car, hand in hand, and she let me in on her secret that she had a huge sweet tooth. *No kidding! Really? I never noticed.*

As soon as we were buckled in, I started driving back to the interstate while she opened up one of her bags. "Want one? I don't mind giving you one if you want to try."

I glanced over and I could tell she meant one in the singular sense, and I was determined to fuck with her a little on the rest of the drive.

"Aww, thanks. I'd love one. I've never tried them before." She handed me one and I popped it in my mouth and began acting like I was trying to decide if I liked them or not.

"Chewy, yet creamy. It's interesting for sure. I don't know what all the hype is about, Kylie." I swallowed it and could feel her staring at me.

"They're amazing! You get vanilla cream wrapped in silky caramel. It's perfectly sweet without being overwhelming and light enough to not feel guilty afterward."

"I didn't really taste the vanilla. Here, let me see if I taste it now." My hand slid over into her bag and I smiled when I felt the wrapper between my fingertips.

Before she could protest, I had it in my mouth and moaned, letting her know the vanilla flavor does come out if you're looking for it.

"I think I like them a little more every time I try one. You may be able to get me addicted to those things if you're not careful, Kylie." I saw her look in the bag, trying to gauge how many she had left.

"Thank you for trying them, but don't worry, you don't have to love them. I know you'll be happy with your candy buttons and gummies. Thank you for taking me there, Ryder. I haven't been to a candy store since I was little."

She was sweet. Possessive with her candy, but sweet. We drove the rest of the way in near silence. I was ready to see Tristen and wanted to meet McKenna. I knew it was going to be hard for Tristen to let Cami go but it would be good for him.

"I wasn't sure if this was going to be a big deal or not, but I should probably let you know before we meet up with McKenna." We were driving through the city, just a few minutes from the hotel.

"Why does that not sound comforting, Ky? Spill." My over-analytical brain started going over worst-case scenarios and the probabilities of them actually occurring. McKenna used to be a dude... McKenna is married to the mob... McKenna and I are lesbian lovers... Well, the last one wouldn't be so bad.

"She has a daughter. The daddy left before Bailey was born and she's raised her alone for the past four years. I don't know Tristen, but I know some guys don't want to deal with another guy's child. I'm sorry I didn't tell you sooner, I just really want her to get back out there and start dating and Tristen seems really nice." I don't think she took a breath that whole time. She looked at me with a nervous face and I thought about how Tristen would react when he found out. He was excited to be a father with Cami. I knew he loved kids. I didn't think he'd have a problem with it but I could have eased him into it if I'd known.

"It should be fine, babe. McKenna can tell him once she's comfortable around him but he deserves to know what he's getting into. I'm sure he'll be okay with it." With a loud sigh, I could see her relax out of the corner of my eye.

We decided to check into the hotel and 'freshen up', per Kylie's words, before meeting with Tristen. "I'm so excited to be here with you right now, Ryder. I needed a break from life for a few days." Kylie was talking to me from the bathroom and I was lying on the bed, waiting for her to get ready since I knew I just needed to throw on a clean shirt and shoes before I was ready. I closed my

Sinfully

eyes, just relaxing for a moment before I heard the lightest pitter-patter coming toward me.

Peeking one eye open, my mouth dropped open as I took in the sight before me. Kylie was facing me with a neon orange lacy thong and nothing else. Her nipples were already hard and she had tousled her hair. Looking at me from underneath those thick black eyelashes as if she was purely innocent was my undoing. She waited patiently for me to take action, but when I kept my position with a wide grin, she gave in.

Prancing over toward the bed, she climbed up on her knees, straddling me in an instant. Without saying a word, she began kissing my chest at a leisurely pace and I couldn't help but lift my hips up to meet her firm ass. While flicking and sucking on my nipples, her hands roamed my lower abdomen, moving slowly back up my arms.

A giggle escaped her lips when she suddenly sat back down on my lap, making me wince at the harshness of her actions. She must have noticed, because to make it better, she began gliding over my hard cock at a soothing, erotic pace. I never knew what to expect out of her. She could be gentle and sweet in bed, but she was damn insatiable, and I wasn't complaining. I had no idea what was coming next.

"Tristen is expecting us in an hour, babe. I don't do late. Make this quick if you want it." She lifted herself off of me and padded over to the end of our bed where our suitcases were. I wasn't giving her an option to leave me hanging. Maybe I needed to be clearer with my choice of words.

"Kylie, you have three seconds to get your fine ass back on this bed or I'm coming to get you." *There. Maybe now she understands.*

"I'm coming back, don't worry. I just wanted to…to show you something. We haven't talked about stuff like this but I figured why wait any longer?" With that, she made her way back to the bed with her hands behind her back. When she reached our bed, I could only wonder what could be back there. Handcuffs? Double-headed purple dildo? Chocolate syrup and whipped cream? No idea.

136

"Have an open mind, 'k, babe?"

"Uhh huh." I hated waiting for surprises, and this seemed a very good one.

She pulled a black silk tie from behind her and I noticed it was mine. I immediately envisioned Payton tied up to my bed and all the naughty things I could do to her. *Damn it! No thoughts of Payton while Kylie is pretty much naked in front of me.*

As she draped the tie around her neck so it ended between her tits, I made my way over and grabbed hold of the material. She looked at me with innocent, yet knowing eyes. *The things I could do with this tie.* Grasping the material in both hands, I had an idea of one thing I wanted to do with her.

"Go stand near the windows, facing away from the room." *I can get into this.* I wasn't that surprised that Kylie wanted to spice things up. I watched her hesitantly walk over to the window, looking back once she reached her destination, waiting for the next set of directions.

"Spread your legs for me. Hands behind your back." She gave me a smirk, and I knew it was turning her on just as much as it was me.

Walking up behind her with my tie in hand, I grabbed hold of her wrists and wrapped them together, firm and snug. I had taken off my shirt and shoes shortly after arriving. Unbuckling my pants while still behind her, she began squirming in need. "Patience, babe. I'll make you feel real good, it's a promise."

With her hands secured behind her, I walked around to her front and knelt down so that her mound was eye level. I lifted one of her legs and let it rest over the top of my shoulder, my tongue had a brief swipe of her wetness, and I began teasing her clit with one finger. "Mmm, baby, I need more. I want your mouth on me."

Sliding one finger inside of her, I used the flat of my tongue against her clit. Her moans were loud and raw. I wanted to fuck her so badly, but with her hands tied, I had to take advantage of the power I had. After lapping up her juices from her first orgasm, I

Sinfully

bent her over and stood behind her. I was glad I had packed a decent supply of condoms for the trip.

I gripped the silk tie, along with her hands to give me leverage, as I slid into her warmth. She was powerless and quickly began pushing herself back toward my cock as I pushed forward. Filling her to the hilt felt fucking amazing.

"You like that, baby? I love fucking your tight pussy."

We had a good rhythm going. "Slowly bring your legs back together, Kylie. Just like that, so fucking tight, babe." She cried out my name as she came. Her muscles contracted around me, causing me to join in on an eye-blurring orgasm.

"So good, baby. So good." I gently unwrapped her wrists and helped her upright. I left a few sweet kisses on her shoulders, followed by a quick swat of the ass. "Time to go get ready." With that, I walked to the shower and knew she would be right behind me to join.

We met Tristen at Gloria's. It was our go-to place back in college. Cheap margaritas brought the ladies out and the brisket tacos were delicious. It had a homey atmosphere with murals painted on the wall and intimate seating.

"What's new, man? Glad to see you again after you ran out on me." I hadn't filled Tristen in on how Kylie and I didn't talk personal details and hoped I could give him the hint he needed.

"It's all in the past. Kylie here lives in LA and makes the best French toast in the world. She cooks for me and the guys when we are watching a game and even sticks around and watches it with us. Can it get any better?" I gave him a wink and hoped that I was obvious enough that we weren't about to bring up Payton or how much of a pussy I turned into while trying to get her.

"Sounds like you got something good going on. You got any friends as beautiful as yourself, Kylie?" Tristen nonchalantly asked as he sipped his beer.

"He's exaggerating on the French toast. I add a little cinnamon and he thinks it's gourmet. I went to college down here so I still have a few single friends who are pretty nice catches. I could—*we*

138

could—set you up with one of them if you'd like. The one I have in mind is McKenna. Beach blonde wavy hair, tanned skin, awesome sense of humor, and she's a second grade teacher." The way she described her friend was why Kylie was a realtor. She showcased the best assets and marketed them well. I doubted Tristen had it in him to say no. He was too nice and definitely a people pleaser.

I could tell he was indecisive but I knew it was because it was a big step for him. I couldn't fathom how hard it would be to start dating again after the love of your life passed away tragically, and I hoped he could make it past the hurdle. I set my hand on Kylie's thigh as she waited for a response. She wasn't one to press an issue but Tristen might need a nudge, or shove.

"She sounds like your type. Why not give it a try? Take her down to the festival at the beach so it's a casual setting, and if there's not a connection, at least you can hang out and enjoy the night. This would be good for you, Tristen."

He was still contemplating. I thought, deep down, he was ready. I just wasn't sure *he* believed he was ready for action. He was always so damn secretive about his relationships and women, though; I wasn't positive where his head was with the situation at hand.

"Sure, why not. Does she live around here? I'm not guaranteeing anything but I wanted to go to the festival, anyway, and her company would be nice."

Atta boy.

"Perfect. You'll love her." Kylie thought she had succeeded, but seeing Tristen's face when she brought up loving someone, I noticed he had zoned out. I knew he was going back to memories of Cami and I truly felt for him. It would definitely be a difficult process, but taking that first step was huge for him.

We ate, for the most part, in an awkward silence. I did let Kylie know Tristen and I went to college together and used to go surfing all the time. I blamed work on being the reason I didn't surf anymore. Tristen was friendly but distant with Kylie. He was a good guy and wasn't one to make someone feel uncomfortable if he could help it. The three of us parted ways with plans to meet up at the festival on Saturday. I figured I would help Tristen out if the date was going poorly, but if all was well, we could run into each other but part ways after a few minutes. My plan seemed to put Tristen at ease.

The drive back to the hotel was quiet. We discussed meeting up with McKenna and Bailey for an afternoon at the zoo before her date with Tristen. I had no set plans so it worked for me.

"Did I do something wrong? I thought it was a great idea setting Tristen up with McKenna. You said he needed to get back out there, and she's a sweetheart. I just left dinner feeling like I was in trouble or something." She had already gotten ready for bed and was sliding under the covers. She liked to keep it fucking freezing in the room at night, so she was always under a thick comforter and cuddled close to me. I wasn't used to the brisk temperature but having her in my arms felt nice.

"You're fine, Ky. Tristen has gone through stuff no one should ever have to go through. Sometimes little things bring up memories that he has done a good job of hiding. There's no need to bring it up, just understand that he might have triggers that pull him back to a darker place. I don't want to bring it up tomorrow with McKenna, though; it should be his place to talk to her if he chooses to. 'K, babe?"

"Of course. I understand. Thank you for letting me in a little. Sometimes I feel like such an outsider in your life. I am never one to pry for information, but the little bits that I do find out, I cherish. You can always come to me, Ryder. I won't judge or think of you differently if you talk to me about your past. We all have them and they aren't perfect."

I was not expecting that. What happened to being casual with no questions asked? I needed to reevaluate what Kylie and I were doing or I might be going down a road I wasn't prepared to travel.

"Sure thing. 'Night." I turned off the lights and lay in bed on my back. Kylie looked at me a moment since I always curled up

Leighton Riley

behind her. After a moment, she turned back on her side and fell asleep, without me behind her.

She needed to get used to that feeling again. It was the first step to easing her out of the comfortable place I had created with her.

Sinfully

Payton

Chloe had been my partner in crime over the last two weeks, trying to set me up on dates with friends of friends of coworkers and so on. I had come to the conclusion that she hadn't met half of the guys from judging how awful they were on our 'dates'. One was thirty-two and still living at home. Another worked at a morgue—which creeped me out—and the last guy I met had four different children under the age of three with four different women. I didn't mind a man with a child, but that situation was not for me.

My neighbor had somehow overheard Chloe and me talking about my dates while we were taking a walk around the neighborhood and offered himself up. He wasn't unattractive and seemed decently normal but it was very unexpected. He was maybe a few years older than me and had lived on my street for a few years. I caught numerous women doing the walk of shame from his house so he obviously had something going for him.

We went out for coffee, but the amount of information he knew about me made me uneasy. I shook it off as just looking out for your neighbors but something wasn't quite right. He noticed when I went out of town and knew I lived alone, which wasn't all that hard to ascertain. He also knew I wrote children's books and didn't do many relationships. I wasn't one who had men over at my place, so I figured that was how he came up with that conclusion. He was sweet enough to walk me up to my door and gave me a sweet, lingering kiss on the cheek before heading over to his house.

With all my dates, I let them know I'd call them, but of course *that* never happened. Being single suited me just fine and I had come to terms with the fact that Ryder and I were not right for each other.

I made Chloe promise that the weekend would be date free, and we planned on going to the zoo for some best friend time before dressing up and going dancing that night. I missed hanging out with her, just the two of us.

142

Leighton Riley

Pulling up to Chloe and Grayson's place, I was excited to go to the San Diego Zoo. I hadn't been since I was ten, with my adoptive parents, and loved seeing all the animals, *especially* the monkeys. Making my way up to her door, I felt like I was finally in a good place and was ready for the weekend to begin. A random, yet insanely attractive, man opened Chloe's door and I stood there in awe.

His hair was tousled perfectly and he was built like a hockey player—broad shoulders, tall as hell, and a defined jawline. I probably looked mute since I was pretty sure he was introducing himself, and I made no effort to move or talk.

"-you okay?" Shaking myself out of my trance, I heard Chloe's voice coming from behind all the muscle. *Who is this guy?*

"Uhh, yeah. Who are you? Who is he?" I asked both the sex god in front of me and Chloe.

"This would be Tucker. He's a friend of Grayson's. Grayson wanted to go to the zoo with us but didn't want to make it weird so he invited Tuck here. Hope that's okay, Payton." She was giving me the *'you don't have a choice so you better enjoy this fine piece of ass since I can't'* look. I couldn't help but let out a slight laugh at Chloe's expression behind Tucker's arm. This was so not what I planned for our *girls' day* but couldn't deny myself a day of hanging out with such a hot gift to women.

"Sounds like fun, Chloe. Hey, would you mind helping me get something from my car since it sounds like one of the guys will be driving now instead of me?" I didn't really give her an option as I pulled her arm and effectively dislodged her from the safe location behind Tucker. "Be right back, Tucker!"

After making our way to my car, I finally let her go, still pissed off at the situation. "You said no more meddling! How is inviting sex-on-a-stick to the zoo with us not meddling, Chloe?!"

"See?! You *do* find him attractive! Hell, *I'd* sleep with him if I wasn't worried about him telling Grayson. You need a little Tuck in your life, Payton, nothing serious, but just a good old-fashioned

143

fucking from a fine man. After the zoo, you can head back to his place and finish your date."

I saw so many things wrong with what Chloe had just said that it took me a minute to process it. I could see her having her way with Tucker if she had an opportunity, but I knew it could backfire on her if Tucker had a big mouth. *Did she just say I could fuck Tucker today?* Is that what Tucker signed up for? Hanging out for a few hours at the zoo and expecting to claim his prize afterward? I was irritated and turned on at the same time. He was exceptionally sexy.

"Let's just get going, okay? I'm tired of overanalyzing the situation, and I want to see some damn monkeys. Your scheme to find me a man will not hinder my plans today, friend."

Chloe jumped in delight and squealed as she grabbed my arm and started tugging me back to her home. The boys were ready to go, Grayson seemingly in charge and Tucker hanging back with me. He was quiet so far, but the more I thought about it, the more exhilarating the day seemed.

"I was told you love the zoo but haven't been since you were a kid. I think it's pretty cute if you ask me. Did you have any exhibits that you are dying to see? We can break away and spend a little more time at those if you want." Tucker sat next to me in the backseat of Grayson's black Yukon and had his right arm hung over the back of my seat. He hadn't tried anything with me yet but seemed conservative or just a really sweet gentleman. From how Chloe described the plans for the day, I expected the opposite. Just thinking of the hidden places Tuck and I could fuck at the zoo made my panties wet. He was one of those guys who oozed sex appeal and you knew for a fact that he was a powerhouse in bed.

"I want to see the wombats and the monkeys! Chloe thinks wombats are ugly so I doubt they'd linger with us. They're just so damn adorable and exotic. I used to name my favorite monkeys when I was little. I'm pretty sure there was a Grumpy, Happy, Sleepy, and Dopey last time. Disney movies were my babysitters back then. My parents could pop in any Disney movie and leave me alone for ninety minutes without me moving once." He had a goofy grin on his face as I realized how much I had just shared with him, a complete stranger. "Umm, sorry. Yeah, we can do whatever you want. I didn't mean to spill my life story. I'm not usually like that."

"You don't have to worry and I'd rather you be genuine and silly than stuck-up and fake any day. Just let me know when you want to hang back and we can, deal?" He was being very nice. I briefly wondered what Chloe had said to him and if he was acting that way for a certain reason.

The four of us walked through the zoo at a leisurely pace, taking random pictures in front of the exhibits. In front of the baboons, Chloe and I bared our 'pink butts' to the camera. We also climbed on the back of the boys' backs to mimic the monkeys holding their babies on their backs. Tucker shared a sweet photo with a tiger whose paw was held up against the glass and he high fived the tiger. When we finally made it to the wombats, Tucker and I hunched down to their level and Chloe took a pretty cute pic of us. Grayson and Chloe left us and let us know to meet them at the front an hour later.

"It feels good to act like a kid again. I haven't laughed this hard in forever!" Tucker slid his hand close to mine and waited as if he was asking permission. I knocked my hand into his and found my fingers interlocked seconds later. We sat on a bench and watched the wombats a few minutes longer in comfortable silence. I silently thought how perfect of a time it would be while we were alone to get better acquainted but Tucker didn't seem to be on the same level of horniness as I was. *Can't a guy throw me a bone here?* Literally. I was tempted to pull him into the reptile exhibit and bring him up to speed with my ideas but thought better of it.

"Why did you decide to come out with us today?" I blurted the question out without really thinking about it. I was curious, though.

"Grayson has mentioned you a few times. Said you were beautiful and hard to tame. I didn't have plans today, so when he asked and said you'd be joining us, I had to jump at the chance. I love a good challenge and he spoke of you in high regards. He also wasn't wrong when he said you were beautiful, although I'd probably use stunning or breathtaking when referring to your beauty, Payton."

Yep. Wasn't expecting *that* answer. I was thinking more along the lines of Chloe saying I was great in bed and it'd be worth his time to come out and join us.

"That's sweet of you." I wasn't used to moments like this. While he was ridiculously good looking, I didn't feel a spark when I was around him. Don't get me wrong, I wouldn't mind having sex with him, but I didn't think it'd be anything long-term.

He stood quickly, pulling me up with him by the hand. We began walking aimlessly around the zoo, killing time and enjoying each other's company. As we were walking by the elephants, I suddenly felt like I had eyes on me. It was the weirdest feeling and I couldn't help but look around. It was when I turned toward the giraffes that I saw them. *Him.*

He was crouched down low, laughing, as a little girl hopped up on his back for a piggyback ride. There were two women with him who were gorgeous. Both girls were blond—one with more beach-kissed hair—and neither looked like they had ever had a child. They were perfectly fit and slim with cut-off shorts and casual shirts that still showed off their curves. The little girl must have been four or five and was laughing at something Ryder had said.

"Payton? You okay, girl?" Tucker's voice had a hint of concern but I didn't have time to deal with that. I pulled him off to an area uneasily seen by those passing by so I could see the only guy who I constantly had on my brain and who I was still upset and unsettled with. He looked like was enjoying himself. I couldn't tell if he was with either girl because he wasn't touching them in any way, but the thought that Ryder was with someone made my stomach uneasy. No sooner had they appeared did they disappear.

"I don't mind playing a secret agent but I kind of need to know the specifics. Are we hiding from someone or are we scoping them out?" Tucker was trying to lighten the mood but I could tell from the confusion in his eyes that he was curious about what made me duck and cover at a zoo.

"I just saw someone I wasn't planning on seeing. Caught me off guard. Ready to go?" I needed to get away and needed to find Chloe and Grayson, pronto.

Heading toward the exit, I thanked the heavens that Chloe and Grayson were already there, sitting on a bench, sharing a cup of Dippin' Dots. We walked toward them and I swung an arm out to grab Chloe and kept walking toward the exit. I wasn't about to wait for them to finish their ice cream or ask questions. I was sick to my stomach and my damn heart was hurting. My bed, a tub of Dutch chocolate ice cream, and a *Sons of Anarchy* marathon were what I needed. That show always reminded me that I had to take care of myself and not count on others. If you did, you got screwed. Or killed. Or sent to jail. Or pregnant. Regardless, our girls' day was officially over.

"What the hell, Payton? We were ready to leave and just waiting on you! Can't you give us two minutes to finish our banana split Dippin' Dots?" I could hear footsteps behind me and kept walking toward the car. I kept telling myself I would not break down, but I was hanging on by a thread.

The drive home was filled with silence and as soon as the car was shifted to Park, I was out the door and heading to my car. I would deal with the repercussions later. I wasn't going to start crying in front of them. *He's fucking moved on!* I knew it had been months but didn't realize how much seeing it would hurt and how much I missed him. I felt like I had been robbed of a real chance with Ryder and suddenly hated those two women. It didn't even matter if they were with him romantically or not. They got to spend quality time with him and hear his laugh.

I sat in my car for a few minutes, not crying, but just staring out the window, trying to figure out why Ryder was brought into my life for such a short period of time before tearing what little we had to pieces. I didn't think we had any type of chance, and knew I should give up, but my heart was more stubborn and wanted to hold on to hope. *Stupid heart.*

Sinfully

Ryder

I wasn't quite sure what Kylie thought of our relationship, but I wasn't about to deal with it in San Diego. We were there to have a good time, set my best friend up with a decent date, and get away from life's problems for a few days. I also didn't want to have to stay in a hotel or drive back to Los Angeles with a girl who'd just had her heart broken. There would be hatred, name calling, and bawling like a baby. I didn't want to deal with that shit. I was smart enough to know I should handle it back at her place so that she couldn't throw my belongings if she, for some reason, thought we were more than casual fuck buddies.

Waking up Saturday morning, I had a plan to check out McKenna to see how well of a match she and Tristen would be and not think about the misinterpretations that Kylie might have. The night before, we fucked like nothing was wrong but I didn't cuddle with her afterward. Our day at the zoo would go as planned, and if she wanted a little public affection, who was I to deny her? At that point, I didn't care if it all blew up in my face. Kylie was a great girl, but she wasn't *the* girl.

We pulled up to McKenna's home and out came a girl who belonged on a surfboard. She had natural sun-kissed blond hair and was wearing shorts and a sweatshirt. Behind her was an adult version of her and I instantly knew she would be Tristen's type. She opened the door of her Chevy Avalanche so Bailey could get in and proceeded to head over to my car. Kylie unbuckled her seatbelt and started getting out of the car and I followed suit to meet Tristen's new date.

"McKenna, Ryder. Ryder, this is McKenna. You got everything you need from the car, babe?"

"Nice to meet you, McKenna. What? I figured we'd take separate cars." I was given a look by both women that told me it wasn't something I could argue about and headed back to the car to

148

grab my phone and wallet. "Sure is a nice ride, McKenna. Girls in good looking trucks are sexy. Tristen is going to love you."

"That's sweet of you. It's my second baby, right after Bailey. You can call me Kenna by the way. Ready for a day at the zoo, everyone?" Bailey let out a holler and as soon as her mom started backing out of the driveway, Bailey started asking for the dirty talking tummy song.

I gave a questioning glance over to Kylie who shrugged her shoulders, letting me know she was as clueless as I was. Soon enough, though, we heard *Talk Dirty* by Jason Derulo come on and the little girl started jamming out. She was shimmying, bouncing her head, closing her eyes, and just going with the music. When the 'talk dirty to me' lyric began, she opened her eyes and put her hands on her belly. We could hear her saying 'talk dirty tummy' as if she was commanding the body part to start talking. I covered my mouth to cover my laugh as she started dancing around in the back of the truck when the saxophones followed. Throughout the song, she talked about her passport having kissies on it and told her dolly to sit comfortably on her lap in first class, but the best was her demanding that her tummy talk dirty to her. She was in her own little bubble and nothing could distract her when that song was on. By the time the song was over, Kylie was hunched over in hysterics and I had tears running down my cheeks in laughter.

"You might just have the coolest daughter ever, Kenna!" I looked over at Bailey and she nodded in confirmation.

"Pound it." Bailey held her fist out toward me and waited for me to clue in on what the four-year-old was asking.

"Uhh." Kylie slid over and fist bumped Bailey and the little girl squealed in delight. "Ohh, I gotcha." I held my hand out for Bailey but she gave me a mean glare and I wondered what I had done wrong. Not more than a few seconds later, though, did her smile come back right along with her fist.

"Just kiddin'. Are you and Kylie married? Do you kiss and have babies?" Did four-year-olds normally ask those types of questions? I didn't have a clue how to answer the kissing question.

"We aren't married and don't have any babies, Bailey. What's your favorite animal at the zoo?" Distractions. It worked with women so it had to work on girls. It was science.

"The dolphins!"

"Baby, you know they don't have dolphins there. They live in the ocean, where mommy goes to surf and where you build sandy castles."

"Aww, fine. I wanna see the alligators and snakes!"

I was excited to hang out with the little girl. She would break some hearts one day. I knew for a fact that Tristen would take to her quickly.

"Louder please! And Momma? You never answered my question yesterday. Why do they want the dirty tummy to talk? Mine never does and I dunno how to make it." Bailey's forehead was scrunched up as she tried to figure out the anomaly.

We drove the rest of the way listening to Katy Perry, Pitbull, and more Jason Derulo. Bailey might not have known or understood all the words, but she sure knew how to move to the beat and sing the chorus, albeit butchering the actual words. Once we parked and got out of the car, Kylie pulled her sunscreen out of her purse and applied it to Bailey's face. "Beautiful, sweetie. You are now officially ready for a day out at the zoo! Let's go!"

The weather outside was perfect. The breeze was light and the sun was shining down to provide us just the right amount of warmth. That was one of the things I loved about San Diego—the amazing weather.

Bailey led the way to her favorite exhibits while the three of us strolled behind her and I was able to get to know McKenna a lot better. She loved teaching and surfing. Bailey apparently already had the surfing itch, so Kenna was contemplating how soon was *too* soon for Bailey to start practicing and if she was being a bad mom by letting her baby surf so young. Tristen and I both learned at a very early age and that comforted her. At the mention of Tristen's name, her eyes widened and I knew that Kylie had spoken to her about him. She was curious about him and didn't seem like she dated much.

We stopped at the meerkats upon Kylie's request and the koalas upon Kenna's. Bailey kept dragging me over to the glass separating the people from the animals to tell me everything she knew about them. It was cute how much random information a child so small knew. She was so full of life and confidence. The fact that she loved the alligators and snakes was amusing, too.

I found Kylie sneaking her arm around me and interlocking our fingers as we walked along, and while I wanted to pull away, I made an effort not to show it. I knew dragging it out and letting her think we were good together would only make things worse later but the day was about Bailey and not our non-existent relationship.

As we made our way to the elephants and giraffes, I tried to focus more so on the little girl in front of us, making sure she had the time of her life. I could overhear her singing as she walked along the path but wasn't quite sure if I was hearing her right. I kept hearing her repeat, "They have it, they want it, they give it away" and assumed that she had no idea what she was talking about actually giving away.

"Hey, Kenna? What's she singing up there?"

"Ugh, *Lost Kitten* by Metric. I was playing it in the car when I thought she was playing on my Kindle but she caught on to the lyrics."

"Has she ever asked what the words meant? Bailey sings about giving it away like she knows."

"A slice of cake. I told her that the girl singing has a slice of cake that she shares with people who want some. Don't give me that look, Ryder. It was the best I could come up with at the time and now she's thinks it's a sweet song about sharing dessert when it's really a sex song." As Kenna explained, I tried and failed at holding in my laughter. Bailey was getting even more awesome as the day wore on.

I snuck up behind her and made the best elephant noise I could come up with, using my extended arm as the elephant's trunk.

She burst out laughing and told me I needed to work on my animal noises, but that she would teach me. I tried to give my best monkey and lion impression but her giggles made me start laughing right along with her. I hunched down in front of her and held my arms behind me to hold her effectively as she jumped on my back. I twirled her around and around, eliciting more fits of giggles from Bailey, the smile on my face making my cheeks actually hurt. On one of the turns, I thought I noticed a familiar face but couldn't shake the feeling in my stomach at the thought that it was her. I missed her smile and her spunk.

I slowed down the spinning and was able to get a better look. She was walking to a secluded area with some guy and I was instantly livid. I was never anything to her. She wasn't one to settle down and only looked for the short-term. I didn't want her to know I had seen her so I slowed to a stop, faced away from Payton, and grabbed Bailey's hand as we headed over to see the pandas before heading home. I was done with Payton. The only problem was that I felt like I was done with Kylie, too. I needed to get back to LA and away from both women.

Chapter 11

Payton

It was sad how just seeing him again tore me apart. I felt like I was in a good place and was suddenly back to square one. Going out on dates with the men Chloe set me up with was only a temporary distraction—Ryder was still on my mind every day.

Chloe and a few friends repeatedly asked me to go out with them throughout the week, but I wasn't up for it. I stayed at home, in shorts and a tank top, caught up on *America's Next Top Model*, *The Originals*, and reruns of *Gossip Girl* to fill my time. Each night, after I couldn't stand to watch any more TV, I would pull out my laptop and begin writing whatever came to mind. I wasn't writing for a purpose, but it felt good to get my thoughts out. I wasn't a pen and paper type of girl and it was kind of like an online diary.

After a week of writing like that, I had thirty-two pages of thoughts. I missed the feeling of writing and creating my own world for your characters and began thinking of what I could write about that wasn't my life or geared toward pre-teens. I liked dark romances with hit men, the mafia, and cold-blooded killers, but wasn't sure how much I knew about actually writing that genre. I would probably get the jargon all sorts of wrong and didn't want to piss those types of people off.

I could have a girl who's on the run from her abusive CEO of a husband who had the resources to find her no matter how far

Sinfully

away she traveled. The alpha male character could be accused of murdering his fiancée and had flown somewhere exotic to get away from being prosecuted. I wasn't sure where they would meet but he could make her feel safe, then break the news that he really *did* kill his soon-to-be-bride, giving a random explanation that somehow made sense. They would be on the run together but have close run-ins here and there.

I thought about it and started coming up with an outline and thrived on the feeling of having the power to create a man any girl would fall in love with, one who left you wanting more. I had the power to make him confident and masculine, with humor and sweetness mixed in. The girl could be weak but grow stronger throughout the story. They would get their happy ending but not before many trials and tribulations.

I woke up—realizing I had passed out with my laptop on my lap, screen still open to Microsoft Word—and realized I was all alone. Not just in my home alone, but I had no one significant in my life besides Chloe, and even then, she had Grayson. My thoughts went back to my childhood days when I was in the system, getting passed over for younger and cuter kids. I had no one to rely on then and it was my norm. After my adoptive parents died, I went back to that lonely place and felt like I deserved to be alone for whatever reason I chose that day.

Chloe taught me that everyone who entered my life wasn't going to leave me, but I always wondered when and why friends and boyfriends were going to leave me. I had hit the 'bottom' quite a few times over the years, where I wasn't talking to any guys and my friends were more like acquaintances. What I really wanted was a damn whiskey and Coke cupcake, but Swizzlesticks was closed, and I was still too scared and confused to confront Thomas. My whole creeper situation was another ordeal that I didn't want to have to deal with.

The next morning, I felt refreshed and ready to deal with whatever life happened to bring me. I went to my kickboxing class and got a massage shortly afterward. It was too cold to head to the beach and I needed to relieve some of my tension. It was sad, but I loved the feeling of being touched, and since I didn't currently have a man to satisfy that need, I settled for frequent massages by attractive male masseuses. They were professional, sadly. I would have totally been open to a more thorough massage but I respected that they were skilled at their job and left customers feeling satisfied, *non*-sexually.

The afternoon breezed by with errands I needed to run and I felt a sense of accomplishment as I headed back home. I could be single, have friends to go out with, and not wallow at home. As I was unpacking groceries, I thought out how I would spend the rest of the night. Hopefully, Chloe would be up for getting drinks with me. I was curious to know if Tucker ever asked about me, but figured my freak out might have steered him in the opposite direction. Regardless, I wanted a night out to have fun and flirt with some hot guys.

After everything was put away, I slipped out of my jeans and put on a pair of workout shorts. I settled into my recliner and started up my laptop on one knee and placed a stack of mail on the other. I knew there would be a few bills I'd have to pay, so I figured why not take care of it now and be done? Logging into Facebook, I went through messages and caught up on the latest gossip and a book-turned-movie. Thirty minutes later, I finally got to my mail. I hated paying bills. At the bottom of the stack, there was a letter with no return address but had all my information included.

My heart skipped a beat. I was terrified when I turned it over and saw the wax 'R' on the seal. I hadn't received a letter or anything since Vegas and figured Ryder or whoever sent it had given up. I mean, I hadn't been to Vegas anymore, which I thought was what bothered him…them?

The tips of my fingers moved uneasily over the hardened wax and I was suddenly enraged at whoever sent it. Why couldn't they just leave me the fuck alone? I wasn't interesting enough to earn me a stalker, damn it!

Sinfully

I ripped open the envelope, eager to find out what twisted and cryptic saying they had for me that time. I was yet again confused by a simple, yet powerful, statement.

WATCHING FROM AFAR IS GETTING HARDER AND HARDER TO DO, MY SWEET PAYTON.

YOU CAN'T HIDE FROM ME

Why couldn't my stalker just tell me in normal terms what I was doing wrong or what he wanted? It'd make the whole process easier. Just saying. I wasn't sure if Ryder had seen me at the zoo but the note pretty much confirmed it. He hadn't tried texting or calling me once since Vegas. We probably could have worked things out if he had tried to talk with me. The letters were too over the top, though, and I was tired of dealing with them.

I remembered from his emails to 'Reece' that he worked for Warrington Strom. Typing it in the search box, I looked up the address and typed it into my phone. He didn't get to be secretive about shit anymore and I was ready for some confrontation.

I texted Chloe and let her know I was heading up to Los Angeles for a few days and that I would explain after I got back. If I told her before I found Ryder, she would try to talk some sense into me and I wasn't in need of that. I threw some clothes, makeup, and my charger into an overnight bag and headed for my car. I would have a few hours to figure out what I wanted to say to Ryder. I needed to hear *his* side of the story but *mine* needed to get out there, too.

During my stop to get gas, I checked my messages and found I had four unread texts.

Chloe: Better not be going after nerd boy.

Chloe: Love you girl. I know you've got a good head on your shoulders and whatever you're going to LA

for, I trust your instincts. Thomas said he misses you by the way. I couldn't stay away from those Buttery Nipple truffles.

Unknown: I got your number from Chloe. Hope you don't mind. It's Tucker. Maybe you'd like to go out with me again sometime?

Tate: Hey baby, I'll be in Vegas in two weeks. Let me know if you want to meet up. Miss you girl

I figured I'd text Chloe back later. Tucker? I was about to text him back when I saw Tate's name underneath. I missed him, too, but in more of a friendly, occasional fuck buddy kind of way. I messaged Tate back first, smiling at the fact that he truly cared about me and wanted to spend time with me.

Me: I'll see if I can make it up there. Save me a dance?

I thought about how I should respond to Tucker and wasn't sure how the next few hours were going to play out with Ryder. I placed my phone back on the console and started the drive again, realizing the man I really wanted to text and talk to was only forty-five minutes away from me. I would deal with Tucker later. First priority was figuring out what the fuck I was going to do when I saw Ryder and how I had to promise myself that I wouldn't give in to his good looks and devastatingly handsome smile.

As I neared Los Angeles, I was still angry as hell. I wanted to see Ryder insanely bad but I needed to get my shit together. I knew I probably looked like hell from the drive but I didn't give a fuck anymore. Ryder could see me 'as is' and take it or leave it. I pulled into a nearby parking lot and headed into Warrington Strom Publishing Agency's building.

The building was immaculate inside. The light marble flooring led you to a sparkling turquoise water fountain in the center of the foyer. Two banks of elevators were hidden in their respective corners and I wasn't quite sure where I was headed. I couldn't find Ryder's suite number or anything, just the general address. I took a chance and headed for the elevators to my right and hoped I would find my way.

As I waited for the next available car, a short and stout man in his fifties came up beside me. "I haven't seen you around before. Do you need any help getting around? I wouldn't mind giving you a tour, beautiful." *Gross.* The dude smelled like stinky cheese and mushroom ravioli, and I couldn't tell if he still had some on his graying beard. He might be able to help me, though, unfortunately.

"I'm actually coming to surprise my...uh...my sister's boyfriend. He works here but I can't remember what floor she told me." I feigned disappointment. *Sister's boyfriend? Good job, Payton, that'll convince him.*

"What's his name, sweetie? I can't say I'm not excited that you're not here to see your own boyfriend, which you have I assume. Right?" *This might not be worth it.* I could feel the bile rising in my throat. The man was sleazy and repulsive. Luckily, the elevator bell dinged and I was saved by the bell.

"Ryder Strom. I'm sorry, but I'm kind of in a hurry. You see, he has a meeting in five minutes and I need to get him his paperwork for it. It really is urgent. Can you help me?" *Please just give me the office number. Don't drag this out any longer.*

"Eleventh floor. Corner office on the right. You'll make it, sweets. I'm down on the third floor, in the second cubicle on the left. Come find me afterward and I'll show you...*everything.*"

Yep. I could feel the vomit and swallowed it back down uneasily. When the door opened to the third floor, I thanked the heavens and finally took a breath of fresh smelling air.

As the elevator ascended higher, I felt nervous and anxious to see him but forgot that I was supposed to be angry. I stepped out into Warrington Strom's offices and headed to his office on autopilot. I kept replaying the reasons why I was supposed to be mad in the first place, and by the time I got to his door, I was remembering seeing him at the zoo with skankasaurus.

Leighton Riley

I raised my hand up to knock but decided he hadn't earned the option to let me in or not. Twisting the handle, I peeked in and saw a distraught Ryder at his desk with his hands covering his face. He looked defeated. A glass of whiskey sat next to his computer, and he had yet to look up at me. I wanted to run my hands along his back to comfort him and kiss his worries away, but I knew it wasn't the time or place. Realizing I needed to let him know I was there, I pulled the letter out of my purse, walked quietly over to his desk, and slid the letter toward him. It took him a moment to glance up, and when he did, he looked even more confused.

Sinfully

Ryder

After getting back to Los Angeles, I knew without a doubt that I needed to end things with Kylie. She kept talking about meeting her parents next time we were down in San Diego and that was a no-go for me. She didn't mean enough to me for a sit down with her parents. The more distance I gave, the more she clung on.

After work one day, I met her over at her place to talk. I let her know I had already eaten and I wasn't going to be staying long. I broke the news to her and waited for some sort of yelling or breaking of objects, but nothing came. She walked into her bedroom and locked it without so much as a word out of her mouth. I waited five or six minutes before heading out myself. I didn't need to console her or make her feel better in the situation. I just hated that it didn't give the finality that it should have.

We saw each other in passing for the next week but said nothing to one another. I assumed she had gotten the hint when I noticed her walking by me and a cute redhead talking in front of my building. We were just being friendly, but when the new girl took hold of my phone, adding her number to it, I figured why not play it up a bit? I whispered in the girl's ear about how exhilarating a night with me would be and she giggled in response. I could hear Kylie's 'hmph' from ten feet away and thought to myself, *mission accomplished*.

I never called the redhead but I *did* successfully get rid of Kylie, or so I thought. I was at work when I got a text from her.

> **Kylie: I overreacted that night at my place. You said you didn't want serious and I pushed you. I don't care if we're just fuck buddies again, come over tonight?**

Well, I thought I had made it clear to her. I knew going back to just fucking her wasn't an option. If she had feelings for me, I needed to let her go. Otherwise, I would just keep hurting her, and if I was honest, the sex wasn't all the great. I could find better pussy to satisfy my needs.

I hated dealing with shit like that at work. It was distracting and I needed a moment to deal with my thoughts. I still wanted Payton. I hated that I did, but my dick got hard just thinking about her sweet, luscious lips on mine. I could almost feel her with me if I tried hard enough. I fucked up with her and I needed to figure out a way to mend things between us. It was crazy how I felt her presence when I thought about her. Things weren't normally like that with me.

All of a sudden, I heard the swoosh and saw the letter land on my desk. Confused, I looked at the unfamiliar piece of paper. Looking up at who was in my office, I was pretty sure my heart skipped a beat. *That was why I felt her presence.* I was too consumed in my thoughts to hear her come in. What was she doing there? Looking at the note, I instantly became worried for her. It wasn't a friendly letter from a friend. It was from someone sick and twisted.

I felt the urge to bend her over my desk and spank her for making me leave. Even with casual clothes on and bare minimum makeup, she looked stunning. My memories of her didn't do her justice. I wasn't sure what to say and was worried that if I opened my mouth to speak, I wouldn't be able to control myself.

"Why do you keep trying to scare me? You know who I am now. Why do you keep sending these?" I could hear the quiver in her voice, and from one look at her face, I could tell she was holding back the tears. Standing up, I stalked toward her to wrap her in my arms but restrained myself and sat on top of my desk.

"What do you mean ba-Payton? Those aren't from me. Why would you be scared?"

"They have an 'R' on the seal, Ryder! How are they *not* from you?" She was getting upset. I loved a feisty Payton. I adjusted my pants and moved a step closer, only to have her take the same step back. I had a strong urge to hold her in my arms but held myself back again.

Sinfully

"I haven't sent you anything. Now, tell me again, why would you be scared of them?" I was curious about the damn letters.

"Th-they talk about how they know my secret, and how they are tired of just sitting back and watching me, saying I can't hide. I don't think they liked me going to Vegas but I stopped! They know where I live, Ryder. They knew where I was staying in Vegas." Her tears were flowing freely by that point. Poor thing. I closed the gap between us and took her in my arms.

My mind wandered to what she had been through with the letters since it wasn't the first one she'd received. The idea of her being alone and scared of someone, whether it be me or a stranger, made my stomach churn.

"I swear to you that it wasn't me but I'll help find out whoever this sick fucker is, Payton. Man, I missed you so much. I'm sorry for finding out you were Reece, but I wasn't going to do anything you didn't want me to. I would do whatever you asked." I kissed a tear on her cheek and looked into her stunned and confused eyes.

I held her tightly and hoped that she wasn't about to pull away. "I figured it had to be you. You knew I was in Vegas and you knew my secret. The only other person who I've told is Chloe and she wouldn't tell anyone. I thought you came to Vegas because I was Reece and you wanted that side of me. I can't tell you how much that hurt me." She twisted my dress shirt into her fists and held on for dear life. I remembered her saying something about a letter during her scream-fest in Las Vegas but I didn't have the chance to question it then.

Did she just come here because of the letter or was it also because she wanted to see me? The way she gave in to my touch left me wondering and I craved being close to her again, smelling her sweet strawberry shampoo as I drew closer. The past few months had made me realize how much I cared for her and wanted to change for her.

"You were with that girl at the zoo. I saw you, and the little girl."

"Yes. She was a fling, to help me move on from you. We aren't talking anymore and the little girl was her friend's. We set her up

162

with Tristen, my best friend back in San Diego. I saw you with him, Payton. Just so you know."

Her eyes shot up to mine, guilt and sorrow showing through. "I didn't even know he was coming with us. Chloe's been trying to set me up. I met him that day."

"Please don't run, Payton. Whatever you do, face whatever fears you have with me right here beside you."

"I came here to yell at you. I thought you were my stalker and had already moved on to someone newer and prettier than me. I thought you wanted Reece, not Payton. You kinda messed up my argument. Jerk." She couldn't hide the faint grin that was beginning to form. Reaching up on her tippy toes, she kissed me ever so softly and I begged for more.

"I tried finding Reece, but found you instead. I was captivated by your book. You didn't hold back on the details or emotions involved and I know readers would enjoy it, too. I went to San Diego to find a way to sign the mysterious Reece Edwards but once I realized it was you, I knew I had to pick having you signed or having a chance with you. When you went to Vegas, I thought you were running into a stranger's arms and was pissed beyond belief. I don't want to share you. I choose you, not Reece, by the way. I couldn't care less about your sexual creativeness or landing you as an author. I want you in my life, for good. I missed you so much, Payton. When I still had a chance with you, I wanted to be a better person. Hell, I started looking ahead to the future instead of living in the present after I met you."

She looked around my office curiously. "Do you have any appointments or meetings in the next hour?" I could tell she was nervous, and I still wasn't quite sure where her head was.

"No, I just finished with a meeting before lunch and was just going to read some manuscripts and email some clients for the rest of the day. Why?"

"I need you." Her lips were on my neck, her tongue flicking out, moving up toward my jawline. I hadn't expected it, but my cock was pleasantly excited at her actions. My hands slowly moved from her back down to her hips, massaging them firmly before reaching to grip her ass. I missed her touch. Being with her felt so different than with any other woman I'd been with.

I guided her over to the couch settled against the window and sat down beside her. While I wanted to take things further with her, I needed to know she was truly in it with me. I couldn't handle her leaving again when things got rough.

"You changed me, Payton. I don't want one-night stands anymore. I want to see where this can go between us. I haven't felt this way with any of my other girlfriends and that's gotta be something. I need to know how you feel, though. I need to know you're going to be with me, giving me a hundred percent. It's not going to be easy, and I know we're going to fuck up here and there, but I promise to fight for this."

"Whenever I'm with you, I want to let you in more than anyone else. I want to tell you things I don't tell anyone besides Chloe. I still get flighty, but when I'm not with you, my heart aches. I've gone on dates and tried writing to get my mind off you, but you're always there. I wake up smiling because I dream of you, and then frown when I realize I'm in bed alone. I don't want to have meaningless hookups anymore. I want something steady and more permanent than what I've had in the past. You help me and I'll help you?"

Chapter 12

Payton

Holy fuck. I was disappointed at myself over how quickly I let my anger dissipate. I had a plan! Sort of. When he told me it wasn't him who sent the letters, I could see in his eyes that he was telling the truth. The fact that he got angry and protective when I talked about them made me feel giddy. I probably should have been more worried that I still had no clue who sent them, but I liked the idea that he was wanting to keep me safe. I missed his smell, so clean and masculine.

"Ryder? This isn't fair for you. It had become second nature not to let people get close to me. I get urges to push you away to protect myself but I want to work on fighting those urges." I knew I would mess it up somehow. I knew distance. I knew how to walk away. What I didn't know was how to stay.

He needed to know what he was getting himself into but I wasn't ready to divulge my past. The look of pity I received after people found out my story was one I'd seen all too often and didn't feel like seeing again anytime soon. I didn't really think about my birth parents anymore, but that look was enough to bring back the flood of emotions of my tragic history.

"You can take time, get used to the idea of trying things with me. Are you planning on staying in Los Angeles for a while? You could come home with me and stay the night, in my arms, safe from harm." I gave him a look, letting him know it was too soon for that, and his face turned into a slight frown as he sighed and nodded.

"I'll stay a few days at a hotel. I won't run from you, but I have to get used to this idea of having someone to confide in and tell everything to. I can write anywhere so it's not like I have to be in San Diego for my job. I think LA could be my new Vegas."

His angry expression told me I had said something wrong. "No! No! No! I meant to get away and have some 'me' time. Not for being with other guys! I just need to get away from San Diego on occasion. Don't worry; I'll come to *you* when I need my fix." I couldn't help but giggle at his cheesy grin he gave me at that.

"Damn right you will. I promise to always give you your fix, my little sex junkie. So if I don't get to take you home, do I get to see you tomorrow? Maybe lunch?"

I sat up and straightened my clothes, leaning against his arm for support. The last hour was not planned and I needed to process. "Sure, just call me. I should get going, though. Thank you for not being the douche that I had made you out to be." At that, I stood to walk away. I was starting to freak out at what I had just agreed to and was determined to get out of his building before I broke down.

Just as I turned the handle, I felt strong hands surround my waist and pull me into him. "Thank you, Payton. Whatever hell you've been through to make yourself scared to let people in, I'm determined to help you through it. Have faith in me, and us."

Ryder

She was back. I just needed to figure out how to make her stay. Once she got in that pretty little head of hers, she'd begin over-analyzing the day. Feeling her lips wrapped around my cock was a thought I kept playing over and over in my mind. Sitting at my desk, I was positive that I would be useless for the rest of the day. I never expected to see Payton walk into my office, nor did I really ever expect to see her again. What racked my brain more so were those letters. I felt a twinge of anger that she would think it was me, but with the wax 'R', I could see where she'd come up with that conclusion. We needed to get back to San Diego so I could figure out who the asshole was and kick his ass. Payton said she planned on staying in town a few days, but I hoped she'd be alright with heading back early, with me in tow.

I texted her at nine that night, hoping she was awake and bored in her hotel room.

> **Me: I picked up some brownies and chocolate covered strawberries at the bakery down the street. If only I had someone to share with ;)**
>
> **Payton: You're crazy. You picking up sweets doesn't sound like your normal routine. Your body is way too perfect for brownies. Address?**
>
> **Me: Maybe I'm learning to change my ways too. Not that I plan on becoming a fat ass though. Maybe I just planned on working off those calories later tonight Miss Davenport**

Twenty minutes later, I had her pinned against the wall in my foyer. She brought out something carnal in me that made me want to mark her and make her mine. With her legs wrapped around my hips, I lifted her arms above her head and ground myself against her core. God bless sundresses. And those cowboy boots? Staying on for a while. The image of those boots being jostled in the air as I fucked her was a fantasy that I planned on playing out.

With need in her eyes, I grinned when I slipped my hand into her panties and found her clit. Those beautiful eyes fluttered closed, her head tossed back against the wall. I increased the pressure and speed of my fingers as they massaged between her legs. Her moans weren't held back as she came against me.

"Hey, stranger. If you greet all your guests this way, we might have a problem." Her smile was evident as she laid her head against my shoulder. That was just a warm-up, though, so she better just have been saving her energy.

"Only ones I have wet dreams about every night. Do you know how nice it is to go to bed and dream about having sex with a beautiful woman each night? I catch myself trying to make myself tired just so I can see you in my dreams again. It's sad really." She shook with laughter but still hadn't raised her head to meet me. I missed that carefree laugh of hers. Leisurely, I lowered her back down to the ground and led the way to the kitchen.

"I'd be a bad host if I didn't offer you a strawberry. After all, you came here for the brownies and chocolate covered strawberries, right?" She took a strawberry out of the box and sucked slightly before taking a bite. My eyes were focused on her juicy lips as she licked her bottom lip, tasting the leftover juices.

"Mhmm. But since your greeting back there, I have other ideas. Vegas feels like forever ago. I've been such a good girl since then, too. Every date I went on sucked ass and I had to go home by myself to get my fix. It's not the same, though, Ryder. You may have had Malibu Barbie to keep you satisfied but I never found my Ken." Damn, her pout was cute. She gave me those sad eyes and all I wanted to do was make her feel better. I pulled her into my bedroom and she stopped as soon as she hit the threshold.

Looking back, I asked "Everything okay, babe? I thought this was what you were not so subtly hinting at." Her eyes spanned the entire area but landed on my photo on the wall near the bathroom. Once I realized why she'd stopped, I knew I needed to explain.

Leighton Riley

"I love books and women. This photo encompasses them both in a seductive manner and I fell in love with the piece." It was of a nude woman laying on a chaise lounge with books surrounding her. Her hair was fanned out and her intimate areas were vaguely hidden. I bought it after my first author hit the New York Times Best Seller list when I was seventeen.

"It's magnificent, Ryder. You can see how captivated she is by the story and her love of reading. Her body is perfection but doesn't feel erotic; it's almost…romantic."

I couldn't help but smile as I saw the same passion in her eyes for books that I had. I could envision the woman in the photo being Payton.

"I love that you enjoy it as much as I do." I encased her in my arms, hands meeting at her lower stomach as I began kissing her left shoulder. Her head tilted involuntarily to the right side, granting me permission. My lips met her spot just behind her ear, followed by nipping her ear, eliciting a whimper from her mouth. My erection was already pressing firmly against her lower back and I could feel her slight swaying movement. I ached to be inside her but wanted to cherish her being in my arms. I couldn't help the feeling that I would lose her at a moment's notice.

Guiding her closer to the bed, I felt her nervous presence and hoped I could make her feel comfortable enough with me to let it go. Pulling at the hem of her dress, I slid it over her head and bit my lip when I saw the deep purple lacy push-up bra and matching thong. She looked at me as if memorizing every fine detail of my face. We were both scared of losing one another. My need for her was growing, and it was getting harder to hold back. Kneeling slightly, I showered her stomach in kisses, moving lower ever so slowly.

On my knees, I placed a trail of kisses along her panty line, edging it lower to reveal her bare pussy. She was breathtaking and it didn't take long for me to fully undress her. She allowed me to worship her body, as if sensing my need to relearn every inch of her.

Sinfully

While playing with my hair in her hands, she confessed, "I'm not leaving, Ryder. You are acting like I'm going to disappear tomorrow. I want to try this…this thing…with you, but you gotta stop acting like I'm dying. Plus, I can't bear another minute with you not being inside of me. I love you worshipping my body, but I need this." Pulling me to a standing position, she grabbed my bulging erection and began stroking firmly through my pants. I didn't need to be told again. Reaching down to unbuckle my belt and pants, I watched as Payton bit her lip after chancing a glance toward my dick that was peeking out of my boxers. After sliding both sets of material down and off my legs, I pulled her into an embrace and moaned as my rough lips collided with her silky smooth ones. Our kisses told each other what we weren't able to say out loud; I felt as if I was finally breaking down her wall.

Payton's hands slid up my chest and when she reached the top of my shirt, she pulled, effectively popping the buttons off my shirt. Gently laying her down on her side, I lay behind her, teasing her entrance with the tip of my dick. I could feel her wetness coating me. It was a turn on to know she wanted me as bad I did her. Just as I was about to enter her, she scooted forward and turned around to face me. "What's wrong, baby?" My face must have been etched with worry because right after she saw my expression, she smiled and caressed my cheek.

"It's nothing bad, Ryder, don't worry. I just…I have to ask you something, but I don't really want to."

"Okay-y? What is it, babe?"

"I want to feel you inside me, but I worry. I know you weren't exactly celibate while we were separated, and to be honest, we've never really talked about it before since you always used condoms. I know I'm on the NuvaRing, but that doesn't protect me from…from those women." She let out a loud sigh as she finished speaking.

"I'm clean, baby. After the last girl I was with, I knew I was done messing around. I was going to try to get you back; you just

170

Leighton Riley

beat me to it." I smiled, hoping that was all that was on her mind so we could get back to me making love to her.

"Really? I didn't know that, babe. I'm clean, too. I went on a few dates since I was tested last, but I never did anything with them. I'm so glad I came back and we sorted everything out, Ryder." She kissed me passionately but didn't take long before she turned again so her back was facing me and lifted her right leg, making room for me to slide into her.

Her tight warmth welcomed my hardness as I entered her slick core. With her lying on her side, I was able to get unbelievably deep; her moans informed me she enjoyed the position as well.

"Just like that. You feel so good inside me. My tight pussy missed you, baby. Oh, harder, Ryder."

"You can't say those things to me, Payt. You feel too good, look too delicious, and sound like an angel. Mmm, fuck, babe, get on your knees." She was turned over and I began taking her from behind. I pulled her into me by gripping her hips but soon she was pushing back onto me and I was done. Coming all over her sweet little ass, I felt like a jerk for not getting her off beforehand. "I'm so sorry. Give me a few minutes and I'll make you feel real good. You pushing into me was so hot, I couldn't hold back."

"So it's my fault, huh? Don't worry. I have full faith that you'll bring me to bliss again. Can we snuggle for a little while? It's new for me not to be wondering which one of us is going to say they have to leave first. Normally, I'd be thinking of reasons to leave that sounded real enough. If I know it'll only be a one night type of deal, I set up that app to call me two hours after I get there and I usually pretend Chloe's boyfriend broke up with her and I need to get to her. They don't ask too many questions, and I can be out of there quick. If the date's going well, I just let them know it was a crazy ex-boyfriend trying to get me back. "

"Seems like you had a good system going for you. Hey, can I ask you something? You don't have to answer but I've been curious." I wrapped an arm around her waist and pulled her close to me. Payton wiggled her butt, getting comfortable and snug beside me.

"Umm, sure?" She seemed hesitant and I wasn't positive I'd get an answer from her but it kept popping up in my mind.

"What made you not want to get attached to anyone? You seem like you want to connect with people but then you put a barrier up and walk away. What happened?"

She stiffened in my arms and her breathing quickened. I knew something had caused her to be that way but had no idea what it could have been. She never talked about her past.

Massaging her sides, I whispered into her ear, "There's no rush, baby. It's okay to let your guard down with me."

"My parents."

"Did they hurt you?" I wasn't sure what she meant but I had a feeling I wasn't prepared for whatever she had to tell me.

"No, nothing like that. They died. So did the next set. I'm jinxed." I could hear her sniffling but was still confused. I wrapped my arms a little tighter and kissed her shoulder.

"I'm so sorry. What do you mean next set?" Twisting to face me, the pain and loneliness was evident in her eyes. I wanted nothing but to console her and make the pain go away but I had a feeling it was something she never talked about. Letting it out might help her so I waited, giving her a kiss of reassurance. A single tear dropped onto my arm, soon followed by a steady flow. I felt the urge to kiss her tears away but stayed still, willing her to keep going.

"My-my mom caught my dad cheating on her and killed him and the girl. She took her own life shortly after while she was holding me in her arms. I was just a few weeks old and a neighbor heard my crying and called the police. It was all over the news so it wasn't hard for me to research when I got older. I was in a foster home until I was seven and my adoptive parents took me in. They were sweet and I saw them as my true family."

She pivoted her head so it was hidden in my arm and she really let it out. I caressed her back, listening to her quietly weep, her body shaking as she cried. She was a fighter. I couldn't fathom the idea of my mother killing my father and then killing herself. Not to mention, being in foster care for that many years had to be cruel. It made sense why she didn't want to grow attached to others.

"No one should have to go through that. I know that your past shapes you into who you are today, but you're such a strong woman, Payton. You don't have to be scared of getting close to me, I'm here for you."

I wasn't the best with consoling and hoped my words along with my actions were sufficient to make her feel better.

"They died in a car accident when I was thirteen. After that, the only person I really let in was Chloe. We met when we were seven, and she's my rock. Everyone else was short-term. It's become instinct to walk away when I started feeling things for a guy. This is why Vegas worked for me. I had a natural reason to walk away and it didn't make me feel like I was doing something wrong."

I wasn't quite sure what to say to her last admission. The hand she'd been dealt was unfortunate and I was surprised she was still standing through it all. I made a silent promise to make her feel safe and loved from that point on. With that being said, I needed to figure out who was sending her those letters.

Chapter 13

Payton

I still couldn't believe I told him about my past. Chloe knew not to bring it up and those who *knew* me knew *nothing* about my fucked-up family history. A few friends had questioned me before but I was quick at making up fairytale stories of my happily married parents who lived on the East Coast and retired to travel around the world. It was just enough for them to shut up and not ask again. With Ryder, though, I openly gave him information and I *wanted* to.

He brought out such intense emotions in me that I was constantly reminding myself not to run. My brain was hardwired to revolt when people got close and he was sounding off all the alarms.

I lay in his bed, his scent surrounding me, and I felt content and peaceful. His steady breathing told me he was sound asleep, his arms still wrapped protectively around my waist, and his erection pressed firmly against my ass. My mind was too busy to sleep but I didn't mind staying enveloped by his arm, and now leg, that were draped over me.

I awoke to feather-light touches down my arm and a warm, solid body behind me. Grinning, I tried to feign sleep but I had been caught. I wasn't ready for him to get up yet.

"You're pretty damn adorable when you sleep, Payton, even with your tiny snore. How about we make breakfast together? I can make a mean omelet." He maneuvered himself over me, biceps bulging as he hovered, planting sweet kisses over my neck and chest.

"I know how to make crepes. Or bacon? Sorry, I don't cook too much but I know the crepe recipe by heart. Mom and I used to make it every Saturday." His glance went from curious to hopeful in an instant and it felt good to have him relish in my opening up to him, even if it was only about a childhood memory.

"I would love nothing more than to have crepes, bacon, *and* an omelet, babe. Hop up!" He lifted himself off me and I missed the heat that radiated off his sexy body. I decided to add licking the ridges of his abs to my bucket list that I had just created in my head. With a swat to my ass, I was jolted from the bed, slid on a pair of shorts and tank top that I had packed, and followed behind him to the kitchen. The view of his ass would never get old.

He was at home in the kitchen. I couldn't help but watch as he got out prep bowls and cutting boards, along with fresh spinach, some kind of fancy cheese, peppers, onions, and ham out of the fridge. If he were to look in my fridge, he would find takeout boxes, deli meat, and leftover pasta. Of the few dishes I knew how to prepare, I did them well and often. Pasta with vodka sauce and Italian sausage was my favorite, and I normally had some in my fridge from the last time I made up a batch.

He handed me a mixing bowl, showed me where the flour was, and I got to work. "Hey, Ryder? Would you by chance have Nutella here? It's the best thing to put on these, with a little bit of powdered sugar to top it off."

"I actually do. I sometimes watch my friend's kid and she loves that stuff. It's the only thing I keep readily available that isn't solely for me. Middle shelf in the pantry; think eye level for a six-year-old."

We went about cooking breakfast like we'd been together for years. I wasn't expecting such mundane tasks like making breakfast or getting ready for the day to be so intimate yet comforting. I could get used to it.

Leighton Riley

After setting all the food down at the table, he brought us each a glass of orange juice and settled in across from me. "What are your plans for today? I only have to run into work for a meeting at noon but it'll be quick. Want to head up to Palm Springs for the night? We could also do a movie or walk around and do some shopping."

"Actually, I want to write. I was thinking about heading to Manhattan Beach, lying out on the sand with a notepad, and getting lost in the beauty before me."

"If you wanted to look at beauty for inspiration, I totally would have posed nude for you, baby. Is it another dirty book?" I gave him the angriest look I could muster but failed miserably since my brain automatically started thinking of him posing naked on his bed. The man made me constantly horny.

"Uhh, I'll take my chances at the beach. I'll be home in the afternoon. Go to work!"

As I finished off my orange juice, I felt his foot slide up between my legs and I jumped in surprise, successfully spilling what was left of my drink over the table and on my plate.

"Oops. Guess you're done with breakfast. I think if my memory serves me right, I was a little selfish last night and need to repay you." Ryder stood, moved up beside me, and cradled me in his arms with one arm under my back and the other under my knees. I kicked and giggled but was perfectly accepting of what was to come. He bent down when we came to a stop outside a door to a room I'd never been in before and I was curious what was inside.

Upon twisting the handle, he revealed an elaborate home gym that he'd never mentioned before. One wall was all mirrors and the equipment was top of the line. He had an elliptical, a weight machine, free weights, and a treadmill conveniently showcased around the room and each of the three other walls had mounted flat screen TV's for his viewing pleasure.

"Why do you have all this if you go to a normal gym?" I was impressed and had the urge to try out the elliptical later while he

Sinfully

was gone. It'd been too long since I'd worked out and I could use the cardio.

"I like to come in here when I don't have time to head to the gym. I can knock out an hour in here before or after work and not have to spend the time driving to and from the gym. Makes it easy."

He walked a few more feet and sat me on a large red yoga ball. Steadying myself, I looked up at him in wonder.

"So are we...?"

"Take your shorts off and spread your legs. Turn toward the mirror, sweet girl." He watched my every movement and I could see him hardening under his boxers.

I was too aroused to protest and quickly stood to slide my shorts off and sat back down on the firm yoga ball. Looking to him for more instructions, I imagined him taking me right there on the ball. That would be fun.

"Touch yourself, Payton. Put two fingers in your pussy and bring them back up to coat yourself with your wetness." I did as asked and was getting wildly turned on by his demands. "Good girl, now use your other hand to rub your clit in slow circles." He had freed his erection from his boxers and was now touching himself as he watched.

We watched each other, never taking our eyes off the show before us. Every moan, every grunt, every sigh turned us on more and I was close to climaxing.

"Taste yourself, sweet girl. Bring your fingers up and see how tangy and sweet you are." Hesitantly obliging, I brought my fingers up and licked one finger to try it but soon found myself sucking each finger clean. His groans showed his appreciation, and if I were being honest, it didn't taste so bad. Sure, it was tangy like he said but it had a hint of sweetness to it also.

Before I could slide my fingers back inside myself, Ryder was hovering over me and grabbing hold of my ankles.

"I've got you. Don't fight the swaying of the ball." He lifted my legs high in the air and moved me so that I was lying down on the ball with my head toward the ground. He thrust his cock inside me and the ball swayed back before swinging forward. I lifted forward to watch him plunge into me over and over again but quickly lay back down to enjoy the feeling of his hardness filling me to the hilt, propelling himself as far as he could. He fucked me with little abandon as the deep penetration brought us both to a quick orgasm.

Breathing heavily, he murmured, "Does that help make up for last night?"

I couldn't move but quietly replied, "I think so. Holy shit, that was unreal. How have you not mentioned how amazing yoga ball sex was before?"

Ryder languorously placed a kiss on my lips before sliding out of me and helping me upright. My legs were wobbly and it felt weird being on solid ground again. Sex was always exciting with Ryder and I hoped to never grow tired of it.

The next two weeks were similar. We'd wake up together, make some sort of smoothie or light breakfast, and head our separate ways. After a few days at the beach, I moved my work inside to his living room where he had the fluffiest, most comfortable recliner that could easily fit both of us side by side. I would set a goal of how many words I wanted to write that day but usually went over that number since I was so enraptured with the story.

I decided to write about a guy whose sister passed away from a skiing accident and found solace with her former roommate and sorority sister. The male character had stopped by to start going through his sister's belongings and the roommate was home, going through the same pain. They formed a special bond that turned into love but not before dealing with the anger and pain that they dealt with daily. I had the first six chapters written and kept thinking of new twists that I could intertwine into the storyline.

Sinfully

Getting those pained emotions on paper was a stress reliever for me and I saw just how similar I was to the character I had written. I felt alone and left behind. Having someone show you that you're not alone, that they truly care about you, can change a person. Seeing that change was what inspired me to keep writing. As the chapters progressed, you saw a lost soul find his way to happiness again and the path he took was full of new experiences with a person who wanted to be with him. Of course, there was a lot of flirting and sex—it was what I knew.

Every afternoon I'd come back to Ryder's place, usually an hour or two before he got home. Sometimes I would take a nap or shower, while other days I would run to the market and grab food for us to make for dinner. He was slowly helping me learn my way around the kitchen and he seemed to enjoy the teacher role.

As we ate our steak au poivre and talked about our day, I couldn't help but think how lucky I was for Ryder to give me a chance. He truly was too good for me. He was a kind-hearted and determined man who worked hard for what he wanted.

"I love that you're becoming all domesticated. You didn't even get scared when you flambéed the sauce tonight. I'd definitely call that progress." Ryder leaned over the table and placed a loving, delectable kiss on my lips, followed by an adorable wink.

"Does that mean I get a reward? Oh, can I pick? Please?!" We were still in the honeymoon phase and Ryder had made it his mission to have his way with me in the most random of locations. I felt like it was more of a scavenger hunt of places to fuck and it got me hot just thinking about it.

"Go for it, babe. Your rewards are usually just as rewarding for me." Seeing him happy made me feel all sorts of funny inside. I was still not used to the whole dating thing.

"I was thinking of a run around the park down the street. It's got such luscious trees and is beautiful when lit up at night. You up for it?"

He pretended to think over my suggestion for a few seconds before nodding and heading to his bedroom. I set our dishes in the

Leighton Riley

dishwasher and followed behind, stopping abruptly when I saw him in his black sliders and nothing else. He was looking for a shirt to put on and the view of his ass alone made me want to ditch the park and take him to bed.

He was all muscle but he had a sexy bubble butt for a man. Feeling his hard muscles all over his body was amazing, but when my hands got to his firm and juicy backside, I couldn't help but give a firm squeeze and occasional spank.

The run could wait, my wet pussy couldn't. Tiptoeing closer to him, I wrapped my arms around his hips and slowly started massaging his taught abs, softly stroking the trail of hair running down from his belly and disappearing under the waistband of his shorts. There was something so sensual about running my hands downward along the soft trail that I knew led to the peak of his excitement. Feeling him harden in my hands would never get old. Knowing I was the reason for his arousal was such a turn on. His soft moan only increased my desire and made my nipples so hard and needy that I pressed them up against his back so he could feel how much he was affecting me, too.

I ran my tongue along his shoulder blade while I rubbed his now rock hard cock over the material. The sliders were constricting and couldn't be comfortable while sporting a hard-on. My hands gracefully slid the fabric over his package and stopped once they were resting on his muscular thighs.

"Let me help you get a little more comfortable."

"Mmm, Payton, have you changed your mind about your reward? Reneging comes at a price, baby."

"Well, in that case, if I wanted to change my reward to fucking your brains out on your balcony, what would the price be?" He twisted around to face me, his erection hitting me in the belly, and the devilish grin on his face told me he already had something specific in mind. Although we hadn't ventured away from plain vanilla sex, I knew he was creative and wanted to stretch the limits on how far he could push my 'naughty girl Reece persona'. The

181

thought of giving him control and willingly submitting to his every demand had me pulsing with need.

I wasn't sure what he had in mind, but I trusted that he would make it an enjoyable experience, so I went with it.

"Strip off your clothes for me, baby." He finished removing his sliders and was now completely naked and moving to sit on a chair near the window. "Nice and slow for me, Payton. I know you've done this before."

I could see him wince as soon as the words came out of his mouth and couldn't help but wonder if my past bothered him. I let it go for the moment, but I knew it wouldn't be the last time it would be brought up.

Trying to be sexy, I started shaking my hips as I slid my shirt over my head and turned around before I started with my bra. I unclasped the hooks, pushed both straps off my shoulders, but kept my arm against my chest. He was wrong about my previous striptease experience, and I had my doubts on how sexy it was for him.

With my back turned, it gave me a little more confidence since I didn't have to see his handsome face. My shorts were next to come off, and after giving a slight tease by showing my butt to him, they fell to the floor, pooling around my feet. Stepping out of them, moving closer to Ryder, I bent completely over as I pulled my thong over my cheeks and slowly down my legs, hoping to give a nice view of what he would get later. His hands were suddenly grasping my ass and massaging wonderfully. I couldn't help but lean into his touch. He pulled my hips down until I was sitting in his lap, skin against skin, no barriers between us. I smiled in delight as I felt him grinding himself against my slippery core.

"Balcony, now. Turn facing the city and wait for me." He gave a soft nudge and I was excited and anxious about what was to come, besides us.

I did as I was told and waited what felt like hours for him to find me. He was high enough not to be easily seen, but there was another building across from him that had windows and balconies facing us. There was an absolute possibility of being seen by someone over there.

I felt his presence before I felt his body. One of his silky ties was being wrapped around my eyes before he bent me over the ledge. His balcony had a cast stone ledge that was probably a foot thick and gave me something smooth to rest my chest on. It wouldn't feel so nice against my skin if he took things on the rough side.

His fingers tested my readiness, sliding one at a time into my tightness, and soon I was slowly welcoming two more fingers. I was dripping with arousal and bit my lip to keep from moaning. It wasn't our first time fucking in public but it was the first time we would more than likely be seen. Not being able to see anything made all my other senses heightened and his slightest movement had me on edge. I tried guessing what his next move would be but with Ryder, he was an outside-the-box thinker when it came to sex.

Sliding his fingers out of my pussy, I hoped I would feel his cock taking their place but instead, his fingers found my mouth. I opened without question, sucking his fingers dry while thinking to myself how weird it was to taste myself even though I had done it once before.

Ryder grabbed onto my right thigh and positioned himself at my entrance, as if he was deciding what to do. "Your chest comfortable against the ledge, babe?"

I nodded in response, unsure why he was asking when he should have been fucking.

"Good girl, now grip onto the inside edge with both hands." I started to turn to look at him but his voice halted my movement, "Now, Payton. Don't let go, whatever you do. Say 'bubblegum' if you start to feel unstable."

Before I could process what he meant by using a safe word, he thrust himself inside of me and stilled once again. My right leg was against his hip as he reached with his left hand and grabbed onto my left thigh. I was suspended by the waist with his hands and holding on to the ledge for dear life. He began pounding into me with a steady rocking motion, rubbing the skin on my chest raw with each thrust.

A surge of adrenaline rushed through me with the fear of falling along with being seen like that. I came hard and a scream ripped through my body, taking me by surprise. His deep moan made me quiver and soon I was close again. The second orgasm began coursing through me as he relentlessly kept plunging into me with power and determination. His vice-like grip on my hips made me feel safe enough to never even think about saying 'bubblegum'.

I was in a state of ecstasy and I never wanted to leave. Ryder started gaining speed, losing his rhythm, and I knew he was close.

"Oh shit, Ryder, I'm so close to coming again, baby. Make me come with you." I knew it I was selfish, but I didn't care at the moment.

I gasped as his right hand shifted from my hip to my clit, making us slightly off balance but still connected. He massaged me just the way I needed and I was suddenly completely undone.

"Yes, baby! That's it, oh my…fuck, Ryder."

"I'm with you, girl. Keep pulsing around my dick, baby, milk my cock dry." His thrusts were to the point and harsh as he filled me with his load. "That was unbelievable, Payton. I'm pretty sure that earned us a hot shower together followed up with some lovin', then sleep."

His breath was warm against my glistening skin which was getting cold from the wind. The night air was brisk with winter right around the corner. He brought my legs down one at a time, reluctantly pulling himself out of me.

Placing sweet kisses all over my back, he removed my blindfold and gave a swat to my behind.

"I've never come so hard before in my life. I don't know what you do to me but I like it. This whole public sex thing is mind-blowingly hot."

"With you, I want people to watch; I want to show them you're mine. Sex with you is like nothing I've experienced before. I haven't felt this type of connection with someone that is both emotional and physical. Now that I've had it, I can't give it up."

He walked back to his bedroom and shortly returned with his comforter and held it out to wrap around me. Skin on skin, we kept each other warm under the blanket as we fell asleep on a lounger under the moonlight. When I woke, it was still the middle of the night, and Ryder had half his body on top of me and the faintest smile on his scruffy face.

I let my mind wander to what our life would be like if we stayed together. Would he want kids? Where would we live? Before I could really get into deep thought, I felt him stir.

"Let's go to bed, sweetheart. I love being under the stars but I love having a mattress under me even more." Kissing his forehead, I pried his arm off my stomach and began to get up. I had no doubt he'd follow.

Grabbing me with both hands, he pulled me back on top of him. "My Payton isn't a nature girl, huh? Never would have guessed." He squeezed my sides and I burst into a fit of laughter. When did he fully wake up?

"I'm a beach girl. In fact, I was thinking about heading back to San Diego soon. I know you have work here, but wouldn't mind you coming back down with me."

"Just tell me when and I'll be there. Lorelei is a great assistant and can handle everything while I'm gone. Do I get to meet Chloe while we're down there?"

"I don't see why not. She was always in your corner before Vegas. I'm sure she'd love to meet you. She tends to ask some rather personal questions with any potential date, though, so be prepared."

Chapter 14

Ryder

She'd gotten to me. I craved her day and night and couldn't imagine not having Payton in my life. Our conversations were on a deeper level and I hung on every word she said. I was officially pussy whipped.

We headed down to San Diego the Saturday before Thanksgiving and planned on having Thanksgiving dinner at Chloe's. Payton and I hadn't talked about giving us a label but it felt very much like a boyfriend/girlfriend thing. The thought alone made me smile.

"Anything I should know before we get there? Are there any topics I need to avoid?" I felt like I knew Chloe but I wasn't positive what I was getting myself into.

"Well, for starters, Chloe knows about Reece but her boyfriend and anyone else there has no idea. I'd like to keep it that way. Chloe hates the Lakers, Dodgers, and well, anything LA related. Other than that, you should be good."

Payton synced her phone to my car, letting me know that she had some of the best music on there and I would be lucky to listen. What she failed to mention was how random her selection was. We started off with Halestorm before listening to Rob Zombie, Jana Kramer, Red Light King, and Jason Derulo. Every single song she couldn't help but sing along to. Her impression of Rob Zombie was priceless but her Jana Kramer rendition was heartfelt and sincere.

She poured her soul into singing that song and I couldn't help but look over every few seconds while she got lost in the lyrics. Her voice was spot on and I hoped she had a playlist of songs just like that.

I wasn't sure how long we had in town but I wanted to get together with Tristen if we had time. He seemed to be in a good place but he seemed unsure of how things went with Kenna. I didn't exactly have the 'in' anymore to find out what Kenna thought about Tristen and couldn't help but wonder if Tristen was sabotaging a good thing.

Once we made it into town, Payton thought it'd be best if we showered and headed over to see Chloe and her boyfriend. What she meant by that was that she thought it'd be best if we had sex in the shower before heading over to meet her friends so we'd behave until we got back to her place. Not one to put up an argument, I did as I was told and we left her place satisfied and only twenty minutes late.

"Payton! You're not allowed to leave for that long ever again. I'm tired of you just up and leaving, only telling me once you're on the road or on a plane. I missed you, bitch!" I waited behind Payton, patiently waiting to be introduced. I knew it was Chloe but I really wanted to see how Payton would introduce me. Boyfriend, friend, or fill in the blank?

"I always come back, Chlo, and we always drink and catch up afterward, so who cares? Oh, this is Ryder. Chloe, behave." There was some type of silent communication going on between the two of them and me and the guy behind Chloe were not worthy of being included. Catching each other's eyes, we gave a head nod and watched the show before us.

"Nice to meet you, Chloe, right?" I tried a handshake, but she was instantly pulling me into an embrace, which was sweet, until I felt her fondle my ass cheek. To be fair, I was warned, but I hadn't mentally prepared myself for that. I could feel daggers being thrown my way as I pulled out of her grasp and didn't need to look behind her to confirm it.

"Damn, he's even better in person. You suck at describing him by the way. It's okay, though, we'll work on it later." Chloe gave Payton a wink and headed back inside, everyone following behind her. Payton shrugged her shoulders and mouthed *sorry* before intertwining our fingers and following Chloe and the guy she was with. I still hadn't caught his name.

"Grayson and Chloe, this is Ryder. Ryder, Grayson and Chloe." We were almost to the kitchen when Payton threw out the introductions but something felt off.

"Are they together, like a couple?" I whispered into Payton's ear as we neared the kitchen island.

"Mhmm. For a while now, why?"

I pulled her in close to me by the waist and shook my head. "No reason."

Grayson handed me a beer and I took it happily. I needed something to take the edge off so I could relax with Payton's friends. It was a big deal to me and I didn't want to mess it up.

I had to admit, the food was excellent but I wasn't sure who actually cooked it. Chloe didn't seem like the domesticated type and Grayson looked like he wouldn't want to get his hands dirty. My bet was on them picking it up at a restaurant and heating it up once they threw away the to-go boxes.

"Ryder, I heard you're a big time editor. Read any good books lately?" Chloe questioned me while biting down on a piece of asparagus.

"Yes, actually. I've had quite the luck recently with some amazing authors. They were right under my nose and I nearly missed the chance, though. In the end, they knew I'd be a good match for them so it worked out."

"Chloe, Ryder's been working like crazy the past few weeks. Let's give him a break from work. Chloe, how was Lake Tahoe with Grayson last weekend?"

That effectively shut her up, although I wasn't sure why. Grayson ending up speaking for the couple as Chloe gave him a stern glare.

Sinfully

"It was fun, until we got on the hill and Miss Priss pussed out. She ended up sliding down the bunny hill on her ass because she was too scared to stand up once we got off the lift. We practiced for nearly an hour at the bottom of the hill with an instructor and she seemed to be fine, gliding along and everything. When we got back to the lodge, her butt was still numb because she got snow in her panties."

"You forgot to mention how hot the instructor was. He had these killer dimples and bright green eyes. His hands were around my waist while I 'glided'. Who knew I would be scared shitless once I got on top of the huge hill?"

"Bunny hill. It was the *bunny hill*, baby! The kids learn on that one before heading to the bigger ones. Next time, I guess we'll go tubing with the lazy people." Grayson didn't seem too affectionate with Chloe but enjoyed telling her story. I wasn't one to judge, but Chloe could do way better than that dickface.

"Maybe when you take her next time, Grayson, you'll be there to support her more on top of the hill. You could have held her waist and made her more at ease. Chloe and I had been skiing when we were younger once and she did fine as long as you stayed close and coaxed her down." Payton had a way of putting him in his place that I thought was needed. She somehow managed not to sound like a raging bitch while she said it, though.

"You should come with us next time. The more the merrier. Maybe we can work together to get her down on her feet then," Grayson said with a slimy confidence.

"Sure, we'd love to join you and Chloe. Ryder, have you ever skied before?" Payton leaned in and pressed a savory kiss to my lips before looking up into my eyes, showing her affection through them.

I rested my arm over her shoulder and gave a light squeeze. "I have, actually. My best friend and, uhh, other friends would head to Beaver Creek every winter break. I haven't been in over a year, though."

190

Leighton Riley

That was close. I knew I needed to tell Payton about my sister but there had never been a good time. I couldn't break the news to her right after she told me about her parents but I knew it could possibly draw us closer with us both losing people we loved. I wasn't as obvious as her when it came to not letting people get close to me but we were one in the same, afraid of being hurt again. Afraid of losing someone you loved and couldn't get back.

I could hear Grayson's audible grumble as he excused himself from the table. Whatever the hell his problem was, he needed to get it in check. I hated seeing someone Payton cared about treated so poorly. His whole demeanor during dinner was cold and calloused.

Chloe looked mortified. "I guess dinner's officially over. I'm glad you were able to come, Ryder. We should set up a day at the beach or something soon. Seems like a little stress relief would do us all some good." She kept glancing back in the direction Grayson stormed off in but didn't make a move to go after him. Her cheeks had a slight blush to them, more than likely a combination of embarrassment and anger if I had to guess.

"Go deal with that, girl. I'll lock the door on the way out. Text me later?" I could tell from Payton's worried face that she wouldn't be able to sleep until she heard from her best friend later. Payton seemed confident in us leaving them to handle their own problems and that was fine with me. I just hated seeing Payton distraught.

As soon as we got in the car, Payton was talking non-stop. I glanced over a few times while I drove us to her place and could see her processing everything without even processing what had just happened.

"What exactly happened in there, babe? And how is Chloe with that douche?"

She looked at me with a storm brewing in her eyes. I could see her anger mixed with confusion and a touch of helplessness. I wanted nothing more than to pull her over the console and protect her from her thoughts. She knew Chloe and Grayson, which gave her more knowledge to what was going on. I was left in the dark not

191

knowing if Chloe was safe to be alone with him or if that was a normal dinner for them.

She seemed miles away from me. I grabbed her hand and rubbed my thumb over her knuckles before giving it a gentle squeeze. I was going to be here with her through whatever was going on, and I needed her to know it.

"Let's get you home and we can talk more about it. I can tell something's bothering you. I'm here if you want to talk but don't feel like you need to right now. You're sure it was okay that we left them alone, right?"

"Something's wrong, but I don't know what. Chloe and Grayson have this weird relationship but he isn't normally that indifferent with her. He's usually smothering her with affection to the point that I want to barf. I'll call Chloe when we get home and see if things have cooled off. I don't think he'd do anything irrational. He loves her too much."

"Thank you for letting me meet Chloe, baby. It means a lot that you're letting me into your world. I want to do everyday things with you, including hanging out with your friends."

"She's my only permanent friend, Ryder. I have other acquaintances but they're mainly Chloe's friends and they talk to me because I'm with her. I don't hang out with them without her. I guess I'm pretty lame, huh? Saying it out loud makes it sound worse than it feels."

"I don't think you're lame. I had friends from school and work but I'd only consider a handful of them close. My closest friend actually lives down here and I don't get to hang with him nearly as often as I wish. Maybe we could catch up with him while we're down here?" Maybe that would get her attention off her friend and all the random and illogical scenarios that were probably running through her head.

We were on her street and I couldn't wait to get her alone behind those walls. I know I should be more comforting but the protectiveness I was feeling for her made me want her badly.

Leighton Riley

"Sure thing. I'd love that. When we get back to my place I'm going to call Chloe and it'll probably be an hour of girl talk. I don't want you to be bored, though." She was being considerate of my time. I didn't mind hanging out in a different room while she tended to her friend but got the hint that she didn't prefer me to be close while she dealt with Chloe.

"How about I go get us some dessert? I'll drop you off and get some ice cream or something to bring back. Any favorites?"

She bit her lip but had hope in her eyes and I knew instantly that she had something in mind for me to get her. "There's this bakery a few blocks away that I'm addicted to. They're open late and have the most delicious desserts that have an alcoholic twist to them. It's called Swizzlesticks and I love the whiskey and Coke cupcakes and the Buttery Nipple truffles. Get extras. For later. Please."

I couldn't help but laugh at her innocent expression. She was serious about me running over there, and if that would make her happy, I had no problem buying some Buttery Nipple truffles.

"Sounds like a plan. I'll be back in a few." With that, I gave her a kiss to show her how much I wanted her. Her lips opened up for me with ease as my tongue slipped inside. I grabbed her hand and pulled it over to the bulge in my pants. "For later, baby. This is what you do to me, all the time. Take care of what you need to because I'll be coming for you after I get back. I can't wait to strip you down and fuck you 'til you pass out, Payton." One more chaste kiss and I pulled away.

"Dick! You can't get me all horny and then leave me! I can wait to call her if you come inside." I knew what she was hinting at and almost gave in. She had no self control and I loved it. I would take care of us later but she needed to be a good friend and I needed to show her I could be her support.

"Go, baby girl. I'll be back soon with treats. Maybe I'll pick up some extra icing or whipped cream for the bedroom. Chloe could probably use a friend right now."

193

Sinfully

"Ugh, fine. See you soon. Hurry back, though. I plan on collecting my prize as soon as your sexy ass walks in the door." She started to get out of my car and I gave a swat to her ass as a parting gift.

Payton

Just as I slid the key into the lock, I felt my phone buzz. Ryder had just pulled away but I wouldn't put it past him to send a text before leaving. I walked inside and sat my purse down on the counter to dig through it and find my phone. *Damn big purses.* We had a love-hate relationship. After scrounging for it at the bottom of everything that had been thrown in over the past two weeks, I pulled it out and found I had one new message from Chloe.

Chloe: Hey! Mind coming back over alone? I need you <3

I had planned on just talking to her on the phone but didn't mind heading back over there. Maybe Grayson had left and we would really be able to talk. I didn't see them as a perfect couple, but Chloe seemed happy with him, so I let it be and supported her the best I could. I needed to know what was going on, though.

I decided to walk back over to Chloe's since it was such a short distance and Ryder had my car. I wanted to get back to Ryder quickly since he left me wanting him and I needed to change my panties. I had no self control around that man. The walk to Chloe's was quick and I was on her street within five minutes of receiving her message. Walking up the stairs, I wondered what I'd be walking into. She hadn't told me they were having problems and I couldn't read her at dinner.

I knocked on the door and waited patiently. After a minute, I texted her to let her know I was there. I had a key but wasn't about to take a chance on me walking in on them *making up.*

Me: I'm here. Open up bitch

I texted Ryder, letting him know I had headed over to Chloe's and would be home soon and not to eat all of the truffles. In less than a minute, I had a response from both of them.

Chloe: Doors open. In my room

Ryder: I make no promises. You're a good friend to her Payton. I may or may not be dressed when you get home.

The second message had me smiling and hoping that I would be able to figure out the situation with Chloe quickly. I opened the door and didn't hear any noise which was odd because there was always some type of music on in the background when she was home alone. She didn't do well with silence and had her iPod set on a deck in the kitchen that could be heard throughout every room.

I quietly walked back to her bedroom and stopped dead in my tracks when I saw Grayson lying on Chloe's bed with no sight of Chloe anywhere.

"Wh-where's Chloe? She told me to come over?" I could hear the nervousness in my voice. He had his jeans on but had taken off his shirt since Ryder and I had left. He had a decent body but it was nothing compared to Ryder's chiseled chest and broad shoulders.

"She went out. I was the one who needed you to come over." He sat up on the bed and placed his head in his hands. "Why are you with that guy? He's not right for you. I thought you were going to listen."

I was thoroughly confused and frightened. Grayson and I had never talked about the men in my life so I wasn't sure where things were going.

"Who I am with is none of your damn business. Where's Chloe?" I demanded. I didn't want to be alone with him and hoped she would be coming back soon.

"I. Said. She went out. I gave you time, Payton. I let you have your fun with those guys in Vegas. I consider myself a patient man but I'm done with your slutty ways. I tried to warn you but you are obviously too stupid to take the hint."

I knew I needed to get away from him. His voice was getting more agitated and he was pulling his hair. He hadn't looked me in the eye since he sat up, though, which I couldn't figure out if it was a good thing or bad. He wanted me there alone with him. He knew about Vegas. *I was fucked.*

I had set my purse down by the door when I walked in and my phone was stuck in there. Ryder knew I was at Chloe's house but there wasn't a reason for him to drop by unannounced. Who the fuck knew where Chloe was; I just hoped she was okay. I needed to play things out right. Grayson wasn't a violent person; I could talk to him and figure out what he wanted. I needed to stay calm.

"Did you send me those letters?" *Damn it! I shouldn't have asked that. I'm supposed to be talking him down, not pissing him off more.*

"Ding ding ding, we have a winner! Your prize will be coming shortly, sweetheart, don't you worry. I'm surprised it took you this long to figure it out. I should have taken what I wanted while you were in Vegas. You were all alone up there after your *boyfriend* left; I should have been there for you. I knew he wasn't right for you, baby, but it'll all be okay now. I'll take care of everything." *This is very, very bad.* Grayson was delusional and I was what he wanted. He was looking up at me with crazed eyes that made me want to back away. I couldn't let him know I was frightened.

I leaned against the wall, still close to the door. I didn't want to get comfortable and felt safer knowing I could try to run if it came to that.

"What about the wax 'R'? How did you know about Vegas and Reece?"

"Chloe is very forthcoming when she drinks. After a few glasses of wine, I can pretty much ask her anything I want. She had told me about your book right after it was released. She calls you Reece sometimes if she's drunk enough. Chloe envies how free you are but I see the walls you've put up. Hearing her talk about the men you slept with without even thinking of the people back home and who it affects, that's not very nice, Payton. The 'R' was for Reece; just another hint that I knew who you were and what you were doing in the city of sin. It was very selfish of you, but I gave you time. I thought you'd come around, but that guy you brought to dinner is telling me otherwise. I saw him with you in Vegas. Have you fucked him? Does he know your filthy secrets?"

Why would people back home care about who I slept with? Chloe didn't and she was all I had.

"Yes, he knows about them. What are you talking about coming around, Grayson? I'm confused."

"Really? I've been with Chloe for years so that I could stay close to you. I watched you fuck around with other men and it killed me inside. I knew one day you'd be mine, though. I'm done waiting for you. I never wanted Chloe. I wanted you."

This is so not good. I had never shown interest in him, and I didn't think he even liked me. He was always distant and secretive, only talking to me when he had to.

"I had no idea, Grayson. I stopped going to Vegas but I'm *not* going to stop seeing Ryder. *He's* who I want to be with." He stood up and took a step toward me. He towered over me and I kept waiting for my survival instincts to kick in but I was stuck, frozen in place. What did he want from me?

Once he was within a foot in front of me, he reached out and tucked a loose piece of hair behind my ear. I got goosebumps when his hand touched my ear and knew I was in trouble. He leaned in close to my ear and whispered, "I'm going to show you, Payton. You're mine."

I could feel his breath on my neck and his attraction to me against my belly. I was sick to my stomach at the thought of him wanting me that way. "You have a good thing with Chloe. She loves you. Reece may seem interesting and fun but that's who I *used* to be. I'm not like that anymore."

Instead of replying, I felt his hand brush up against my waist and slowly move to my backside. He pulled me in close and ground himself against me. I truly hadn't thought he'd be that aggressive with me. I could handle a guy who was mad, but Grayson wanted something I wasn't willing to give. I just wasn't sure what my next move should be.

"It was never about Chloe, baby." He grabbed the neckline of my v-neck shirt and ripped it in half. I turned my head and shut my eyes as I screamed in fright. His hands were groping my breasts, pulling my bra down with rigid movements. "I need to taste you. In my dreams you're sweet to taste but like it rough in bed. You like it rough, babe? I'll make you scream my name as you come for me."

I had never felt so exposed and fragile. He towered over me and had me against the wall. Without thinking, I brought my knee up swiftly and hit him square in the balls. He stumbled for a moment and I knew it was my chance. I turned quickly and started to run out the door. I had made it to the living room when I felt my hair being pulled back and could hear the ripping of some of the strands out of my head. I was yanked back and had an arm around my neck.

"Tsk, tsk, sweetheart. I guess this answers my question if you like it rough or not."

That was the last thing I heard before everything went black.

Chapter 15

Ryder

I was falling for her. I just needed to find the perfect time to tell her. We'd finally gotten to a place where I didn't think she'd run, even if I opened up and told her how I felt. As I drove to Swizzlesticks, I couldn't help but grin at how I could show her how much she meant to me. Seeing her worry about Chloe's relationship broke me. That was her family. I could see it in her eyes that she would move heaven and hell to make sure Chloe was okay.

I would be there for her when she got home to talk to if needed. I wanted to bring her down to the beach. I wanted to tell her about Cami. We both had gone through something no one should have to go through.

As I pulled up to the bakery, I could see why Payton loved the place. The black chalkboard had neon writing noting the alcoholic flavors of the day. I put the car in park and headed inside, curious what my options would be. I stayed in shape but had a sweet tooth that I gave in to every so often. I decided on ordering a half dozen whiskey and Coke cupcakes and picked out an assortment to bring home as well. I got a few of the Buttery Nipple truffles, some Chocolate Martini bon bons, and some chocolate covered strawberries that were dipped in mocha flavored liquor.

As I was checking out, I heard the bell chime noting that another customer had walked in. I thought nothing of it until I heard Chloe's distinct voice call me name.

Sinfully

"Ryder? What are you doing here?" She walked up to me and peeked into the container that had been put together for me. "You'll want at least another five or six truffles if you plan on trying them. Payton may be little but she can eat that entire container in a night and not gain a pound.

"I can run out and see if this is what she wanted. Why didn't she come inside?" I was suddenly worried that I hadn't gotten enough of what she liked.

"What are you talking about? She isn't with me, isn't she with you?" The look in her eyes was genuine. Chloe had no idea where Payton was. My mind starting thinking of all the worst case scenarios and I had a bad feeling in my gut.

"She's supposed to be with you. She said she was headed to your place, Chloe."

"I figured I would call her when I got home. I knew she'd want to talk with me, but I needed some sweets after dealing with dickhead all night, so I left to grab a box for myself. I was actually tempted to head to the liquor store after stopping here so that'd I'd be on a sugar high and tipsy when I bitched out my sucky-ass boyfriend."

I pulled out my phone and called Payton's phone. After a few rings it went straight to voicemail. I looked back at Chloe, and she still didn't seem fazed that Payton said she was headed to her house. Payton had told me she would just call Chloe once she got inside so I wasn't sure what made her decide to walk back over.

Chloe must have realized my confusion and worry because she put her hand on my forearm and calmly stated, "She's fine. I'll head home now and we'll be sharing a bottle of wine and some cupcakes in no time. Stop worrying over nothing. What's the worst that could happen? She has to wait for me with Grayson?"

We both left with our boxes of sweets but I couldn't shake the feeling that something wasn't right. I tried Payton's phone again but it still went to voicemail. She had texted me from it not even a half hour before, so I knew she had it on her.

I ended up following Chloe over to her house and got a sense that something was wrong. Maybe she was just inside waiting. I was probably overreacting and kept reassuring myself that I would be able to see her in a minute and make sweet love to her once I got her safely home.

I followed Chloe up the steps and waited for her to dig her keys out of her purse. After what felt like hours, she finally got the door open and I could hear a male voice grunting from one of the rooms in back. I didn't hear anything else, though, and Payton wasn't in sight.

"Babe? You here?" I pushed past Chloe and started looking through the rooms.

"Grayson, have you seen Payton?" She was walking toward the master bedroom, and after checking the other rooms, I stepped up behind her. The door was shut, and when she tried to open it, she was met with resistance.

"It's locked. We never lock the door, Ryder," Chloe whispered, her voice laced with worry. Her eyes were wide and her hands were fidgety.

I put my ear up to the door and could hear shuffling near the floor and what sounded like Grayson struggling with something.

"Open the damn door! Payton? Are you in there, baby? I'm right outside but I need to know if you're okay. Please say something."

I was about to lose my shit and bust down the door. "You never meant anything to her! She's mine and always has been. I just need to put her in her place." Grayson's voice didn't sound the same as it had at dinner. It was lower, void of emotion.

I turned to Chloe, needing her to back away while I got through the door. "Can you go around to the window outside and see if you can see anything? Keep your phone on you and be prepared to call for help."

"That's my boyfriend you're talking about. Watch it!"

"Well, that's the love of my life in there and I can't get her to say anything while your *boyfriend* is claiming her as his! Now go to the window!" I growled the last part.

I took a few steps back and tried mentally preparing myself for whatever I was about to see as I kicked the door in. Looking inside the room, I took in the scene. The bed was rumpled but empty. My vision turned to the floor, and close to the door, I saw Grayson. He was on his knees with his pants undone. I was about to tackle him when I saw Payton's body, only it wasn't moving.

She was positioned in an unnatural position and I could see the gash to her head and stomach. Her shirt was torn to shreds and her bra was pulled below her chest, exposing her bruised skin. Blood was all over her body and I wasn't positive where it was coming from. There was a pool of it starting under her head and her stomach was already turning a deep purple. I looked away from her body and remembered where I was and what was happening.

"CHLOE! Call 9-1-1 now!" I yelled as I ran forward and punched him straight in his face, hearing the distinct crack of bone breaking. Blood sprayed onto my clothes and the ground. Two more punches to the gut knocked Grayson to the ground and I knew I had to get to my girl. "Stay the fuck away from her, or so help me, I'll kill you with my bare hands. You're a sick piece of shit!"

Kneeling next to her, I took her hand in mine and it was limp. I could see her chest moving up and down but it was labored. Her jeans were still on and I silently said a *thank you* that he hadn't gotten that far. *What did she do to deserve this?*

A sudden force to my back knocked me over, but I was careful not to fall on her. Another to the side and I was hunched over, feet away from where I needed to be. I needed to protect her. Just as Grayson's foot was about to slam down on my stomach, I grabbed hold of his foot and twisted. He collapsed near us and I took the opportunity to jab him in the stomach a few times while he was down.

Leighton Riley

I came up behind her and pulled her close to me. I felt a few tears run down my cheek as I held her in my arms, hoping and praying that she was going to be okay. We had just found each other, I couldn't lose her. In the background, I could hear Grayson stumbling to get up, and as much as I wanted to beat him unconscious, I wasn't going to leave Payton.

I moved the stray hairs away from her face and whispered how much I loved her and needed her. "I'm here for you now. Be strong, my precious girl. He won't hurt you anymore, I promise. I need for you to open up your eyes for me, sweet angel."

Not a sound came from her. I kept watching and hoping that she'd open her eyes or make some type of noise but there was nothing but silence.

Chloe walked in the room and took in what she saw. Grayson was still hovering around like he was scared to leave. She walked straight over to him and kicked him in the balls. "You lying, disturbed, cunt face whore! That's my best friend! What did you do to her?" She kept kicking him over and over again and he just stood there and took it. Chloe was bawling as she kept screaming at him. "You're a monster! How could I have ever thought I loved you? You deserve to rot in hell!

"Sh-she was meant for me. I needed her to see that I was the right one for her but she started fighting me. *You* don't deserve her love, *I* do! She's my soul mate and I need to be with her." What he was saying wasn't making sense. I chanced a glance over to Chloe just as I heard the sirens and she looked like she was in shock.

Grayson stood awkwardly in the middle of the room, watching Payton. I couldn't stand for his eyes to be on her. "You need to back the fuck away. You don't get to look at her like she's your reason to breathe. You beat her unconscious!" I could hear the footsteps nearing the front door and Chloe yelled out that we were in the back.

I still wasn't sure why Grayson didn't run but I was glad he was easily apprehended by the cops. He kept muttering how he couldn't leave her as he was escorted away.

205

Sinfully

The paramedics forced me to back away from Payton as they worked on her. Chloe was sobbing on the floor with her knees up to her chest. I crouched down behind her and held her as we both cried for the one we loved who was helpless before us.

I couldn't lose her. We had both been through enough heartache in our lives and we deserved our happy ending. The paramedics kept talking in medical jargon and soon she was being lifted onto a stretcher and taken outside.

"I need to be with her. Please." The young paramedic gave me a grave look and nodded solemnly.

Present

Payton has been in a coma for two weeks. Two weeks I've sat by her side, hoping to see her condition improve. Two weeks I have been told to go home and they'd call if anything changed. The medically induced coma was only for the first week, now it's all up to her. They say her body is protecting itself by shutting down so its vital organs can heal. When she's ready, she'll wake up. She has to.

Chloe has been by every single day. She filled me in on the sexual assault and attempted murder charges against Grayson. He is being held on a one million dollar bond and would likely see lengthy jail time as long as he doesn't prove to be clinically insane. His DNA under her fingernails that matched the scrapes to his face is enough to put him away for now. Grayson had a few broken ribs, internal bruising, a nasty black eye, and a broken nose to top it all off. She's a fighter. *My* fighter.

My baby girl had massive internal bleeding and a cracked skull, among other more minor injuries. Doctors believe she put up a good fight while standing up, but when he knocked her to the ground, she most likely hit her head on the baseboard which caused the fracture. The swelling on her brain has gone down significantly. After three surgeries to stop the internal bleeding and to repair a ruptured spleen, fractured ribs, and a collapsed lung, she's finally stabilized.

Watching her chest move by machine is terrifying. She looks so lifeless with a tube down her throat and wires everywhere. Her head is wrapped in gauze and her stomach is bandaged from her recent surgeries. The bruises are turning a nice shade of green now and her cuts have scabbed over.

Doctors worry that with the swelling to her brain there may be permanent brain damage when she wakes up. Her main physician seems optimistic about Payton waking up, and I won't leave her side until she does.

I never got to tell her how much I love her. Even though I've told her a hundred times since the accident, I need to tell her when she is conscious. I can't let another person I love slip away.

With Cami, there was the terrible unknown because her body was never found. We held on to hope that we would spot her, but after four days, the search party was called off. I was never able to say goodbye. I was with Cami and Tristen when it happened and not being able to save her wrecked me. Tristen and I were riding the wave ahead of her, and by the time we were out, she had gone under. She wanted to wait on the perfect wave and was waiting for it while Tristen and I rode as many as we could handle.

I felt helpless searching for Cami in the vast ocean and stayed out in the water for hours searching for her. After it got dark, I waited at the beach, desperately hoping that she would find her way back. I couldn't leave her out there.

I now feel the same helplessness that I did that day in the water. At least Payton is still with me. Chloe was sweet enough to bring me some shower products and a razor but I couldn't care less about how I look at the moment. I haven't shaved in two weeks and have only showered a few times using the shower in the hospital room. The nurses aren't pleased but I'm not going to leave her so I can freshen up. I make Chloe sit beside her bed while I quickly get the grime off my body and make myself presentable.

Her vitals haven't changed in three days. They keep her comfortable with pain meds but she looks so alone in the hospital bed. The wires surround her and make me timid to get close to her but I need to feel her against me. I hold her hand constantly, rubbing her dry skin with my thumb, hoping to solicit movement from her.

It's late in the night and I'm restless sitting next to her. With most of her wounds being to her abdomen and head, I'm scared to move her the slightest bit. She has just a few inches on her right side. I stand up and examine where the IV, machines, and wires are to make sure I'm not going to mess anything up. I gently move her hand to rest on her stomach and climb in beside her. Watching the monitors, I make sure I haven't disturbed her before settling down.

It feels unnatural to have her body up against mine and not feel that connection to her. I keep waiting for her to curl up against me and push her butt up to my groin. I fight the urge to wrap my arm around her waist or under her head.

I'm shaken awake by an older nurse with graying hair. "I have to check her vitals and give her medicine. You can stay there but be careful when you get up." My eyes are still groggy but I nod, trying to wake myself up to see how she is doing. Looking at the clock, it's three in the morning.

"Has anything changed? I didn't notice anything when I got in bed with her. I needed to be close to her."

"The doctor is planning on reducing some of her dosages. We'll still keep her comfortable but this might help her regain consciousness. Sometimes people get too comfortable with the medicine and don't fight to wake up. Dr. Bills will be here in the morning to discuss this more. Are you sure there isn't any family to call?" I know her parents are dead and she doesn't have any siblings. She had mentioned an aunt named Katy but it didn't seem like they were close.

"I don't think so, but I'll double check with her best friend. She'll be here in the morning." The nurse went about her business but I can't fall back asleep. I keep watching Payton sleep peacefully and I feel lost without her. She is *it* for me, I don't want anyone else. I just need to see her beautiful blue eyes again.

"Payton, baby, I don't know if you can hear me but I need you to fight. I can't imagine my life without you in it. I was thinking that after you get out of here, we could go to some exotic beach and get away for a while so you can heal. Just imagine the white sand, turquoise water, and warm breeze. I won't ever let anyone hurt you again, sweet angel. I'll be here for you no matter what." My tears fall onto her hospital gown as I silently weep. The cards that had been dealt to us were unfair and cruel but I'm not giving up on her, on us.

Over the next week, Payton's doctor eases her off her medications and her vitals are looking better. The furthest I venture from her is the cafeteria downstairs. I know a dozen of the nurses by name and they are kind to me. Visiting hours never apply to me and they make sure to keep me informed of the slightest new information.

On my way back from grabbing a sandwich, I see Dr. Bills and a handful of nurses running toward Payton's room. My heart drops and I start sprinting toward her room. *What happened?* I wasn't there and something happened.

I walk in and see they've reclined her bed so she's now lying flat. Her arms are tugging at the tube and she keeps making coughing noises. I'm pushed away by Brittany, one of the dayshift nurses I had grown close to. "Ryder, you have to back up. They're working on her now. You can stay in here but stay against the wall and prepare yourself for what you may see."

What am I seeing right now? They are giving her more medicine and Dr. Bills is instructing her to keep coughing but not to touch the tube. Seeing her struggle is the hardest thing to see but she's conscious. Her eyes aren't open but she *is* moving and I can't wait to get close to her.

Sinfully

"Ahhhh-ow! Make it stop, it hurts too much, make it stop!" Her crackly voice is soft but determined. She is in pain and all I can do is watch. What's hurting her?

Brittany is near Payton's side now. "I just gave you more pain medicine. It will make you sleepy but don't fight it and try not to move. Alright, sweetie?" She's cleaning the residue left around her mouth from the tape that kept the tube in place. "Everything's alright now. Ryder is here with you, Payton. He's been with you the whole time."

I watch the one-sided conversation and am happy that I made friends with the nurses here. I may not be able to get close to her yet, but she knows I've been here.

It feels like hours have passed by the time Dr. Bills and her crew of nurses finally start filing out of the room. Payton had gone back to sleep moments after she was given the medicine but they stayed to make sure everything was okay with her. Her doctor tries to get me to talk outside but I refuse and she settles on talking quietly by the door.

"Her brain activity looks good. We won't know if there's any permanent damage until she's fully awake, but with the pain level she's still in, we are going to ease her back slowly. When she wakes again, we'll try to keep her awake to do a more thorough examination on her, but she'll be sleeping a lot for the next few days. Don't rush her or expect her to know anything she did before the accident. We haven't been able to check her short-term or long-term memory, and that can be difficult for loved ones to see. We don't know what she'll remember at this point. I suggest you take the next few hours to call anyone you need to let them know her progress and prepare yourself for what's to come. She's going to be okay, though."

Chapter 16

Payton

I can hear his voice. He seems so far away, though. Through the blackness, I can feel his presence with me but I can't see him. I try moving toward him but fall short. I try speaking to him and fail again.

My body is useless and the only thing I can do is listen to his words. He tells me that he loves me. That he will never leave me. That we are meant to be and have only begun to live our lives together. I'm still so sleepy. It doesn't take long for me to give in to the blackness again.

When I wake up again, I can hear a female voice talking to Ryder. It sounds like Chloe but I'm not positive. "You need to prepare for the worst. There is a chance she might never wake up, and if she does, she might not be the same."

Where am I?

"She WILL wake up. Her body just needs more time to heal. She's my everything, so stop talking about what-ifs and tell me her progress for today." I can hear the desperation in his voice.

I attempt to speak to him again, but nothing comes out. I want him closer to me but he is still talking to that woman. *Why can't I open my eyes?* My head is throbbing and the rest of my body feels heavy.

Soon enough, the female voice is gone and Ryder slips in beside me.

Are we in my bed? I have missed his touch and hope he'll stay a while because I'm getting sleepy again.

My throat is itching. *Why am I still so tired?* I need to scratch the itch! I attempt to pull my hand up and am surprised when it slowly complies. My neck is the first thing I feel but it isn't where I need relief. Moving further up, I feel plastic and begin to panic. Upon closer inspection, I can make out tape keeping a plastic tube in place in my throat. *What is happening!?*

I try tugging but the tape is holding it tightly in position. I need to see what's going on. My eyelids are sticky, but I manage to open them to see through a small slit.

The walls are stark white and I hear commotion from the distance. Two slender figures are moving around me, uttering for me to stop moving and to wait. I don't know what I'm supposed to wait on, though.

"Page Dr. Bills now!" *Doctor? Who's sick?*

The tube is still bothering me like no other and I need to cough but I'm scared. Just as I'm reaching for it again, I hear loud footsteps come toward me and a woman with a stern but soft voice tells me she's going to help me.

"I need you to put your arms down, Payton, and cough for me. We'll get the tube out, but you need to keep coughing until I tell you to stop. Ready?" As long as I'll be able to breathe freely I'll do anything. The tube scratches and tickles as it comes up and suddenly I'm free, and exhausted.

They have me lying flat on my back, but I want to sit up. My abdomen feels like it's being torn apart when I try pushing up and I can't stifle the scream of pain that erupts from me. I can now feel my throbbing head and the pain is becoming overbearing. After yelling for them to make it stop, I finally feel relief start to take over my body. The last words I hear are from someone telling me that Ryder is with me and everything will be alright. The blackness returns and I welcome it.

Ryder

Payton's going to be okay. She's asleep again, but I feel like I can finally breathe for the first time in over two weeks. After seeing her wake up for those few brief moments, I feel the need to be close to her, in case she wakes up again. Lying in her hospital bed is never comfortable, and my body is protesting, but I need to feel her against me. I feel her hand twitch and the motion startles me. Looking her over, I whisper, "I'm here with you, baby. I'm here."

I place a gentle kiss on her forehead and the corners of her lips turn up. It's only a small movement but means the world to me. I lower my head and press a tender kiss to her lips, and after a moment, I feel her respond. I open my teary eyes and see her smile growing. She really *is* going to be okay.

"You're squishing my arm." *Oh shit.* I hadn't realized when I moved, I had settled back down and was leaning against her arm. I can't help but chuckle at that being the first thing to come out of her mouth. I scoot off of her, suddenly having no idea what to say. *Will she remember me?*

"Do you need me to get a nurse? Are you in pain?" Her eyes are fluttering but not quite open yet. I want her to stay awake and talk to me but not if she's hurting.

"Kiss me again. Please." I really hope she knows who I am since she's asking for more kisses. I'm not going to deny her, though.

I lean in again, bringing my hand behind her head, being careful of the bandages, and leisurely kiss her on the lips again. Just as she tries moving her hands up, she breaks the kiss off with a pained expression and a quiet whimper.

"What hurts, baby?" I press the nurse's call button and request that they come in. "Your stomach and head were banged up the worst but they said any movement might hurt you for the next few days. Just try to relax until a nurse comes."

Sinfully

"What happened to me? How long have I been here?" Confusion and worry is written all over her face and my stomach sinks at the thought of having to tell her what happened that night at Chloe's home. I hate just *thinking* about it and seeing her reaction will completely break me.

"You were assaulted, sweet girl. You've been sleeping for a few weeks but you're doing awesome now. That's what matters." I hold her hand as I sit up, wondering if the nurses heard my request.

"Sleeping for weeks? Like in a coma, Ryder?" Her voice is getting stronger and more agitated now. I don't want to upset her but I know she's going to ask for more information.

"Yes. You're going to be okay now, though. Dr. Bills will be by soon and we'll know more then. I missed you so much, Payton. You scared me there for a while and I can't imagine not having you with me. I wish I could take your pain away." She gives a sweet smile and I hope that my answer will pacify her questions for a while.

Brittany, our daytime nurse, and Dr. Bills stop by a little while later and let us know they'd like to keep her under their supervision for the next day or so, but then she'll be able to go home under bed rest because her abdomen will still need time to heal.

"Hold me?" Payton is just about passed out when she requests that I lie next to her. I'm more than grateful that she remembers me and who we are together, but I'm still dreading telling her what really happened. I just want to focus on her getting better, not on what brought her here in the first place. I hold her for hours as she sleeps peacefully while my inner turmoil is breaking me down.

214

Chapter 17

Payton

It's been almost three months since my accident. I call it an accident because it doesn't sound as terrifying as *assaulted by my stalker*. My injuries don't hinder me in everyday activities anymore but I *do* take naps more frequently. Chloe has apologized a million times, blaming herself for ever dating Grayson to begin with, but I know not to blame her. He would have found another way to get close to me if it hadn't been her. Psychiatrists diagnosed Grayson with attachment disorder and borderline personality disorder but say he is fit for trial.

Ryder, over time, has given me the details of that horrible night. I can see his own pain while he goes over some of the more disturbing details. After ripping my shirt in half, Grayson left bruises in the shape of handprints on my breasts and also on my upper chest while he held me down.

Paramedics found that the button on my jeans was ripped off but my zipper had gotten stuck so Grayson couldn't pull them down over my ass. All of my internal bleeding was from him punching me in the stomach and holding me down as I fought him. Apparently, people like Grayson can totally black out and not realize how badly they are hurting someone until someone intervenes. Even his 'love' for me didn't stop him from almost beating me to death. Fighting back helped keep me alive but made my injuries more severe. They said if it had gone on another couple of minutes, it would have been much worse. I'm grateful that Ryder and Chloe were there to save me because I truly don't believe I would be here if it weren't for them.

Ryder hasn't been back to Los Angeles and has been working from my home whenever I'm asleep or preoccupied. He's been with me the entire time and I realize now how foolish I was for fighting my feelings to be with him in the first place. He's the only one who gives me butterflies in my stomach just by looking my way. Ryder makes me feel like the most beautiful woman around and I never want to lose him.

Today, we are headed down to the beach for a peaceful day together. He says he wants to talk to me while we're down there and I can't help but wonder what needs to be said there and not at home.

I miss the ocean and can't wait to feel the sand between my toes and the cool water against my skin. I'm waiting on Ryder to finish getting ready while I cut up some fruit and cheese to take down to the shore with us along with some crackers. We're meeting his friend, Tristen, for dinner afterward so I figured a snack would be sufficient.

"Hey, babe, do you remember where I put my phone? I need to text Tristen to tell him what time we'll meet him and I can't find it." I chuckle, remembering last night's events.

"You threw it across the room last night when it kept going off as I was riding you. It's probably close to the hamper if I remember correctly."

He blushes as he remembers last night as well.

"Oh yeah. Thanks, baby. You ready?"

"Sure am. I'm bringing a picnic basket for a snack and already have the towels down in the car." I move in to kiss him and his arms wrap around my waist and hoist me up onto the island.

Between kisses, I manage to tell him we don't have time for this. "I can be quick. I'll make it up to you tonight in bed, sweet girl." He's already unbuckling his pants so I don't see a reason to argue.

My beach cover-up leaves my bikini bottoms as the only thing standing in the way of him filling me, and he takes full advantage. He moves the fabric harshly over to the side and plunges two fingers inside me and roughly rubs his thumb over my clit. "So wet. Damn, baby." He brings his fingers to his lips and licks them before grabbing his cock with his fist and ramming inside my tightness. He feels so amazing inside me that I know I'll be coming right along with him soon enough.

"Harder, Ryder! You feel so good inside me, baby. Mmm...fuck me."

"Ride my dick, sweet girl. That's it...so good, Payton. I'm close..."

I'm about to explode but want us to finish together. "Come with me, Ryder. I'm there, baby, fuck...right there. Don't stop! Mmm...come with me, baby."

That was enough for him and I feel him jerk inside me as I come undone around him.

Pure bliss.

Ryder

My girl is back. The past month has been filled with new experiences for us. Doctor appointments, pain, fatigue, and confusion are part of Payton's daily routine but we're getting through it together. The doctors and confusion have slowly become less frequent and her pain and fatigue aren't a deciding factor anymore in what she has planned for the day. We see time together as a gift and try not to take it for granted. I haven't been back to Los Angeles, and thankfully have been able to work while I'm down here with Payton.

Tristen has been there for me when I need someone to talk to. He reminds me that she is still here and to cherish every moment with her. We haven't been able to spend as much time together but we've been talking almost every day. He seems happy but won't go into details about McKenna or dating in general.

I'm ready to tell Payton about Cami. I've wanted to tell her for a while now but it's never been the right time. As we make our way down to the warm sand, I try to think of how I should approach the subject. The beach is where I feel closest to Cami and I need for Payton to know about my sister and the heartache I've felt, too.

"We should go surfing soon, babe. I miss the waves and the rush! Dr. Bills finally cleared me so I can technically go now." My stomach twists into knots. I don't know if I'll ever surf again. Too many painful memories plague me when I think of surfing. I'm terrified that something will happen to Payton if we go out together. *How do I ease her into this conversation?*

"Maybe in a few weeks. I, uhh, need to get a new board." Such a lame excuse, and from the look on her face, she isn't buying it.

"What's going on, baby? You've told me about how you used to surf all the time with Tristen but I don't ever hear you talk about going out there. You seem more content with getting sun on the beach than feeling the adrenaline rush of catching a massive wave."

Leighton Riley

She sits down in the sand beside me and lays her hand on top of mine.

"I had a sister, Cami, she was my twin." Memories of our childhood come racing back to me—building forts, playing soccer together, and baking cookies with grandma. I feel the sting behind my eyes and will myself to hold it together.

"I didn't know. You haven't talked about her before. Did something happen?" She spreads my knees open and climbs over to sit between them. I wrap my arms around her and instantly feel more settled.

"We were surfing—Tristen, Cami, and I. The swells were high but the current was decently strong. Tristen and I rode this one wave together while Cami waited for the perfect one. By the time we paddled back, she was gone." I feel the tears running down my face and don't bother to wipe them. Payton turns her body so her legs are dangling on one side and she wraps her arms around my neck.

She needs to see this. She isn't the only one who's lost someone and I need her to know how Cami's death affected my life, just like her parents had hers.

"What do you mean gone?" Her brows come together and I can see that she knows what I mean but hopes she misheard. She looks into my eyes and sees everything she needs to see.

"We looked for hours out there, Tristen and I. We even brought in search and rescue teams but never found anything. They said a lot of bodies wash up within the next few days but she never came back."

"Baby, I'm so sorry. For you to be out there with her when it happened, it must have been devastating." She's clutching onto me harder now. She doesn't realize it, but her touch grounds me.

"She and Tristen were in a relationship. Payton, she was going to be a mom. I didn't know at the time that they were serious but they would be been great parents together. Tristen and I both closed ourselves off to the world for a while after it happened. I had no idea he was going through such a tragic loss of the love of his life and his unborn baby. I feel like a shitty friend. We're in a better place now but it's still hard sometimes. I feel her when I'm down here by the water but I don't know if I'll ever surf again."

"You didn't know. What matters is that you're there for him now. Everyone deals with death in their own way. Thank you for telling me. I guess we're both a little broken, huh?" She manages a smile but it doesn't meet her glistening eyes.

"Not anymore, babe. We have scars from our past but we aren't broken anymore. You make me want to be a better person. I haven't been this happy since before Cami's accident, and even then, it's not the same kind of happiness. Every morning when I wake up, you're the first thing I think of, even when you aren't beside me. I don't want to go another day without you knowing how much I care about you. I *love* you, Payton."

Payton shifts again so that each leg is wrapped around my waist, straddling me. Staring into my eyes for what feels like minutes, she thrusts her mouth onto mine and kisses me like our lives depend on it. Finally breaking the kiss, she moves back, teary eyed, but with a grin.

"You love me? Like *love* love me?" Her hands come up to hold in her chuckle and she seems surprised by my confession.

"Yes, sweet girl, I *love* love you. I wanted to say it before your incident but never found the right time. You don't have to say it back but I needed you to know. I'm in this with you for the long haul if you want me."

Her smile fades away and my hearts skips a beat. *Oh no.*

"Ryder? I've never told anyone that I love them." She looks unsure of herself and I just want to hold her and reassure her that everything's okay.

"Never, baby? What about other guys or your parents?"

"I never had that type of relationship with them. My foster parents were just adults who kept us in the same house but they weren't nurturing. My adoptive parents were loving, but I never told them I loved them and they never said it, either. I guess I love Chloe but that doesn't count."

I lift her chin up she can see me when I tell her, "You are loved, Payton. Not just by me, but by Chloe and Thomas—who, by the way, is in love with you—and your adoptive parents. You are so easy to fall in love with and you don't even realize it. You're beautiful inside and out, sweet girl."

"I love you, too, Ryder. You've stood by me while I figured out how to be vulnerable and you've shown me it's worth it to open up more to friends. I don't want to live in fear anymore. You know, I heard you a little bit in the hospital, while I was still asleep. I thought you should know." She has a sly grin that tells me she heard me confess my love weeks ago and hasn't said a word.

I move my hands to her waist and begin tickling her and she falls backward onto the sand. Getting up and hovering over her delicate body, careful not to put too much pressure on her, I bend down and softly kiss her lips.

"I love you, Payton Davenport."

"Mmm, say it again." A smile erupts from my face as she seems suddenly more carefree.

"I love you, Payton Davenport, and all your other aliases that you might come up with in the future. Now, let's go meet Tristen."

I am so ready for Tristen and Payton to meet so that we can all hang out together, and hopefully McKenna would round it out to a foursome. My life is coming together and I can't help but smile at how things are turning out.

Chapter 18

Payton

He loves me. *Holy shit.*

I don't deserve him, but I'm selfish and I'm not letting him go anytime soon. Walking up to the restaurant, hands intertwined and matching smiles, nothing can ruin this moment. My past is in my past and my future is standing beside me.

Tristen and Ryder both agreed that I need to try this hole-in-the-wall seafood restaurant that they used to go to after a day out in the water. The chef picks out fresh fish from the docks each morning, so the menu is always different. From the looks of it, you can tell it's been here forever from the rusting metal due to being near the ocean, and the place is packed with locals.

"Psst." I stop right before we walk into the restaurant and turn toward Ryder.

"Yeah, babe?" He's assessing me with his eyes and I know he's thinking I'll want a quickie before we head inside. Not saying he's wrong, but that's beside the point.

"Not that."

"Oh, well could you be persuaded? I can be *hard* to resist."

"You're so cheesy. No, I just wanted to let you know that I feel completely happy and have never felt this…euphoric. And now, when we go to Vegas, we can be that happily in love couple that everyone hates."

"Sounds perfect, Payton. Anywhere you want to go, I'll be by your side, unless I'm behind you." He gives me a wink and I know we need to get inside so he'll settle down.

"I was thinking about how we haven't christened the media room yet. Just something to think about while we're at dinner." With that, I walk in, but have to wait for Ryder so he can look to see if Tristen is here.

Ryder looks toward the back left corner and immediately starts heading that direction and I follow suit.

"How'd you know where he'd be?" I hadn't seen him texting his friend, but with the amount of people and tables in this place, it's like *Where's Waldo* in here.

"We kinda have our own table. It's not necessarily reserved, but if Karissa knows we're coming, she doesn't let anyone sit here. Jackson, her husband, runs the kitchen and Karissa runs the front. From our table, you can see the ocean without obstruction and watch the surfers during lunch time."

As we get closer, my eyes land on a lean but muscular surfer boy with beach-blond hair and the most striking green eyes I've ever seen. The problem is, I recognize those eyes. *Shit. Fucking shit.*

My instincts to run kick in and I back up a step before realizing I can't run from this. Tristen is his best friend. *How do I have the worst luck ever?* Me and my stupid slutty ways. This is going to look bad.

"Payton? No way, this is *your* Payton?" I can hear the surprise in Tristen's voice.

"Wait, you…you know her? You know each other?" Ryder asks, standing between his best friend and me. I'm looking down, scared to look into Ryder's eyes and willing Tristen to disappear. I can feel them staring at me.

This is *so* not going to be good. Will Ryder believe me? I just got him and am now going to lose him. *I shouldn't have let him in.* I need to get this over with, to rip it off like a Band-Aid. A really big Band-Aid that might leave me raw and exposed afterward.

Leighton Riley

"We met in Vegas. It was a while back, though, before we met. But we didn't sleep together, I promise!" I yell it out a little too loudly and a few people at nearby tables turn to see what's going on.

Neither of them say anything and I finally work up the nerve to look up. Tristen seems apologetic yet silent and Ryder looks crushed.

My eyes stay focused on Ryder and I wish we were alone so we can talk about what happened. He's staring into my soul and I hope he sees my despair and regret.

"Let's have a seat. And a drink." Tristen motions for us to sit down and I'm not in the position to argue.

"I want her to explain. Then you, Tristen. No bullshit, either." Ryder is calm but his fists are clenching and unclenching slowly.

"We met back in September I think? He was sad and lonely so we had dinner and walked around together. He said he didn't want to talk about his problems but wanted to just have a day without having to deal with the past. We went to Serendipity 3, shared a deep-fried Oreos and ice cream sundae, and went to see the Jabbawockeez show before finishing off the night by me teaching him how to play Texas Hold 'Em against the dealer. Pure, innocent fun. He needed an escape and that's the whole reason I was there, anyway."

"Really?" Ryder looks at Tristen incredulously while Tristen nods in confirmation.

"The pants stayed on, man. Scout's honor. I was in a bad place and she made me forget for a few hours." Tristen is relaxed as can be. I envy him.

"Waiter, two beers and a margarita, please." Ryder looks back at me after ordering and asks, "That okay, babe? You're not on any more pills, right?" He seems concerned with my well-being which is a good sign.

"I'm dying for a margarita, baby, but I shouldn't right now." His hand finds its way over to mine and he intertwines our fingers gently. Maybe everything will be okay.

225

Sinfully

Once our drinks are served, Ryder takes a sip of the margarita and moves his beer aside. "What? Liquor before beer and you're in the clear. I'll drink the beer afterward." He acts like the bomb we just laid on him is no big deal and is ready to move on.

I bring my lips to his ear and whisper, "I love you, baby, always and forever." Squeezing my hand just a little tighter, he murmurs, "Always and forever, Payton."

I hold out my water for a toast. "To our past, which will stay in our memories, and to our present, which has created our future." I'm not quite sure how obvious or subtle my toast is, but I get confused stares from both men at the table.

Tristen doesn't dare say a word, but Ryder squints his eyes as if it will help him figure it out.

"Uhh, babe? Whatcha mean by created our future?"

I just chuckle and move our clasped hands over my stomach. His jaw drops open and I nod in response.

"Really? Like...for real?"

"I'm only six weeks along, so it's still early. I never put my NuvaRing back in after the accident. Surprise?" I look into Ryder's eyes and he is almost teary eyed.

"We're gonna have a baby? Tristen, we're gonna...*oh shit*. Bro, I'm so sorry. I didn't think about how this might affect you but I had no idea."

I sit here, unmoving, confused by what they are talking about. Then I remember how Cami was pregnant with Tristen's baby when she died. I'm a shitty person. I doubt Tristen knows that I know, though.

"I'm sorry. I wasn't expecting to announce it so soon, but I thought maybe you could be his or her godfather?" Worry consumes me as I wait for Tristen's response.

With a laugh, he comes back with, "Hell, I'm going to be his uncle. Welcome to the family, Payton."

"Thanks, Tristen. It really means a lot that you want to be there. Looks like I'll be moving down to San Diego permanently. The city could use a new publisher in town, anyway."

226

"So you're okay with this, baby? I know it wasn't planned, but you're the one for me and I can't wait to have a mini-Ryder running around one day." I wasn't sure how Ryder would react to our news but he is ecstatic.

"Okay with this? I'm in love with you and lil-bit. Thank you, Payton, for showing me how much life there is to live and how sharing it with the people you love makes everything worth it." Ryder pulls me close to him and kisses my forehead.

Everything is going to be okay. I took the chance and fell in love with the man of my dreams, or emails, whichever.

Sneak Peek of Tristen's story…

Regretfully

by

Leighton Riley

Tristen

My best friend is going to be a dad. I should be a husband *and* a dad right now but it was taken away from me. Not that I'm bitter, it's just not fair. Cami was my soul mate, my everything. While we hadn't told everyone about our relationship, we had been together for years and before that we were best friends. She was my first; I thought she'd be my last.

How do you move on after your whole world is swept away from you? Sure, girls are available for me if I want them, offering to get my mind off her for an hour or two. I've never been the guy to hook up with some random girl at a bar—it isn't my style.

Ryder and I had grown distant after Cami's death and I am partly to blame. Every time I see him, I see Cami. It was hard to deal with seeing so much of her in his mannerisms, his face, and his personality. Being twins, they were more alike than different. I haven't been a good friend, and I probably would have dealt with her death better if he'd been around, but that didn't happen. I've made some mistakes but I'm learning from them.

Meeting Payton in Vegas had been by chance and it was like she recognized my pain and knew what I needed. She was genuine and passionate about Vegas—she said that it was her place to escape.

After that short weekend in Vegas, I felt a weight lifted off my shoulders. Cami ruined me for other women. I compare every girl I come close to having feelings for to her. It isn't fair to me or the girls. There is this one girl. She scares the shit out of me. Well, the feelings I have scare me. She's incredible, but I've probably fucked that up, too. Can you love two people? Is it betrayal?

Sneak Peek of...

Fatefully

by

Leighton Riley

V

Sneak Peek — Fatefully

Authors Note

Chloe's story takes place after her and Grayson break up. For those who have not read the Sinfully series yet, there will be no spoilers within this story, only added snippets into the life of Chloe and her best friend Payton, who is the main female character in *Sinfully*.

This story takes place after *Sinfully*.

Enjoy

Chapter 1

Walking into the hotel with my best friend, I can't help but have butterflies in my stomach. Payton brought me along to today's book signing so that I can get a sense of what I'd be agreeing to if I were on the cover of one of her upcoming books. Owen, her current cover model, is going to be here too—she wants me on the next cover, *with him*.

"Payton, how the hell are you so calm right now? I mean, in just a few hours, girls are going to be fangirling all over you!" I look around and catch a few girls watching us from afar. It may have taken her awhile, but she's finally embracing her career as an erotic romance author. This is her fourth signing this year, but only the second that she will have Owen with her.

"I might get a few fangirls this weekend. Owen is the one who gets bombarded. Readers recognize him instantly, and since he's known for being sweet and engaging with them, they don't mind coming up and asking for a photo with him. Last month in Little Rock, it took us forty-five minutes to get to the restaurant downstairs. He loves interacting with the fans and can be quite the flirt."

Quite the flirt? I could use a weekend being next to a flirt. Ideas swirl around my head, playing out different ways the weekend could end. We were supposed to have chemistry on the next cover.

This could be fun.

Sneak Peek — Fatefully

"When's he supposed to get here anyway?" I ask, as we make our way up to our room. After the flight from San Diego to Tulsa with a layover in Dallas, I pray that I have time to freshen up before he arrives.

"I texted him our room number; he just landed so it won't be too long. Chloe, I'm warning you, he *is* a charmer. He is the all-in-one package. He's an EMT during the day and bouncer at a nightclub on the weekends. Owen knows how to talk to the ladies and will make you feel as if you're the only one he cares about. Don't get too enthralled with him, sweetie. You're still newly single and need to take baby steps," Payton calls out from the bed. She's already pulled out her laptop and is going to work on emails and messages I'm sure.

"I'm not a little kid, Payt. I can handle him. Plus, after Grayson, I deserve to be a little reckless and carefree. You will not cockblock me, Payton! You hear me?" I lift my suitcase onto the bed and quickly find exactly what I need. Pulling out a pair of white designer shorts and a midnight blue blouse, I decide on pairing them with a cute pair of sandals, just in case he isn't on the tall side.

Just as I pull my top off, I hear the knock on the door. *Shit!*

"Payton, stall him!"

"I will do no such thing," Payton calls out as she heads to the door, laughing at the scene before her.

I rush to pull on my new top and nearly fall over trying to slip on my sandals. My makeup hasn't been touched since this morning, and I'm sure I look like a hot mess.

"Mornin', sweetheart." I hear the deep voice reverberate throughout the room and my core clenches with need.

"Hey, Owen. How was the flight? You can come in if you want, or your room is right down the hall." I watch by the bed as Payton opens the door wide to let our guest in. I'm staring like a deer in headlights. I take in his toned and tanned body. Broad shoulders, a lean waist, and gym shorts that are hugging his massive thighs. He's got stunning hazel eyes and short, dark brown hair. He is beautiful.

Sneak Peek — Fatefully

Owen moves into the room with confidence and eyes me immediately. Licking his lower lip, he does a full take of what's in front of him.

"You, my dear, are gorgeous. I'm Owen." He stalks over to me and stops within an inch of touching me. My body is on fire, and I'm regretting not wearing heels. He is easily ten inches taller than my short five-foot three-inch frame. He towers over me and I watch as his chest rises and falls. Looking up, I'm met with striking eyes that are filled with…lust?

"Chloe. I'm your other half." I say without thinking and hold out my hand. Right now, all I care about is feeling his warmth radiate off him and how if Payton wasn't in the room, this might have a different outcome.

His handshake is firm, but his thumb caresses my hand gently. "You sound confident in your admission. Personally, I like to, *get to know*, the woman a little before I commit. I'd make an exception for you though."

"I mean, I meant- for the cover. Your other half for the cover." I snap out of the spell he has me under and back up a step, causing me to fall onto the bed.

"Mhmm. Whatever you say, gorgeous."

I'm in trouble.

Chapter 2

"So, do the assistants get assistants too because I could really use a Diet Coke right now." I'm sitting in Payton's chair watching her arrange her table just right. I had offered to help, but she quickly fired me from the task, saying I wasn't doing it right.

"You have about ten minutes before the bloggers come in for interviews. Can you grab me a Diet Pepsi while you're at it?" She responds without looking up.

"I'm taking a ten out of your money bag. Just so you know. Be back in a few." I hurry along, wondering where all the man candy is. The ballroom is filled with authors, volunteers, assistants, and event coordinators, but no men. I'd be lying if I said it wasn't motivation to run into one of them.

After waiting in line in the gift shop, I finally have our drinks along with Laffy Taffy for me and Peanut Butter M&Ms for Payton. Checking the time on my phone, I realize I only have two minutes before they open the doors. Picking up the pace, I'm slightly disappointed at not running into at least one hottie.

Just before I reach the doors, strong arms envelope my waist, and I'm hoisted off the ground. "What the...!"

Hearing his laugh and looking down at the strong cords of muscle that run up his forearms, I instantly relax, knowing whose bulge I'm feeling behind me. "I like the chase, sweetheart. Do you need some help?"

He places me back on the ground and turns me to face him. Nodding silently, I've lost all ability to form words.

Laughing quietly, he grabs the bag of refreshments and places his hand on my lower back. "I have a few ideas of poses we could do for the photo shoot. You have to trust me on them though. Is that alright?" His deep timbre makes me want to do anything the man asks.

"I can do that. You've been doing this longer than I have, you're actually my first."

Stopping dead in his tracks, he eyes me as if I were a rainbow unicorn. It's only then that I realize what I said.

"No! You're not my first, *that*! I've never been on a cover or modeled before. You know more about it than me, therefore I trust you." Ducking my head in shame, I wonder how in the world this attractive man is still talking to me.

"Don't hide, especially from me." He lifts my chin up with his finger, leaning in close to my ear. "There are more unconventional ways to expose you, Chloe," he whispers softly. Pulling away, he brushes a loose tendril of hair away and winks.

Getting to the table, Payton smirks when she catches how flush I am. The moment Owen has his back turned from us, she mouths *what did you do?!*

Shrugging my shoulders, I can't hold back on the huge smile I have currently. That boy. Correction, that *man*.

I've been watching Owen take pictures with fans for the past three hours, and if I see him kiss one more cheek, I might cut a bitch. He may not be mine, but I feel oddly possessive over him. Payton has a good handle on the signing and doesn't need me to do much so

Sneak Peek — Fatefully

I'm left gawking at his chiseled chest, six-pack abs, and amazing V of which I'm curious where it ends. His black Armani boxer briefs are peeking out of his jeans, and he wears them perfectly.

I want to lick him.

Moving my gaze back up, I choke when I meet his gorgeous hazel eyes. He's been watching me gawk at him! *Shit.*

I look down at my phone in my lap, welcoming any distraction, but I hear him tell the girls waiting in line to hold just a second.

I feel him behind me, hovering behind my chair, his lips brushing against my ear. "I might be kissing their cheeks, but they aren't who's occupying all my thoughts. Patience." Kissing my cheek swiftly, he returns and carries on his duties of being the hottest cover model at the event.

Holy hell. What did he mean? I wasn't anything to him. He could get any girl he wanted to.

"I don't know what you did, but that boy wants in your pants. You ready to let go of your past and live a little? If so, I think Owen might be the perfect match for you," Payton observes, as she pulls out her lip gloss from her purse, waiting for the next round of readers.

Chapter 3

By the time the signing is over, I'm all hot and bothered. Owen's quick glances my way have me giddy like a school girl and he's consuming my thoughts.

"We're supposed to be getting ready for the after party, but I gotta stop by Kailie Hill's table and get a book from her. She wrote this fantastic dark alpha male story and I told her it *needs* to be on my shelf. I'll meet you up in the room soon," Payton explains, as she starts undoing her banner. "I got this, you go get prettied up for Owen." She shoos me off, and I'm left wondering what the night will bring.

Walking into the elevator, I slouch back against the wall, hoping that I'm not in over my head with this one. He's got to be the most handsome man I've ever seen in person and there's this draw to him that's undeniable. Closing my eyes, I think through different outfits I can wear tonight when I feel the elevator come to a stop. When I open my eyes, I'm met with those damn hazel eyes again.

Where was he just at?

Dressed in a different pair of jeans, lime green tennis shoes, and a black button-down shirt, he looks purely delectable. My eyes take in his bulging biceps and thick, tight chest.

"Perfect timing. How are you doing, sweet girl?" He steps into the elevator and leans against the opposite wall. He continues to watch me, and I am taken aback by his down to earth personality and devilish good looks.

When I fail to respond, he moves slightly closer to me, quietly mentioning, "You know, you can talk to me. Anything and everything, just say what's on your mind." Smiling sweetly, he nods gently, giving me the reassurance that I need.

"You don't want to know what's on my mind." I can't hide the blush as I realize how perverse and downright naughty my thoughts are. The elevator comes to a halt and I step out, not realizing his room is on the same floor.

"This way. And I very much would like to know. I don't like having to guess." He lends his hand and leads me down the opposite hallway. Following without really giving it thought, it only dawns on me once we stop at his room.

He thinks he can have his way with me, without any thought or question. Was I giving off *those* vibes? I mean, I don't think I'd turn him down, but isn't he supposed to at least put in a little effort first?

"Stop thinking and come in. I didn't bring you here for that. *Yet*, at least." He holds the door open, waiting for me to follow suit.

"Was I that obvious?" I quickly walk past him and stop when I see the king-size bed. Thoughts of him hovering over me—skin gliding against mine, taking what he wants—fill my brain.

"Little bit." He laughs, moving to sit on the desk chair. "Make yourself comfortable, babe. It's hard being in the public eye constantly, I just needed to get away for a few. What'd you think of the signing?" He props his ankle on the opposite knee, getting comfortable. I move to the bed and have a seat on the edge, crisscrossing my legs.

"The readers were amazing! The love and support they have for Payton and the other authors is incredible. Being here and seeing the interactions, definitely puts it in perspective. Now watching the girls with you, that's another story. Do you ever get tired of it?"

"Do I get tired of having girls want their picture with me? Nope, can't say I do. Without Payton and the support of her fans, I wouldn't be here. Being able to spend a few minutes with them and have their picture taken with me, it's my small way of saying thanks. Plus, my life would be fucking boring without these random trips to events."

"Didn't one of them ask to lick your nipples?" I question with a flirtatious smile.

"You heard that?" He rubs his eyebrow, hiding his snicker.

"Mhmm."

"It's all in good fun. I try to keep it with kisses on the cheek because if one reader sees it, then they all want the nipple lick. I learned that the hard way."

"What if I asked?" Looking into his eyes, I hope the courage I suddenly found doesn't dissipate too quickly.

"I don't think I could deny you anything you asked, especially behind closed doors." Dropping his knee and leaning forward, his eyes move between my lips and eyes. His deep, masculine voice sends tingles down to my core.

"What if I didn't want just a kiss on the cheek?" I scoot so my feet touch the floor, and I watch as his chest rises and falls.

"I'd say we have very similar thoughts. I need you to know though; this wasn't why I brought you in here. I just wanted to talk more privately, without prying eyes."

I hear my phone going off in my purse, but ignore it. His stare is too intense, and I just want to get lost in it, and in him. He stands up and takes the two steps needed to be directly in front of me. I look up so I'm not staring straight at his obvious arousal.

As he begins to bend over to kiss me, there's a knock on the door. He lowers his head in defeat, but keeps a calm face as he stalks over to the door. I lay back, no clue what I'm doing or what was about to happen. I just know I don't want it to stop.

"Uhh, am I interrupting something?" Payton's distinct voice booms through the room and I jerk into a sitting position.

Fuck. Wait, don't I have her approval for this?

Sneak Peek — Fatefully

"We were just getting away for a few minutes. Don't go all momma bear on us. We weren't doing anything wrong," Owen explains for the two of us.

"Momma bear? I'm the same age as both of you! Chloe wasn't answering her phone and I got worried." Payton bit her nail, and I instantly feel like shit.

She didn't worry like this too much anymore, but her anxiety of people leaving her is still in there, coming out just when she's in a good place in her life. She should know by now I'm not leaving her side, but the fact that I made her worry kills me.

Moving over to the door, I wrap my arms around her stomach and embrace her tightly. "I'm sorry. I didn't mean to frighten you," I murmur quietly so only she can hear.

Nodding her head, we take a moment to gather ourselves. I can feel Owen watching our strange interaction, but I don't care at the moment. She needs me just like I need her. She's gotten so strong lately that I forget she still has demons she fights daily.

"I can leave if you want me to? I feel like I'm watching something intimate." Owen starts heading for the door and I can't help but burst out in a fit of laughter. Turning around, his confused face is priceless.

"Owen, let's just say Chloe and I go back a ways. We've been through some tough shit. It wasn't about to get intimate though, you perv. Owen, we'll meet you downstairs in twenty?" Payton asks as she starts to head out the door.

Looking back, I see the lust and desire in his eyes and I mouth *later* to him before walking away.

"Why do I have the feeling I just cockblocked you?" Payton inquires as we walk back to our room.

"I plead the fifth?" I look over and, from the look on her face, she knows all she needs to.

"Mhmm. Well, how about I accidently lose the both of you later at the party and since I know where you'll be, I'll just assume I'll see you both for breakfast?" she plans out as we start touching up our makeup.

XVIII

Sneak Peek — Fatefully

"Are you pimping me out? You're basically telling us to go fool around. Aren't you supposed to tell me to wait and be a good girl or something?" I pull out a short black dress and some cream heels for the night but get stuck on which lingerie to wear. Sexy? Slutty? Classy? I don't know him well enough to know what he'll like and end up choosing a black lacy push up bra with matching panties. Simple but sexy.

"It's not pimping. It's just giving my blessing to have the best sex of your life. Not that I know how he is in bed, but have you seen him? He has to be a rock star in the sack."

"You. Are. Incorrigible. But I love you anyways. So, how do I look?" Twirling around, I wait for her approval but when I hear nothing, I twist to face her and see her rummaging through her bag.

"Here." Handing me a pair of handcuffs.

"Umm, why do you have these in your suitcase?" Staring, I wait for her to elaborate.

"You never know when you'll need handcuffs. And I kinda forgot to take them out last time we had a vacation."

"That's enough of an explanation for me. No explicit details needed!" I cut her off, knowing full well she wouldn't mind giving the exact details of her last rendezvous involving them.

"Ugh. You are both hot, why not have some fun? Just put them in your purse in case. We use them in bed occasionally, and it's fucking hot as hell." She shrugs her shoulders as if this is completely normal for her to share.

"I'm going to pretend I didn't just hear that and stick them in my purse, just in case. Anything else, momma bear?"

"Nope. You look gorgeous. Let's go downstairs together and then I'll find another group to hang out with. You deserve to have fun and be a little reckless and Owen won't hurt you. He's one of the good ones. Just don't hurt him or I'll have to find another model. Got it?" She moves a stray piece of hair away from my face and grabs a Kleenex for me to blot my lip gloss.

XIX

"Yes ma'am. Let's go before I back out." I head for the door and hear her laughing as I she picks up her purse. "What's so funny?"

"It's like your first day of school. I'm sending you off to bigger and better things, literally. I bet Grayson was tiny, am I right?" She shudders, and I can't help but show how average he really was with the use of my fingers.

"Can we go now? I don't want to miss nap time." I grin as she gives me a funny face, knowing full well what I meant.

"Go, go. I'm right behind you. Owen just texted me and said he's at the bar. How about I just bow out now and you show up alone?" she suggests with a smile.

"I can do that. Thank you, Payton. I owe you."

Chapter 4

eeing him at the bar in gray dress slacks and a black button-down makes my knees go weak. He's sipping a dark amber liquid and is on his phone, unaware of me just a few feet behind him. Payton gave me his number before we left the room so I decide to have a little fun.

Me: Is that seat taken?

Owen: Depends... who's asking?

I have a seat on one of the couches behind him, surprised that he hasn't once looked around.

Me: Someone who's been having naughty thoughts about you

Owen: That doesn't narrow it down much

Owen: Hmm, have I been having naughty thoughts about you too?

Me: How the hell am I supposed to know?

Owen: True.

Me: ...Black, lacy panties

Owen: Uhm.. Yes please?

Me: Come and get it

He finally turns around and smirks as soon as he sees me. Tossing a few bills on the counter, he stalks toward me and my core tingles.

"You look radiant. Where's our friend?" he ponders.

"Busy. Did you want to wait for her?" Pouting slightly, I pray he catches on.

"Not at all, are you ready for the party?" He holds out his elbow for me to take as I stand and begins leading us through the hotel.

"We can stop by for a few minutes." Looking over, he waits a moment before nodding in agreement.

"I thought we'd never get out of there! People don't notice if I leave, but they have an uproar when you head for the door."

"I don't know what you're talking about. Now, where were we before we were interrupted?" Placing my hands in his, he walks me over to the bed and nudges me to sit. "Here?" His lips are inches from mine.

"I think a little bit closer actually." I lean in and wait for him to finish the distance.

"Mmm, here?" He feathers his lips over mine, but doesn't kiss me. I'm dying to have him ravage me right now, but he's in control.

I lick my lips without thinking and my tongue brushes against his lips. "What are we doing?" I toss out there.

Backing up a tad, he sighs in defeat and runs his hand through his hair. "Fuck if I know. I'm not normally like this, I swear. There's this... thing with you that I can't wrap my head around.

Sneak Peek — Fatefully

We don't know each other, but I want to, in a bad way. Not just sexually either."

He moves to have a seat in the chair again, and I finally see a touch of vulnerability in his rugged features. He's not just some piece of man candy, he's truly genuine and a good guy. Most would have taken advantage of the opportunity without another thought.

"I feel it too. I got out of a tumultuous relationship recently, and it's been a struggle for me to find myself again. I got caught up in what the future should be and forgot to live in the present. But I feel the pull with you, and I don't want to fight it. I want to have fun and live a little. Payton said I wasn't allowed to hurt you. Do you know why she would say that?"

"Yes. I do know." Looking up towards the ceiling, he shakes his head and takes a deep breath.

"I have a little girl. She's two and her mom cheated on me before and after she was born. She was fantastic at making up excuses of where she was and I was fucking clueless. When I found out, it tore me to shreds. We'd been together since sophomore year of high school and all of a sudden, I'm a single dad. Payton knows enough of that story to make it clear why she said not to hurt me. I don't need her to protect me though, I know what I'm doing and I'm kind of in the same boat you are. I was so used to having a partner and now being alone, I feel like I'm starting over and don't know how to handle it."

He's more similar to me than I ever imagined. We're both a little broken, but haven't given up. Seeing the softer side to him makes me want him even more, but on a deeper level. I want to know who he is and what he likes. I want to know how to make him smile and how to console him when he's down.

I stand and walk over to the chair, feeling in control as he tries to figure out what my motives are. I run a hand over his short hair, trying to remember every detail of his beautiful face. "She's an idiot. I'm sorry for what you've been through, but not sorry about the fact that it led me to you. Even though we just met, I can already tell that you've got a kind heart and undeniable genuineness that shines through."

Bending down, I place a tender kiss on his soft lips and immediately feel him respond. He grabs my hips and pulls me into him. Straddling him, I wrap my arms around his neck and get lost in how he kisses with expertise.

"You're right. She is an idiot, but I'm thankful to be here with you right now." Resting his head against my chest, he ran his hands up and down my back in a soothing motion. "I really wish I was going to be in town longer or we lived closer. Seems like a cruel joke for us to meet and then have to say goodbye."

I knew it wouldn't be long term from the moment I met him, but my heart hurt hearing Owen say it out loud. "Maybe I can persuade Payton to take me with her to signings you're at. She mentioned you have another four this year that you're going to." Kissing his shoulder, I tried not coming off as clingy, but I didn't want to end things right then.

"I'd love that. And who knows, maybe I'll even go pay my favorite author and her best friend a visit. We kinda owe her for putting us together. Oh! And we have future covers that we need to do shoots for. We'll be together, I promise. I'll make it happen." Giving me a cheesy wink, he pulls off my dress and sucks in a deep breath upon catching sight of me. Giggling quietly, I feel his erection press against my ass. He takes hold of my back and carries me over to the bed. Pulling back the covers, Owen lays me down gently and climbs in beside me after taking off his shirt and slacks.

"Get some sleep, sweet girl," he whispers in my ear.

"Like that's going to happen. You're not exactly hiding the fact that you're rock hard for me." I turn to face him, and he wraps a leg around my thigh, grinding himself against me.

The look on his face tells me everything I need to know.

"I want to throw all logic aside when I'm with you. I want to be vulnerable and to feel again. Being in the public eye has made me skeptical of everyone I meet, but I can't resist you, Chloe. You need to tell me to stop right now if you don't want this going any

Sneak Peek — Fatefully

further," Owen confesses, and waits for my answer. Feeling his hard cock brush against my core is making me crave him. I can't deny either of us what we really want.

"I'm not going to stop you, Owen." Moving in, I kiss him on the lips, and he pulls me on top of him. I can feel his tight cords of muscle between my legs and under my hands and I want to touch him everywhere. "Make me feel again."

With that, he takes control and flips us so I'm underneath him. His body towers over my tiny frame. His magical hands and tongue bring me to a quick and unexpected orgasm before he even enters my wet core. Already, he's attuned to my needs and desires, quickly finding what makes me fall over the edge of bliss.

If this is how it always is with him, I may never let him go. Falling asleep in his warm embrace, I finally have a peaceful night's rest without worries of the past and dream of my future.

Acknowledgments

To Erin, you were the first person I told my crazy idea to on Black Friday about writing a book. You supported me throughout the process and have been my fan since day 1. We met by chance and I treasure our friendship. We've both grown a lot over the past year and can't wait to see what the next year holds for us!

To Ashley, my writing buddy. We both are learning the ropes together and I love how creative and open-minded you are. Having someone to talk to who's also writing their first book has been a great help and I love bouncing ideas off you. Our sprinting sessions and critiquing has made me looking at my writing in a different light and I couldn't have done it without you. The cover turned out amazing and will be using you for Tristen's story! Oh, and thanks for Tristen's name!!!

To Karina, my always happy beta reader. Your excitement and passion for the story kept me writing. I couldn't wait to see what you thought about what I had written that night and you've always been supportive of all my crazy ideas, even though I won't bring people back from the dead! <3 Littlebird

To Dusty, you are hilarious! I love how curious you are and I'm glad you were persistent because I've gained a great friend out of it. You think of things I missed and have given me great ideas

Sinfully

and feedback. I'm glad my location wasn't turned off and you found out where I lived! You're also a friend by chance and I am grateful every day for our friendship.

To Amy, you got my love for reading started by giving me Fifty Shades of Grey and I've become addicted! We're alike in more ways than should be allowed and am so glad you bought a house from me and let me in with open arms. You've seen me grow as a person and remind me to stay focused on what I want and to have fun in the process. You made fun of my word choice and made me describe things I'd rather not describe but it was the right decision and it made the book better. Love you girl!

To Brittany, Michelle, Shelly, Dusty, Anna, and all of my beta readers, you are awesome at catching stuff I never saw and asking all the right questions! I loved your ideas and recommendations and am grateful for each and every one of you. You girls caught the random stuff I looked over and I needed it!

To Tiffany, you are a rock star editor and I am grateful to have found you! You understand my randomness and help keep me in line. Thank you for all your ideas, enthusiasm, and honesty in all of our chats. You've given some really great advice and I'll be putting you to work again soon!

To my mom, for being open enough to read my story and not judge me. I was scared to have you read my sex scenes but after you corrected a grammatical error within one of those scenes, I knew I could come to you with ideas and talk openly with you about it. Thank you for being there for me and supporting me throughout the process! Love you mama

To Yara, Natalie, Jamie and Randi, you are all crazy and fantastic in your own ways and love being able to come to you with ideas and to talk about our favorite book boyfriends. We may not have ever met if it weren't for her, but I'm glad to have you all by my side! ;)

To my street team, you all rock and am forever grateful for your passion and creativity!!

XXVIII

Leighton Riley

To my readers, I never expected anything to come of my idea to write a story but with Payton and Ryder's story, I've realized a lot about myself. There are areas of the story that stem from my life and my experiences which made me take a step back and analyze my choices and path I decided to take. Both of these characters are people you'd actually see in real life and deal with real life issues. Thank you for taking the time to read their story and I can't wait to share Tristen's story next!

Meet Leighton

Texas born and raised, I found my love for dirty books rather recently. I work in real estate for my normal job and I write contemporary romance. *Sinfully* will be the first of three in its series, but they will be able to be read separately if desired. I love sweet tea (made right!), cookie cake, and anything with chocolate and peanut butter. I have a few guys at my gym that are my TDF's (tall, dark, and fuckable) but also have a HSB (Hot Sauna Boy), because let's be honest, they're my motivation while I'm there! I go to Las Vegas often but I swear I don't have as much fun as Payton does. Although, if I found myself a Tate there, I might change my opinion!

Authors such as Katy Evans, SE Hall, Angela Graham, Jasinda Wilder, and Jillian Dodd have been a large influence on me and I'm forever grateful. I decided to write *Sinfully* on Black Friday in November 2013, on a whim. I thought I'd get bored after a few pages but was captivated by the characters and it developed into something I am truly proud of. When it comes to book boyfriends, I love those who are strong but with a little imperfection or tragedy in their past (Remy, Kellan, Q, Twitch are just a few of my favorites). I LOVE talking to my readers so feel free to message me on Facebook. <3

Visit me Online:

Facebook www.facebook.com/leightonrileyauthor
Twitter: @LeightonRiley3
Goodreads: www.goodreads.com/author/show/7992651.Leighton_Riley

XXXI

Leighton's Books

Sinfully

She played the game by her own rules...until he changed them...

Payton wrote a self-published book regaling her encounters with men while visiting Las Vegas. To her horror, life changes in more ways than one when someone finds out her true identity.

Ryder, a successful publisher, is determined to find and sign Reece Edwards. Using what little information he can find on her, he sets out to find her, feeling it will definitely be worth the chase.

While on his search for Reece, Ryder meets Payton and the chemistry is explosive. Payton has done well with not allowing anyone to get close to her, but something is different with Ryder. Ryder can't get Payton out of his head, but he is still on his mission to locate Reece.

With two tragic pasts, Payton and Ryder each have demons to overcome. Will they be able to put those demons to rest or will it be all for nothing?

XXXIII

Sinfully

Regretfully

How do you heal after everything has been ripped away from you?

Completely devastated and alone, Tristen cannot fathom life after losing Cami and his unborn child. He attempts to find normality in his broken world but everything seems wrong.

Aria is compelled to help Tristen and cannot escape the undeniable connection she feels for him, even though Cami was one of her closest friends. She tries to help him move forward by befriending him but quickly realizes that there is more.

Tristen and Aria are both struggling to deal with these confusing emotions. Can they find happiness even when they feel utterly broken?

Regretfully is book 2 in the Sinfully series but can also be read as a standalone

Made in the USA
Charleston, SC
14 December 2015